STORMBRINGERS

STORMBRINGERS
PHILIPPA GREGORY

SIMON AND SCHUSTER

First published in Great Britain in 2013 by Simon & Schuster UK Ltd
A CBS COMPANY

Copyright © 2013 by Philippa Gregory

Map and chapterhead illustrations © Fred van Deelen, 2013

1 3 5 7 9 10 8 6 4 2

Simon & Schuster UK Ltd
1st Floor
222 Gray's Inn Road
London
WC1X 8HB

www.simonandschuster.co.uk

Simon & Schuster Australia, Sydney
Simon & Schuster India, New Delhi

A CIP catalogue copy for this book is available
from the British Library.

PB ISBN: 978-1-4711-4399-1
E-BOOK ISBN: 978-0-85707-737-0

Typeset by M Rules
Printed and bound by CPI Group (UK) Ltd, Croydon, CR0 4YY

CARTA DI PICCOLO

THE ROAD FROM ROME TO PESCARA, ITALY, NOVEMBER 1453

The five travellers on horseback on the rutted track to Pescara made everyone turn and stare: the woman who brought them weak ale in a roadside inn; the peasant building a hewn stone wall by the side of the road; the boy trailing home from school to work in his father's vineyard. Everyone smiled at the radiance of the couple at the front of the little cavalcade, for they were beautiful, young, and – as anyone could see – falling in love.

'But where's it all going to end, d'you think?' Freize asked Ishraq, nodding ahead to Luca and Isolde as they rode along the ruler-straight track that ran due east towards the Adriatic coast.

It was golden autumn weather and, though the deeply scored ruts in the dirt road would be impassable in winter-time, the going was good for now, the horses were strong

3

and they were setting a fair pace to the coast.

Freize, a square-faced young man with a ready smile, only a few years older than his master Luca, didn't wait for Ishraq's response. 'He's head over heels in love with her,' he continued, 'and if he had lived in the world and ever met a girl before, he would know to be on his guard. But he was in the monastery as a skinny child, and so he thinks her an angel descended from heaven. She's as golden-haired and beautiful as any fresco in the monastery. It'll end in tears, she'll break his heart.'

Ishraq hesitated to reply. Her dark eyes were fixed on the two figures ahead of them. 'Why assume it will be him who gets hurt? What if he breaks *her* heart?' she asked. 'For I have never seen Isolde like this with any other boy. And he will be her first love too. For all that she was raised as a lady in the castle, there were no passing knights allowed, and no troubadours came to visit singing of love. Don't think it was like a ballad, with ladies and chevaliers and roses thrown down from a barred window; she was very strictly brought up. Her father trained her up to be the lady of the castle and he expected her to rule his lands. But her brother stole everything and she was bundled into a nunnery. These days on the road are her first chance to be free in the real world – mine too. No wonder she is happy.

'And anyway, I think that it's wonderful that the first man she meets should be Luca. He's about our age, the most handsome man we've – I mean – *she's* ever met; he's kind, he's really charming, and he can't take his eyes off her. What girl *wouldn't* fall in love with him on sight?'

'There is another handsome young man she sees daily,'

Freize suggested. 'Practical, kind, good with animals, strong, willing, useful ... and handsome. Most people would say handsome, I think. Some would probably say irresistible.'

Ishraq delighted in misunderstanding him, looking into his broad smiling face and taking in his blue honest eyes. 'You mean Brother Peter?' she glanced behind them at the older clerk who followed leading the donkey. 'Oh no, he's much too serious for her, and besides he doesn't even like her. He thinks the two of us will distract you from your mission.'

'Well, you do!' Freize gave up teasing Ishraq and returned to his main concern. 'Luca is commissioned by the Pope himself to understand the last days of the world. His mission is to understand the end of days. If it's to be the terrible day of judgement tomorrow or the day after – as they all seem to think – he shouldn't be spending his last moments on earth giggling with an ex-nun.'

'I think he could do nothing better,' Ishraq said stoutly. 'He's a handsome young man, finding his way in the world, and Isolde is a beautiful girl just escaped from the rule of her family and the command of men. What better way could they spend the last days of the world, than falling in love?'

'Well, you only think that because you're not a Christian, but some sort of pagan,' Freize returned roundly, pointing to her pantaloons under her sweeping cape and the sandals on her bare feet. 'And you lack all sense of how important we are. He has to report to the Pope for all the signs that the world is about to end, for all the manifestations of evil in the world. He's young, but he is a member of a most important

5

order. A secret order, a secret papal order.'

She nods. 'I do, so often, lack a sense of how very important men are. You do right to reproach me.'

He heard, at once, the ripple of laughter in her voice, and he could not help but delight in her staunch sense of independence. 'We *are* important,' he insisted. 'We men rule the world, and you should have more respect for me.'

'Aren't you a mere servant?' she teased.

'And you are – a what?' he demanded. 'An Arab slave? A scholar? A heretic? A servant? Nobody seems to know quite what you are. An animal like a unicorn, said to be very strange and marvellous but actually rarely seen and probably good for nothing.'

'Oh, I don't know,' she said comfortably. 'I was raised by my dark-skinned beautiful mother in a strange land to always be sure who I was – even if nobody else knew.'

'A unicorn indeed,' he said.

She smiled. 'Perhaps.'

'You certainly have the air of a young woman who knows her own mind. It's very unmaidenly.'

'But of course, I do wonder what will become of us both,' she conceded more seriously. 'We have to find Isolde's godfather's son, Count Wladislaw, and then we have to convince him to order her brother to give back her castle and lands. What if he refuses to help us? What shall we do then? However will she get home? Really, whether she's in love with Luca or not is the least of our worries.'

Ahead of them, Isolde threw back her head and laughed aloud at something Luca had whispered to her.

'Aye, she looks worried sick,' Freize remarked.

'We are happy, *inshallah*,' she said. 'She is easier in her mind than she has been in months, ever since the death of her father. And if, as your Pope thinks, the world is going to end, then we might as well be happy today, and not worry about the future.'

The fifth member of their party, Brother Peter, brought his horse up alongside them. 'We'll be coming into the village of Piccolo as the sun sets,' he said. 'Brother Luca should not be riding with the woman. It looks ...' He paused, searching for the right reproof ...

'Normal?' Ishraq offered impertinently.

'Happy,' Freize agreed.

'Improper,' Brother Peter corrected them. 'At best it looks informal, and as if he were not a young man promised to the church.' He turned to Ishraq. 'Your lady should ride alongside you, both of you with your heads down and your eyes on the ground like maidens with pure minds, and you should speak only to each other, and that seldom and very quietly. Brother Luca should ride alone in prayer, or with me in thoughtful conversation. And anyway, I have our orders.'

At once, Freize slapped his hand to his forehead. 'The sealed orders!' he exclaimed wrathfully. 'Any time we are minding our own business and going quietly to somewhere, a pleasant inn ahead of us, perhaps a couple of days with nothing to do but feed up the horses and rest ourselves, out come the sealed orders and we are sent off to inquire into God knows what!'

'We are on a mission of inquiry,' Brother Peter said quietly. 'Of course we have sealed orders which I am commanded to open and read at certain times. Of course we are sent to inquire. The very point of this journey is not – what-

7

ever some people may think – to ride from one pleasant inn to another, meeting women; but to discover what signs there are of the end of days, of the end of the world. And I have to open these orders at sunset today, and discover where we are to go next and what we are to inspect.'

Freize put two fingers in his mouth and made an ear-piercing whistle. At once the two lead horses, obedient to his signal, stopped in their tracks. Luca and Isolde turned round and rode the few paces back to where the others were halted under the shade of some thick pine trees. The scent of the resin was as powerful as perfume in the warm evening air. The horses' hooves crunched on the fallen pine cones and their shadows were long on the pale sandy soil.

'New orders,' Freize said to his master Luca, nodding at Brother Peter, who took a cream manuscript, heavily sealed with red wax and ribbons, from the inside pocket of his jacket. To Brother Peter he turned and said curiously, 'How many more of them have you got tucked away in there?'

The older man did not trouble to answer the servant. With the little group watching he broke the seals in silence and unfolded the stiff paper. He read, and they saw him give a little sigh of disappointment.

'Not back to Rome!' Freize begged him, unable to bear the suspense for a moment longer. 'Tell me we don't have to turn round and go back to the old life!' He caught Ishraq's gleam of amusement. 'The inquiry is an arduous duty,' he corrected himself quickly. 'But I don't want to leave it incomplete. I have a sense of duty, of obligation.'

'You'd do anything rather than return to the monastery and be a kitchen lad again,' she said accurately. 'Just as I would rather be here than serving as a lady companion in an isolated castle. At least we are free, and every day we wake up and know that anything could happen.'

'I remind you, we don't travel for our own pleasure,' Brother Peter said sternly, totally ignoring their comments. 'We are commanded to go to the fishing village of Piccolo, take a ship across the sea to Split and travel onwards to Zagreb. We are to take the pilgrim road to the chapels of St. George and St. Martin at Our Lady's church outside Zagreb.'

There was a muffled gasp from Isolde. 'Zagreb!' A quick gesture from Luca as he reached out for her – and then snatched back his hand, remembering that he might not touch her – betrayed him too.

'We travel on your road,' he said, the joy in his voice audible to everyone. 'We can stay together.'

The flash of assent from her dark blue eyes was ignored by Brother Peter who was deep in the new orders. 'We are to inquire on the way as to anything we see that is out of the ordinary,' he read. 'We are to stop and set up an inquiry if we encounter anything that indicates the work of Satan, the rise of unknown fears, the evidence of the wickedness of man, or the end of days.' He stopped reading and refolded the letter, looking at the four young people. 'And so, it seems, that since Zagreb is on the way to Budapest, and since the ladies insist that they must go to Budapest to seek Count Wladislaw, that God Himself wills that we must travel the same road as these young ladies.'

Isolde had herself well under control by the time Brother Peter raised his eyes to her. She kept her gaze down, careful not to look at Luca. 'Of course we would be grateful for your company,' she said demurely. 'But this is a famous pilgrims' road. There will be other people who will be going the same way. We can join them. We don't need to burden you.'

The bright look in Luca's face told her that she was no burden; but Brother Peter answered before anyone else could speak. 'Certainly, I would advise that as soon as you meet with a party with ladies travelling to Budapest you should join them. We cannot be guides and guardians for you. We have to serve a great mission; and you are young women – however much you try to behave with modesty you cannot help but be distracting and misleading.'

'Saved our bacon at Vittorito,' Freize observed quietly. He nodded towards Ishraq. 'She can fight and shoot an arrow, and knows medicine too. Hard to find anyone more useful as a travelling companion. Hard to find a better comrade on a dangerous journey.'

'Clearly distracting,' Peter sternly repeated.

'As they say, they will leave us when they find a suitable party to join,' Luca ruled. His delight that he was to be with Isolde for another night, and another after that, even if it was only a few more nights, was clear to everyone, especially to her. Her dark blue eyes met his hazel ones in a long silent look.

'You don't even ask what we are to do at the sacred site?' Brother Peter demanded reproachfully. 'At the chapels? You don't even want to know that there are reports of heresy that we are to discover?'

'Yes, of course,' Luca said quickly. 'You must tell me what we are to see. I will study. I will need to think about it. I will create a full inquiry and you shall write the report and send it to the lord of our order, for the Pope to see. We shall do our work, as commanded by our lord, by the Pope, and by God Himself.'

'And best of all, we can get a good dinner in Piccolo,' Freize remarked cheerfully, looking at the setting sun. 'And tomorrow morning will be time enough to worry about hiring a boat to sail across to Croatia.'

PICCOLO, ITALY, NOVEMBER 1453

The little fishing village was ringed on the landward side by high walls pierced by a single gate that was officially closed at sunset. Freize shouted up for the porter, who opened the shutter to stick his head out of the window and argue that travellers should show respect for the rules, and might not enter the village after the curfew bell had tolled and the village gates closed for the night.

'The sun's barely down!' Freize complained. 'The sky is still bright!'

'It's down,' the gatekeeper replied. 'How do I know who you are?'

'Because, since it's not darkest night, you can perfectly well see who we are,' Freize replied. 'Now let us in, or it will be the worse for you. My master is an inquirer for the Holy Father himself, we couldn't be more important if we were all cardinals.'

Grumbling, the porter slammed the shutter on his window and came down to the gate. As the travellers waited outside, in the last golden light of the day, they could hear him, complaining bitterly as he heaved the creaking gate open, and they clattered in under the arch.

The village was no more than a few streets running down the hill to the quay. They dismounted once they were inside the walls and led the horses down the narrow way to the quayside, going carefully on the well-worn cobblestones. They had entered by the west gate of the perimeter wall which ran all round the village, pierced by a little bolted doorway on the high north side and a matching door to the south. As they picked their way down to the harbour they saw, facing the darkening sea, the only inn of the village with a welcoming door standing wide open, and bright windows twinkling with candlelight.

The five travellers led their horses to the stable yard, handed them over to the lad, and went into the hallway of the inn. They could hear, through the half-open windows, the slap of the waves against the walls of the quay, and could smell the haunting scent of salt water and the marshy stink of fishing nets. Piccolo was a busy port with nearly a dozen ships in the little harbour, either bobbing at anchor in the bay or tied up to rings set in the harbour wall. The village was noisy even though the autumn darkness was falling. The fishermen were making their way home to their cottages, and the last travellers were disembarking from the boats that plied their trade crossing and recrossing the darkening sea. Croatia was less than a hundred miles due east and people coming into the inn, blowing on their cold fingers, complained of a contrary wind which had prolonged their journey for nearly two days, and had chilled them to the bone. Soon it would be winter, and too late in the year for sea voyages for all but the most fearless.

Ishraq and Isolde took the last private bedroom in the house, a little room under the slanting roof. They could hear the occasional scuffling from mice and probably rats under the tiles, but this did not disturb them. They laid their riding cloaks on the bed and washed their hands and faces in the little earthenware bowl.

Freize, Luca and Brother Peter would bed down in the attic room opposite with half a dozen other men, as was usual when there were many travellers on the road and the inn was crowded. Brother Peter and Luca tossed a coin for the last place in the big shared bed and when Luca lost he had to make do with a straw mattress on the floor. The landlady of the inn apologised to Luca whose good looks and good manners earned him attention everywhere they went, but she said that the inn was busy tonight, and tomorrow it would be even worse as there was a rumour that a mighty pilgrimage was coming into town.

'How we'll feed them all I don't know,' she said. 'They'll have to take fish soup and bread and like it.'

'Where are they all going?' Luca asked, ashamed to find that he was hoping that they were not taking the road to Zagreb. He was anxious to be alone with Isolde, and determined that she should not join another party.

'Jerusalem, they say,' she replied.

'What a journey! What a challenge!' he exclaimed.

She smiled at him. 'Not for me,' she said. 'It's challenge enough making gallons of soup. What will the ladies want for their dinner?'

Freize, who sometimes served their dinner and sometimes ate with them, depending on the size of the inn and whether they needed help in the kitchen, was sent into the private dining room by the landlady and took his place with his friends at the table.

He was greeted with little smiles from both girls. He bowed to Lady Isolde and noticed that her blonde hair was coiled demurely under a plain headdress, and her dark blue eyes were carefully turned away from Luca, who could not stop himself glancing towards her. Brother Peter, ignoring everyone, composed a lengthy grace and Isolde and Luca prayed with him.

Ishraq kept her dark eyes open and sat in quiet thought while the prayer went on. She never recited the Christian prayers, but as Freize noted – peeking through his fingers – she seemed to use the time of Grace for her own silent thoughts. She did not seem to pray to her god either; as far as he knew, she carried no prayer mat with her few clothes and he had never seen her turn to the east. She was in this, as in so much else, a mystery, Freize thought, and a law to herself.

'Amen!' he said loudly, as he realized that Brother Peter had finally finished and that dinner might be served.

The innkeeper's wife had excelled herself, and brought five dishes to the table: two sorts of fish, some stewed mutton, a rather tough roast pheasant, and a local delicacy, pitadine, which was a pancake wrapped around a rich savoury filling. Freize tried it in the spirit of adventure and pronounced it truly excellent. She smiled and told him he could have pitadine for breakfast, dinner and supper, if he liked it so much. The filling changed according to the time of day, but the pancake remained the same. There was coarse brown bread baked hot from the oven with local butter, and some honey cakes for pudding.

The travellers dined well, hungry from their long ride, and easy and companionable together. Even Brother Peter was so warmed by good food and the friendliness of the inn that he poured a glass of wine for the two young women and wished them, '*Salute*.'

After dinner the ladies rose and said goodnight, and Ishraq went up to the little bedroom while Isolde lingered on the stairs. Luca got up casually from the dining table, and heading for the inn's front door, happened to arrive at the foot of the stairs in time to say goodnight to her. She was hesitating on the first two steps, holding her lit candle, and he laid his hand over hers on the stair rail.

'And so it seems we travel together for a little longer,' he said tentatively, looking up at her.

She nodded. 'Though I will have to keep my word to Brother Peter, and go with another party if we meet one,' she reminded him.

'Only a suitable one,' he reminded her.

She dimpled. 'It would have to be very suitable,' she agreed.

'Promise me, you will be very careful who you choose?'

'I shall be extremely careful,' she said, her eyes dancing, and then she lowered her voice and added more seriously, 'I shall not readily leave you, Luca Vero.'

'I can't imagine parting from you,' he exclaimed. 'I really can't imagine not seeing you first thing in the morning, and talking to you through the day. I can't imagine making this journey without you now. I know it is foolish – it's been only a few weeks, but I find you more and more ...'

He broke off, and she came down one step of the stair, so that her head was only a little higher than his. 'More and more?' she whispered.

'Essential,' he said simply, and he stepped up on the bottom step so they were level at last. Tantalisingly, they were so close that they could have kissed if he had leaned only a little more, or if she had turned her face towards him.

Slowly, he leaned a little more; slowly, she turned . . .

'Shall we plan our journey before we go to bed?' Brother Peter asked dryly from the doorway of the dining room. 'Brother Luca? Do you not think we should plan our journey so that we can make an early start tomorrow?'

Luca turned from Isolde with a quiet exclamation. 'Yes,' he said, 'of course.' He stepped back down to Brother Peter. 'Yes, we should. Goodnight, Isolde.'

'Goodnight,' she said sweetly and watched him as he went back into the little dining room and shut the door. Only when he was gone did she put her hand to her mouth as if she had been longing for the kiss that could not happen on this night, and should never happen at all.

In the morning the quayside was alive with noise and bustle. The boats that had been out at sea since dawn were jostling for position in the port. The earliest arrival was tied up alongside the harbour wall, the others tied to it and the farthest ones throwing ropes at bow and stern and the fishermen walking on planks laid across one boat to another with huge round woven baskets of fish dripping on their broad shoulders till they reached the shore and stacked them in their usual place for the buyers to come and see what they had landed.

The air above the boats was filled with seagulls, circling and swooping for offcuts of fish, their cries and screams a constant babel, the flash of their white wings bright in the morning sunshine.

A little auction of the catch was taking place at the harbour wall, a man yelling prices to the crowd, who raised their hands or shouted their names when he reached a price that they could meet, with the winner going forward, paying up, and hefting the basket to their cart to take inland, or carrying it up the stone steps into the town, higher up the hill, to the central market.

Basket after basket heaped with shoals of sardines came ashore, the fish brilliantly shining and stippled black like tarnished silver, and the landlady of the inn came down and bought two baskets and had the lad from the stables carry them home for her. The other women of the town hung back and waited for the buyers to drive down the prices before they approached and offered their money for a single fish. Wives and daughters went to their fathers' boats and took the pick of their catches for a good dinner that night. Individual fishermen had sets of scales on the quayside and leaned from their boats to sling iridescent-scaled fish into the tray, holding the balance to show to the waiting women, who then hooked the fish and dropped them into the bottom of their baskets.

Sleek cats wound their way around the legs of the buyers and sellers alike, waiting for the fish to be gutted and cleaned and scraps dropped down to them. In the sky above, the seagulls still wheeled and cried, the cold sunlight of the early morning shining on them as brightly as on the dazzling scales of the fish, as if the air, the land, and the sea, were all celebrating the richness of the ocean, the courage of the fishermen and the profitable trade of Piccolo.

Freize was strolling through the bustle of the quayside, sniffing the pungent scent of fish, marsh and salt, pulling off his cap to the prettier of the fish wives, stepping around the boxes of fish and the lobster pots, relishing the noise and the joy and the vitality of the port. He revelled in being far from the quiet solitude of the monastery as he made his way through the crowd to find a ship that would take them due east, to the port of Split. He had spoken to one master already and wanted to find another to compare the price. 'Though I don't doubt they'll have seen me coming and fixed the price already,' he grumbled to himself. 'A party on the road from Rome, two beautiful ladies and an inquirer of the church – bound to put the price up. Not to mention Brother Peter's long face. I myself would charge double for him, for the sheer misery of his company.'

As he paused, looking around him, a ginger kitten came and wound herself around his ankles. Freize looked down. 'Hungry?' he asked. The little face came up, the tiny pink mouth opened in a mew. Without thinking twice, Freize bent down and lifted the little animal in one hand. He could feel the little ribs through the soft fur. It was so small its body fitted in his broad palm. It started to purr, its whole body resonating with the deep, happy sound. 'Come on then,' Freize said. 'Let's see what we can find for you.'

In a corner of the harbour, seated on a stone seat and sheltered from the cold morning wind by a roughly built wall, a woman was gutting her fish and throwing the entrails down on the floor where they were snatched at once by bigger cats. 'Too big for you,' Freize remarked to the kitten. 'You'll have to grow before you can fight for your dinner there.' To the woman he said, 'Bless you, Sister, can I have a morsel for this kitten here?'

Without raising her head she cut a little piece off the tail and handed it up to him. 'You'd better have deep pockets if you're going to feed stray cats,' she said disapprovingly.

'No, for see, you are kind to me, and I am kind to her,' Freize pointed out, and sat beside her, put the little cat on his knee, and let her eat the tail of the fish, working from plump flesh to scaly end with remarkable speed.

'Are you planning to sit around all day looking at a kitten? Do you have no work to do?' she asked, as the kitten sat on Freize's knee and started to wash her paws with her little pink tongue.

'There I am! Forgetting myself!' Freize jumped to his feet, snatching up the kitten. 'I have work to do and important work it is too! So thank you, and God bless you, Sister, and I must go.'

She looked up, her face criss-crossed with deep wrinkles. 'And what urgent work do you do, that you have the time and the money to stop and feed stray kittens?'

He laughed. 'I work for the Church, Sister. I serve a young master who is an inquirer for the Pope himself. A brilliant young man, chosen above all the others from his monastery for his ability to study and understand everything – unknown things. He is an inquirer, and I am his friend and servant. I am in the service of God.'

'Not a very jealous God,' she said, showing her black teeth in a smile. 'Not a God who demands good time-keeping.'

'A God who would not see a sparrow fall,' Freize said. 'Praise Him and all the little beings of His creation. Good day.'

He tucked the kitten in his pocket where she curled around and put her paws on the top seam so that her little head was just poking out and she could see her way as they went through the crowd to where the fishermen were spreading out their nets for mending, taking down sails and coiling ropes on the ships.

At last Freize found a master who was prepared to take them across the sea to the town of Split for a reasonable fee. But he would not go until midday. 'I have been fishing half the night, I want my breakfast and dry clothes and then I'll take you,' he said. 'Sail at noon. You'll hear the church bells for Sext.'

They shook hands on the agreement and Freize went back to the inn, pausing at the stables to order the grooms to have the horses ready for sailing at midday. It seemed to him that the crowds at the quayside had grown busier, even though the market had finished trading. At the inn, there were many young people at the front door, peering into the hallway, and in the stable yard about a dozen children were sitting on the mounting block and the wall of the well. One or two of them had hauled up the dripping bucket from the well and were drinking from their cupped hands.

'What are you doing here?' he asked a group of about six boys, none of them more than twelve years old. 'Where are your parents?'

They did not answer him immediately, but solemnly crossed themselves. 'My Father is in heaven,' one of them said.

'Well, God bless you,' Freize said, assuming that they were a party of begging orphans, travelling together for safety. He crossed the yard and went into the inn through the kitchen door, where the landlady was lifting half a dozen good-sized loaves of rough rye bread from the oven.

'Smells good,' Freize said appreciatively.

'Get out of the way,' she returned. 'There is nothing for you until breakfast.'

He laughed and went on to the small stone hall at the entrance of the inn and found Luca and Brother Peter talking with the innkeeper.

Luca turned as he heard Freize's step. 'Oh, there you are. Are there many people outside?' he asked.

'It's getting crowded,' Freize replied. 'Is it a fair or something?'

'It's a crusade,' the innkeeper explained. 'And we're going to have to feed them somehow and get them on their way.'

'Is that what it is? Your wife said yesterday that she was expecting some pilgrims,' Freize volunteered.

'Pilgrims!' the man exclaimed. 'Aye, for that was all that someone told us. But now they are starting to come into town and they say there are hundreds of them, perhaps thousands. It's no ordinary pilgrimage, for they travel all together as an army will march. It's a crusade.'

'Where are they going?' Brother Peter asked.

The innkeeper shook his head. 'I don't know. Their leader walks with them. He must have some idea. I have to go and fetch the priest; he will have to see that they are housed and fed. I'll have to tell the lord of the manor; he'll want to see them moved on. They can't come here, and besides, half of them have no money at all; they're begging their way along the road.'

'If they are in the service of God then He will guide them,' Brother Peter said devoutly. 'I'll come with you to the priest and make sure that he understands that he must offer them hospitality.'

Luca said to Freize, 'Let's take a look outside. I heard they are going to Jerusalem.'

The two young men stepped out of the front door of the inn and found the quayside now crowded with boys and girls, some of them barefoot, some of them dressed in little more than rags, all of them travel-stained and weary. Most were seated, exhausted, on the cobblestones; some of them stood looking out to sea. None were older than sixteen, some as young as six or seven, and more of them were coming in through the town gate all the time, as the gate-keeper watched in bewilderment, racking his brains for an excuse to close the gate and shut them out.

'God save us!' Freize exclaimed. 'What's going on here? They're all children.'

'There's more coming,' Isolde called from the open window above them. She pointed north, over the roofs of the little town where the road wound down the hill. 'I can see them on the road. There must be several hundred of them.'

'Anyone leading them? Any adult in charge?' Luca called up to her, completely distracted by the sight of her tumbled hair and the half-open collar of her shirt.

Isolde shaded her eyes with her hand. 'I can't see anyone. No-one on horseback, just a lot of children walking slowly.'

Almost under their feet a small girl sat down abruptly and started to sob quietly. 'I can't walk,' she said. 'I can't go on. I just can't.'

Freize knelt down beside her, saw that her little feet were bleeding from blisters and cuts. 'Of course you can't,' he said. 'And I don't know what your father was doing letting you out. Where d'you live?'

27

Her face was illuminated at once, sore feet forgotten. 'I live with Johann the Good,' she said.

Luca bent down. 'Johann the Good?'

She nodded. 'He has led us here. He will lead us to the Promised Land.'

The two young men exchanged an anxious glance.

'This Johann,' Luca started, 'where does he come from?'

She frowned. 'Switzerland, I think. God sent him to lead us.'

'Switzerland?' exclaimed Freize. 'And where did he find you?'

'I was working on a farm outside Verona.' She reached for her little feet and chafed them as she spoke. At once her hands were stained red with her blood but she paid no attention. 'Johann the Good and his followers came to the farm to ask for food and to be allowed to sleep in a barn for the night, but my master was a hard man and drove them away. I waited till he was asleep and then my brother and I ran away after them.'

'Your brother's here?' Freize asked, looking round. 'You have an older brother? Someone to look after you?'

She shook her head. 'No, for he's dead now. He took a fever and he died one night and we had to leave him in a village; they said they would bury him in the churchyard.'

Freize put a firm hand on Luca's collar and pulled him back from the child. 'What sort of fever?' he asked suspiciously.

'I don't know, it was weeks ago.'

'Where were you? What was the village?'

'I don't know. It doesn't matter, I am not to grieve for I will see my brother again, when he rises from the dead.

Johann said that he will meet us in the Promised Land where the dead live again and the wicked burn.'

'Johann said that the dead will rise?' Luca asked. 'Rise from their graves and we will see them?'

Freize had his own question. 'So who takes care of you, now that your brother is dead?'

She shrugged her thin shoulders, as if the answer must be obvious. 'God takes care of me,' she said. 'He called me and He guides me. He guides all of us and Johann tells us what He wants.'

Luca straightened up. 'I'd like to speak with this Johann,' he said.

The girl rose to her feet, wincing with the pain. 'There he is,' she said simply, and pointed to a circle of young boys who had come through the town gate all together and were leaning their sticks against the harbour wall and dropping their knapsacks down on the cobbles.

'Get Brother Peter,' Luca said shortly to Freize. 'I'm going to need him to take notes of what this lad says. We should understand what is happening here. It may be a true calling.'

Freize nodded, and put a gentle hand on the little girl's shoulder. 'You stay here,' he said. 'I'll wash your feet when I get back and find you some shoes. What's your name?'

'Rosa,' she said. 'But my feet are all right. God will heal them.'

'I'll help Him,' Freize said firmly. 'He likes a bit of help.'

She laughed, a childish giggle at his impertinence. 'He is all powerful,' she corrected him gravely.

'Then He must get extra help all the time,' Freize said with a warm smile to her.

Luca stood watching the child-pilgrims as Freize jogged up the narrow street from the quayside to the market square, where the church stood, raised above the square by a flight of broad steps. As Freize went upwards, two at a time, the door of the church above him opened, and Brother Peter came out.

'Luca needs you,' Freize said shortly. 'He wants you to take notes as he speaks to the youth who leads the pilgrims. They call him, Johann the Good.'

'An inquiry?' Brother Peter asked eagerly.

'For sure, something strange is going on.'

Brother Peter followed Freize back to the quayside to find it even more crowded. Every moment brought new arrivals through the main gate of the town and through the little gate from the north. Some of them were children of nine or ten, some of them were young men, apprentices who had run from their masters, or farm boys who had left the plough. A group of little girls trailed in last, holding hands in pairs as if they were on their way to school. Luca guessed that at every halt the smaller, weaker children caught up with the others; and sometimes some of them never caught up at all.

Brother Peter spoke to Luca. 'The priest is a good man and has money to buy food for them, and the monastery is baking bread and the brothers will bring it down to the market to give to them.'

'It seems to be a pilgrimage of children led by a young man,' Luca said. 'I thought we should question him.'

Brother Peter nodded. 'He might have a calling,' he said cautiously. 'Or he might have been tempted by Satan himself to steal these children from their parents. Either way, the Lord of our Order would want to know. This is something we should understand. We should inquire into it.'

'He says that the dead will rise,' Luca told Peter.

The rising of the dead was a key sign of the end of days: when the graves would give up their dead and everyone would be judged.

Brother Peter looked startled. 'He is preaching of the end of days?'

'Exactly,' Luca said grimly.

'Which one is he?'

'That one, called Johann,' Luca said, and started to make his way through the weary crowd to the boy who stood alone, his head bowed in prayer. 'The little girl called him Johann the Good.'

There were so many children coming through the gate and down to the quayside now, that Luca could only wait and watch as they passed. He thought there were seven hundred of them in all, most of them exhausted and hungry, but all of them looking hopeful, some of them even inspired, as though driven by a holy determination to press on. Luca saw Freize take the little girl called Rosa to the inn kitchen to bathe her feet, and thought that there must be many little girls like her on the march, barely able to keep up, with no-one looking after them, driven by an unchildlike conviction that they were called by God.

'It could be a miracle,' Brother Peter said uncertainly, struggling through the sea of young people to get to Luca's side. 'I have seen such a thing only once before. When God calls for a pilgrimage and His people answer, it is a miracle. But we have to know how many there are, where they are going, and what they hope to achieve. They may be healers, they may have the Sight, they may have the gift of tongues. Or they might be terribly misguided. Milord will want to know about their leader, and what he preaches.'

'Johann the Good,' Luca repeated. 'From Switzerland, she said. That's him there.'

As if he felt their gaze upon him, the young boy waiting at the gate as his followers went past raised his head and gave them a brilliant smile. He was about fifteen years old, with long blond hair that fell in untidy ringlets down to his shoulders. He had piercing blue eyes and was dressed like a Swiss goatherd, with a short robe over thick leggings laced criss-cross, and strong sandals on his feet. In his hand he had a stick, like a shepherd's crook, carved with a series of crucifixes. As they watched, he kissed a cross, whispered a prayer, and then turned to them.

'God bless and keep you, Masters,' he said.

Brother Peter, who was more accustomed to dispensing blessings than receiving them, said stiffly, 'And God bless you too. What brings you here?'

'God brings me here,' the youth answered. 'And you?'

Luca choked on a little laugh at Brother Peter's surprise at being questioned by a boy. 'We too are engaged on the work of God,' he said. 'Brother Peter and I are inquiring into the well-being of Christendom. We are commissioned by the Holy Father himself to inquire and report to him.'

'The end of days is upon us,' the boy said simply. 'Christendom is over, the end of the world has begun. I have seen the signs. Does the Holy Father know that?'

'What signs have you seen?' Luca asked.

'Enough to be sure,' the lad replied. 'That's why we are on our journey.'

'What have you seen?' Luca repeated. 'Exactly what?'

Johann sighed, as if he were weary of miracles. 'Many, many things. But now I must eat and rest and then pray with my family. These are all my brothers and sisters in the sight of God. We have come far, and we have further still to go.'

'We would like to talk with you,' Brother Peter said. 'It is our mission to know what things you have seen. The Holy Father himself will want to know what you have seen. We have to judge if your visions are true.'

The boy nodded his head as if he were indifferent to their opinion. 'Perhaps later. You must forgive me. But many people want to know what I have seen and what I know. And I have no interest in the judgments of this world. I will preach later. I will stand on the steps of the church and preach to the village people. You can come and listen if you want.'

'Have you taken Holy Orders? Are you a servant of the church?' Brother Peter asked.

The boy smiled and gestured to his poor clothes, his shepherd's crook. 'I am called by God, I have not been taught by His Church. I am a simple goatherd, I don't claim to be more than that. He honoured me with His call as He honoured the fishermen and other poor men. He speaks to me Himself,' the boy said simply. 'I need no other teacher.'

He turned and made the sign of the cross over some children who came through the gate singing a psalm and gathered around him to sit on the stone cobbles of the quay as comfortably as if they were in their own fields.

'Wouldn't you like to come into the inn and break your fast with us?' Luca tempted him. 'Then you can eat, and rest, and tell us of your journey.'

The boy considered them both for a moment. 'I will do that,' he said. He turned and spoke a quick word with one of the children nearest to him and at once they settled down on the quayside and unpacked their knapsacks and started to eat what little they were carrying – a small bread roll and some cheese. The other children, who had nothing, sat dully where they were, as if they were too tired for hunger.

'And your followers?' Luca asked him.

'God will provide for them,' the youth said confidently.

Luca glanced towards Brother Peter. 'Actually, the priest is bringing food for them, the abbey is baking bread,' Brother Peter told him, rather stiffly. 'I see you are not fasting with them.'

'Because I knew that God would provide,' Johann confirmed. 'And now you tell me He has done so. You invite me to breakfast and so God provides for me. Why should I not trust him and praise His holy name?'

'Why not indeed?' Brother Peter said glacially, and led the way to the dining room of the inn.

~

Ishraq and Isolde did not join the men for breakfast. They peeped through the open door to see the boy Johann, and then carried their plates upstairs to their bedroom and ate, sitting at the window, watching the scene on the quayside as children continued to pour into the town, the smallest and the frailest coming last as if they could hardly keep up. Their ragged clothes showed that they were from many different areas. There were children from fishing villages further north up the coast who wore the rough smocks of the region, and there were children who had come from farms and wore the capes and leggings of shepherds and goatherds. There were many girls, some of them dressed as if they had been in service, in worsted gowns with goatskin aprons. Isolde nudged Ishraq as three girls in the robes of novices of a convent came through the gate of the town, their rosaries in their hands, their little veiled heads bowed, and passed under the overhanging window.

'They must have run away from a nunnery,' she said.

'Like us,' Ishraq agreed. 'But where do they think they're going?'

In the dining room the youth prayed in silence over the food, blessed the bread, and then ate a substantial breakfast that Freize brought up from the kitchen. After the boy had finished, he gave thanks in a lengthy prayer to God and a short word of appreciation to Luca. Brother Peter took out his papers from his travelling writing-box desk and dipped his pen in ink.

'I have to report to my lord who in turn reports to the Holy Father,' he explained as the boy looked at his preparations. 'If your journey is blessed by God then the Holy Father will want to know the proofs. If he thinks you have a calling he will support you. If not, he will want to know about you.'

'It is blessed,' the boy said. 'D'you think we could have come all this way if God had not guided us?'

'Why, how far have you come?' Luca asked cautiously.

'I was a goat herder in the canton of Zurich when I heard God's voice,' the boy said simply. 'He told me that a terrible thing had happened in the east. A worse thing than the great flood itself. A greater wrong than the flood that drowned everyone but Noah. He said that the Ottomans had come against Christendom in a mighty wave of men, and had taken Constantinople, our holy city, the heart of the Church in the east, and destroyed it. Did I hear right or no?'

'You did,' Luca said. 'But any passing pedlar could have told you so. It happened in May this year.'

'But it was not a passing pedlar who told me so, for I was up in the hills with my goats. Every dawn I left the village and took the goats up the paths to the higher fields where the grass grows fresh and sweet. Every day I sat in the fields with them, and watched over them. Sometimes I played my pipe, sometimes I lay on my back and watched the clouds. When the sun sat in the top branches of the silver birch tree I ate the bread and cheeses that my mother had tied into a cloth for me. Every evening as the sun started to go down, I brought my flock safe home again and saw them into my neighbours' fields and stables. I saw no-one, I talked to no-one. I had no companion but an angel. Then one day, God spoke to me and He told me that the infidels had taken the holy church of Constantinople. He said that the sea had risen so high that they had rowed their galleys right over the land, over the harbour wall, and into the harbour. He said that the greatest church in the whole world was once called Hagia Sophia and that now it is in the hands of the infidels and they will make it into a mosque, take down the altar and defile its sacred aisles, and that this is a true sign of the end of days. Did I hear right or no?'

'They took the cathedral,' Luca confirmed uneasily. 'They took the city.'

'Did the priests pray at the altar as the infidels came in the door and cut them down?' Johann asked.

Luca glanced to Brother Peter. 'They served the Mass until the last moment,' Brother Peter confirmed.

'Did they row their galleys over the land?'

'It can't be true,' Luca interrupted.

'It wasn't exactly true,' Brother Peter explained. 'It was a trick of war. They mounted the galleys on great rollers and pushed them across the land into the inner harbour. The devil himself guided them to put the rowers to the oars and the drummers to the beat so they looked as if they were rowing through the air. Everyone said it looked like a fleet of galleys sailing along the road.'

Luca shook his head in amazement. He had not heard the story before but the boy nodded, as if he had seen the terrifying sight and then the sacrilege himself. 'God told me that the infidels would come and bring terror to every village in the world, and that just as they have come through Greece they will come on and on, and nothing can stop them. He said they would come into my own canton, they will come to every village in Switzerland. He said that they are led by a young man only a little older than me. Is that right?'

Luca looked at Brother Peter. 'Sultan Mehmet is nineteen years old,' he confirmed.

'God told me that this is a war for young people and for children. The infidels are led by a young man; I heard my calling. I knew that I must leave my home.'

The two men waited.

'I took my crook and my knapsack and I said farewell to my father and mother. The whole village came out to see me leave. They knew that I was inspired by God himself.'

37

'Did anyone leave with you?'

He shook his head and stared at the window as if he could see on the dim pieces of the horn panes the poverty of the dirty village street, the dreary lives of the people who scratched a living from the thin mountain soil, who were hungry and cold every winter and knew, even in the warmth of summer, that the cold and hunger of winter would come again. People who confidently expected that nothing would ever change, that life would go on in the same cycle of hard winters and bright summers in a remorseless unchanging round – until the day that they heard that the Turks were coming and understood that everything had suddenly got worse and would get worse still.

'Children joined me as I walked,' Johann said. 'They heard my voice, they understood. We all know that the end of days is coming. We all want to be in Jerusalem for judgement day.'

'You think you're going to Jerusalem?' Freize demanded incredulously from the doorway. 'You're leading these children to Jerusalem?'

The boy smiled at him. 'God is leading them to Jerusalem,' he said patiently. 'I am only walking with them. I am walking beside them.'

'Then God has chosen an odd route,' Freize said rudely. 'Why would He send you to the east of Italy? Why not go to Rome and get help? Why not take a ship from there? Why walk these children such a long way?'

The boy looked a little shaken at Freize's loud scepticism. 'I don't lead them, I don't choose the route, I go where God tells me,' he said quietly. He looked at Brother

Peter. 'The way is revealed to me, as I walk. Who is this man questioning me?'

'This is Brother Luca's servant,' Brother Peter said irritably. 'You need not answer his questions. He has no part in our inquiry.'

'Oh, beg pardon for interrupting, I'm sure,' Freize said, not sounding at all sorry. 'But am I to give your leavings out at the door? Your followers seem to be hungry. And there are broken meats from your breakfast, and the untouched bread. You dined quite well.'

The boy passed his plate and the bread in the basket without giving it another glance. 'God provides for us,' he said. 'Give it all to them with my blessing.'

'And see that the food is shared fairly when it comes from the monastery,' Brother Peter ordered Freize, who nodded and went out. They could hear him stamping to the kitchen and the back door. Brother Peter turned his attention back to the boy. 'And your name is?'

'Johann Johannson.'

'And your age?'

'I think I am almost sixteen years old. I don't know for sure.'

'Had you seen any miracles or heard anything before this year?'

He smiled. 'I used to hear a singing in the church bells of my village,' he confided. 'When they rang for Mass I used to hear them calling my name, as if God himself wanted me to come to His table. Then sometimes, when I was with the goats in the high pasture in summer, I would hear voices, beautiful voices, calling my name. It was an angel who used to meet me in the highest meadows. I knew that

39

there would be a task for me. But I did not know it would be this.

'God told me of the end of days when I was on my own in the high pasture and I puzzled as to what I should do with this knowledge. I spoke to my priest and he said perhaps it was a revelation; we would have to wait till we could know more. We could not believe that what I had heard in the pasture about the Church of the East could be true. Nobody could believe that a great city like Constantinople could fall. But then a pedlar did, at last, come to the market, and he stood in the village square and there were tears in his eyes as he told us all that the Rome of the East had fallen – that the city had held out as long as it could, a light in the darkness, as the darkness grew darker; but that the Ottoman Turks were too much for it. I knew then, that my vision was true, that the voice I had heard was the voice of God, that the end of days was upon us, and that I must go to Jerusalem.'

'You knew of the fall of Constantinople before the pedlar came and told everyone?' Brother Peter made a note. 'You had reported your vision to your priest?'

'I did,' the boy said with certainty.

'You are certain that you told your priest of the end of days before the pedlar came?'

The boy nodded, not troubling to repeat himself.

'And how do you plan to get to Jerusalem, from here?' Luca asked.

'God has told me that the sea will dry up before us,' the boy said simply. 'As it did before the children of Israel. We will walk to the southernmost point of Italy and then I know that the waves will part and we will walk to the Holy Land.'

Luca and Brother Peter exchanged a wondering look at his confidence. 'It's a long, long way,' Luca suggested gently. 'Do you know the way? Do you know how far?'

'It doesn't matter to me what the road is called, nor how far it is,' the boy said confidently. 'God guides me, not signposts or worldly maps. I walk in faith, I am not the toy of men who draw maps and try to measure the world. I don't follow their vision but that of God.'

'And what will you do, when you get there?' Brother Peter asked.

'This is not a crusade of weapons,' the boy replied. 'It is a children's crusade. When we get there the children of Israel will come to us. The Turk children will come to us. Ottoman children will come. Arab children will come to us and we will all serve the one God. If there are any Christian children left alive in those tragic lands, then they will come to us too. They will all explain to their fathers and their mothers and there will be peace. The children of all the enemies will bring peace to the world. It is a children's crusade and every child will answer the call. Then Jesus will come to Jerusalem and the world will end.'

'You have seen all this in a vision?' Brother Peter confirmed. 'You are certain?'

His face shining with conviction, the boy nodded. 'It is a certainty,' he said. 'How else would all these children have joined me already? They come from the villages and from the little farms. They come from dirty workshops and the backstreets of evil cities. They come with their brothers and sisters. They come with their friends. They come from different countries, they come even if they cannot understand my language, for God speaks to them. The Arab children, the Jewish children will come too.' He wiped his mouth on his sleeve, like the simple peasant boy he was. 'I see you are amazed, my masters, but this is how it is. It is a children's crusade and it is going to change the world.

'And now I must pray with my brothers and sisters,' he said. 'You may join us if you want.' He rose up, picked up his crook, and went to the doorway.

'How will the waters part?' Luca asked him curiously.

Johann made a gesture with his hands, pushing the air away before him. 'As it did before,' he said. 'For Moses. However that was. The waves will part on one side and the other. We will see the sea bed beneath our feet. We will see the wrecks of ships that lie on the bed of the sea and we can pick up their treasure as we walk. We can gather pearls as if they were flowers. We will go dry-shod all the way to Palestine.' He paused. 'Angels will sing,' he said, pleased. He went from the room, leaving Luca and Brother Peter alone.

'What an extraordinary boy!' Luca exclaimed, pushing back his chair from the table. 'He has a gift, it can't be denied.' He brushed his forearm and ran his hand up the nape of his neck. 'My hairs are standing on end. I believe him. I am truly persuaded. I wish I could follow him. If I had heard him when I was a child I would have left a plough in the field and gone after him.'

'A charismatic leader,' Brother Peter decided. 'But whether he is a dreamer or whether he is a prophet, or even a false prophet, I can't tell. We must hear him preach and perhaps question him some more. I'll have to get news of this to Milord at once. This is urgent.'

'He will want to know of such a boy?'

'Of such a boy, and of such a crusade. This could be another sign of the end of days. He will want to know everything. Why, if they get to Palestine and do half of what they promise, then the Ottoman Empire will struggle to deal with them. For them it will be their worst nightmare knocking at their front door. With such a large band of children they'll either have to guard them, or arrest them, attack them, or let them enter into the holiest places. Either way these children could upset everything. This may turn out to be the greatest weapon we could have devised against our enemies. We would never have thought of such a device but they could be far more powerful than any Christian army of grown men. If Johann can appeal to Ottoman children and Turk children and if they join him in a Christian crusade, then the world would be turned upside down.'

'Do you really think they can get all that way to Jerusalem?'

'Who would have thought they could have got here? And yet they have, in their thousands.'

'Certainly hundreds,' Luca said cautiously.

'There are hundreds of children following that boy already. How many more can he recruit as he marches south?'

'You can't think that the sea will part before them?' Luca asked. 'How could such a thing happen?'

'Do you believe that the Red Sea parted for the children of Israel?' the older man put to him.

'I have to believe it. The Bible is clear that it did. To question it would be heresy.'

'Then why should such a miracle not happen again?'

Luca shook his head. 'I suppose it could. I just—' He

broke off. 'I just can't understand how such a thing could be. How it could happen. Don't question my faith, I believe the Bible as I am bound to do. I am not denying one word of it. But this sea rushing back from the sea bed? And these children walking dry-shod to Palestine? Can such a thing be possible?'

'We have to see if it can be done. But if the sea does not part for them it may be that Milord will get them ships.'

'Why would he take the trouble?' Luca hesitated, noticing the excitement in the older man's face. 'Is our inquiry about the end of days, or is the Order more interested in defeating the Ottomans? Are we seeking the truth or forging a weapon?'

'Both, of course, both,' Brother Peter replied roundly. 'Both, always. It is one and the same thing. The world will end when the Ottomans enter the gates of Rome, and at that moment the dead will rise from their graves for judgment. You and I have to travel throughout Christendom to watch for the signs of the dead rising, of Satan emerging, and the Ottoman armies coming ever closer. The infidels in Jerusalem and Jesus descending from heaven is one and the same thing, both signs of the end. What we have to know is when it takes place. These children may be a sign, I really believe that they are a sign. We must write to Milord, and we have to know more.'

~

Luca tapped on the door of Isolde's room and she opened it wide when she saw him. 'I can't stay,' he said. 'But I wanted to warn Ishraq.'

The dark girl appeared behind Isolde. 'Me?'

44

'Yes. You've seen the children, coming into town. They're a crusade, hundreds of children, perhaps more. They're heading south, on their way to Jerusalem to defeat the Ottomans.'

'We've seen them from the window. They look exhausted.'

'Yes, but they are very sure that they are on their way to Palestine, a mighty crusade and a sign of the end of days. They know of the sack of Constantinople by the Ottomans. If you go down into the streets at all, you must not wear your Arab dress. They might turn on you. I don't know what they would think.'

'I should not wear Arab dress? I am not to wear my own clothes? I am to deny my heritage?'

'Not while the Children's Crusade is here. Wear what Lady Isolde wears for now.'

Ishraq gave him a steady look from her dark eyes. 'And what shall I do about my Arab skin?'

Luca flushed. 'You are a beautiful colour, God knows there are few women to match your looks, the colour of heather honey and eyes as dark as midnight,' he said fervently. 'But you cannot wear your pantaloons and your robe and veil until the crusade leaves the town, or until we get the ship out of here. You must dress like Isolde, like a Christian woman, for your own safety.'

'She will,' Isolde ruled, cutting short the argument. 'It makes no difference to you, Ishraq, you wear my gowns just as often as you wear your pantaloons. You prove nothing by wearing your Arab clothes.' She turned to Luca. 'Will we still sail at noon?'

'No. We have to speak more with these children and we

have to send a report to Rome. Brother Peter believes they are inspired by God, but certainly if they can get to Jerusalem with or without His guidance, they will pose a huge challenge to the Ottomans.'

'Are they walking onwards?'

'I expect they'll go on this afternoon. People are giving them food and money to send them on their way. The church here is feeding them. And they are determined to go on. It's a remarkable pilgrimage; I am glad to have seen it. When you talk with the boy, Johann, it's inspiring. You know, I would go too if I were free.'

'D'you think they can possibly get to Jerusalem?' Ishraq wondered.

'Who would have thought they could come this far? Children led by a youth who doesn't even know where Jerusalem is? Brother Peter thinks they are part of the signs that we have been sent out to observe. I'm not sure, but I have to see that it is a sort of miracle. He is an ignorant country lad from Switzerland, and here he is in Italy, on his way to Jerusalem. I have to think it is almost a miracle.'

'But you're not sure,' Ishraq observed.

He shrugged. 'He says the waters will part for them – I can't imagine how. It would be a miracle in this place and time and I can't see how it would happen. But perhaps they will be able to walk to Messina and someone will give them ships. There are many ways that they could get to Jerusalem dry-shod. There are other miracles as great as parting the waters.'

'You believe that this boy can find his way to Messina?' Ishraq asked him sceptically.

Luca frowned. 'It's not your faith,' he said defensively. 'I

46

see that you would not believe these pilgrims. You would think them fools, led by a charlatan. But this boy Johann has great power. He knows things that he could only have learned by revelation. He claims that God speaks to him and I have to believe that He does. And he has already come so far!'

'Can we come and listen to him?' Isolde asked.

Luca nodded. 'He is preaching this afternoon. If you cover your heads and wear your capes, you can join us. I should think half the village will be there to listen to him.'

~

Isolde and Ishraq, wearing their grey gowns with their brown cloaks came out of the front door of the inn and walked along the stone quayside. Most of the fishing ships were moored in the harbour, bobbing on the quiet waves, the men ashore mending their nets or coiling ropes and patching worn sails. The two girls ignored the whistles and catcalls as the men noted the slim, caped figures and guessed that there were pretty faces under the concealing hoods. Isolde blushed and smiled at a shouted compliment but Ishraq turned her head in disdain.

'You need not be so proud, it's not an insult,' Isolde remarked to her.

'It is to me,' Ishraq said. 'Why should they think they can comment on me?'

They turned up one of the narrow alleyways which led up the hill to the market square and walked below criss-cross lines of washing strung from one overhanging balcony to another. A few old ladies sat on their doorsteps, their hands busy with mending or lace-making, and nodded at the girls as they went by, but most of the people were already in the market square to hear Johann preach.

Isolde and Ishraq passed the bakery, with the baker coming out and closing up shop for the day, his face and hair dusted white with flour. The cobbler next door sat cross-legged in his window, a half-made shoe on his anvil, looking out at the gathering crowds. The next shop was a ships' chandlers, the dark interior a jumble of goods from fishing nets to cork floats, fish knives and rowlocks, screws by the handful, nails in jars, blocks of salt and barrels. Next door to him was a hatter and milliner, doing poor trade in a poor town; next to him a saddler.

The girls went past the shops with barely a glance into the shadowy interiors, their eyes drawn to the steps of the church and to the shining fair head of the boy who waited, cheek against his simple crook, as if he were listening for something.

Before him, the crowd gathered, murmuring quietly, attentively. Behind him, in the darkened doorway of the church, stood Brother Peter, Luca and Freize beside the village priest. Many of the fishermen and almost all the women and children of the village had come to hear Johann the Good preach, but Isolde noticed that some of the older children were absent. She guessed they had been sent to sea with their fathers, or ordered to stay at home – not every family wanted to risk its children hearing Johann preach. Many mothers regarded him as a sort of dangerous piper who might dance their children out of town, never to be seen again. Some of them called him a child-stealer who should be feared, especially by mothers who had only one child.

The children of the crusade had been fed on a mean

breakfast of bread and fish. The priest had collected food from his parishioners and the people of the market had handed out the leftovers. The monks in the abbey had sent down baskets of fresh-baked bread and honey scones. Clearly some of the children were still hungry, and many of them would have been hungry for days. But they still showed the same bright faces as when they had first walked into the village of Piccolo.

Ishraq, always sensitive to the mood of a crowd, could almost feel the passionate conviction of the young crusaders: the children wanted to believe that Johann had been called by God, and had convinced themselves that he was leading them to Jerusalem.

'This is not faith,' she whispered to Isolde. 'This is longing: a very different thing.'

'You ask me why we should walk all the long, long way to the Holy Land?' Johann started suddenly, without introduction, without telling them to listen, without a bidding prayer or calling for their attention. He did not even raise his voice, he did not raise his eyes from the ground nor his cheek which was still resting thoughtfully against his shepherd's crook, yet the hundreds of people were immediately silent and attentive. The round-faced priest in the grey unbleached robes of the Cistercian order, who had never in all his life seen a congregation of this size, lowered his gaze to the doorstep of his little church. Brother Peter stepped slightly forwards, as if he did not want to miss a word.

'I will tell you why we must go so far,' Johann said quietly. 'Because we want to. That's all! Because we choose to do so. We want to play our part in the end of days. The infidels have taken all the holy places into their keeping, the infidels have taken the greatest church in Constantinople and the Mass is celebrated no more at the most important altar in the world. We have to go to where Jesus Christ was a child and we have to walk in His footsteps. We have to be as children who enter the kingdom of heaven. He promised that those who come to him as little children will not be forbidden. We, His children, will go to Him and He will come again, as He promised, to judge the living and the dead, the old and the young, and we will be there, in Jerusalem, we will be the children who will enter the kingdom of heaven. D'you see?'

'Yes,' the crowd breathed. The children responded readily, at once, but even the older people, even the villagers who had never heard this message before were persuaded by Johann's quiet authority. 'Yes,' they said.

Johann tossed his head so his blond ringlets fell away from his face. He looked around at them all. Luca had a sudden disconcerting sense that Johann was looking at him with his piercing blue eyes, as if the young preacher knew something of him, had something to say especially to him. 'You are missing your father,' the boy said simply to the crowd. Luca, whose father had disappeared after an Ottoman raid on his village, when Luca was only fourteen, gave a sudden start and looked over the heads of the children to Isolde, whose father had died only five months ago. She was pale, looking intently at Johann.

'I can feel your sorrow,' he said tenderly. Again his blue gaze swept across Luca and then rested on Isolde. 'He did not say goodbye to you,' Johann observed gently. Isolde bit her lip at that deep, constant sorrow and there was a soft moan from the crowd, from the many people who had lost fathers – at sea or to illness, or in the many accidents of daily life. Ishraq, standing beside Isolde, took her hand and found that she was trembling. 'I can see a lord laid cold and pale in his chapel and his son stealing his place,' Johann said. Isolde's face blanched white as he told her story to the world. 'I can see a girl longing for her father and him crying her name on his deathbed but they kept her from him, and now, she can't hear him.'

Luca gave a muffled exclamation and turned to Brother Peter. 'I didn't tell him anything about her.'

'Nor I.'

'Then how does he know this?'

'I can see a bier in a chapel alone,' Johann went on. 'But nobody mourns for the man who has gone.' There was a sob from a woman in the crowd who fell to her knees. Isolde stood like a statue, listening to the young man describing the loss of her father. 'I can see a daughter driven from her home and longing to return.'

Isolde turned to Ishraq. 'He is speaking of me.'

'It seems so,' Ishraq cautiously responded. 'But this could be true of many people.'

'I see a girl whose father died without her at his side, whose brother stole her inheritance, who longs, even now, to be back in her home, to see her father again,' Johann said his voice low and persuasive. 'And I have good news for you. Good news. I see this young woman, her heart broken by her loss, and I can tell you that she will return. She will return and take her place again.'

Isolde clutched at Ishraq's steady hand. 'He says I will return!'

'And I see more,' Johann went on. 'I can see a young man, a boy. A young boy, and his father lost at sea. Oh! I can see that boy waiting and waiting on the quayside and looking for the sails of a boat that never comes home.'

A muffled sob from one youth in the huge crowd was repeated all around the people. Clearly, Johann saw truly. Many people recognised themselves in his vision. Someone cried out for the blessing of God on a fatherless family, and one woman was comforted, softly weeping for her father who would never come back from the sea.

'This is an easy guess in a port,' Ishraq muttered to Isolde and got a burning look in reply.

'I see a boy, a youth, learning that his father has been taken by the infidels themselves. They came at night in their terrible galleys and stole away his father, his mother, and everything they owned, and that boy wants to know why. That boy wants to know how. That boy will spend the rest of his life asking questions.'

Freize, who had been with Luca in the monastery when the Abbot had called him out of chapel to tell him that there had been an Ottoman slaving raid and his mother and father were missing, exchanged one level look with Luca. 'Odd,' was all he said.

'A youth who has lost his father without explanation will ask questions for all his life,' Johann stated.

Luca could not take his eyes from the young preacher; it was as if the boy was describing him, as if he knew Luca at the deepest level.

'I can answer his questions,' the boy reassured the crowd, his voice sweet as if he were quite entranced. 'I can answer that boy who asks, "where is my father?" "Where is my mother?" God will tell me the answers. I can tell you now, that you will hear your father, I can tell you how to hear his voice.'

He looked over towards Isolde who was hidden among the village women, all dressed alike, with her hood completely covering her shining blonde hair. 'I can tell you how to claim your inheritance and sit in your father's chair where he wants you to be. I can tell you how to return home.'

A little cry broke from Isolde, and Luca checked himself from moving towards her.

'Come with us,' the boy said quietly. 'Come to Jerusalem where the dead will rise and your fathers will meet you. Come with me, come with all of us and we will go to Jerusalem and the world will have no end and your father will put his hand on your head with a blessing once more, and you will feel his love and know you are his child.'

Isolde was openly weeping, as was half the crowd. Luca gulped down his emotion, even Freize knuckled his eyes. Johann turned to the priest. 'Now we will pray,' he said. 'Father Benito will hear confession and pray with us. May I confess, Father?'

The priest, deeply moved, nodded, and led the way into the darkness of the church. Most of the crowd knelt where they stood and closed their eyes in prayer. Isolde dropped to her knees on the dirty cobblestones of the market and Ishraq stood beside her, almost as if she would guard her from this revelation, from grief itself. Freize, looking over, met Ishraq's steady dark gaze and knew himself to be shaken and puzzled by what they had heard.

'He knows things that we didn't tell him,' Luca said in a rapid undertone to Brother Peter. 'He knows things that are impossible that he should know other than by revelation. He spoke of me, and of my childhood, and I had said nothing of either to him. He spoke of the Lady Isolde and he hasn't even seen her. Nobody in this village knows anything about any of us.'

'Would Freize . . .' Brother Peter asked doubtfully.

Freize shook his head. 'I'm not the one who gives breakfast to boys begging on the harbour wall,' he said loftily. 'And I don't gossip. I haven't said one word to him that you have not heard. If you ask me, he made a few lucky guesses and saw the response he got.'

'You wept,' Luca said bluntly.

'He said things that would make a stone weep!' Freize returned. 'Just because it makes you cry, doesn't mean that it's true.'

'To speak of an Ottoman raid to me?' Luca challenged him. 'That's not a guess. To speak of Isolde driven from her castle? That's no wild guess, there is no way that he would think of it, no way that he could know such things. He knew nothing of her, she kept out of his way. And yet he spoke of her father laid on a cold bier and her brother stealing her inheritance.'

'I believe he is inspired,' Brother Peter agreed, overruling Freize's scepticism. 'But I shall ask the priest for his opinion. I shall ask him what Johann tells him.' He glanced into the shadowy interior of the church where the priest was kneeling on one side of a carved wooden screen and Johann was kneeling on the other side, reverently whispering his confession with his fair head bowed.

'Johann's confession must be secret,' Luca remarked. 'Between him, the priest and God.'

Brother Peter nodded. 'Of course. But Father Benito is allowed to give me an impression. And as soon as I have spoken with him I shall send our report to Rome. Whether the boy is a visionary or a fraud I should think that Milord will want to help this. It could be very important. It is a crusade of its own making, a rising up of the people. It's much more powerful than the lords ordering their tenants to war. It is the very thing that the Pope has been calling for and getting no response. It could change everything. As Johann goes through Italy he could gather thousands. Now I have seen him preach I understand what he might do. He might make an army of faith – unstoppable. Milord will want to see that they are fed and shipped to the Holy Land. He will want to see that they are guarded and have arms.'

'And he spoke of fathers,' Luca went on, indifferent to Brother Peter's plan for a new great crusade. 'He spoke of me, and my father. He spoke of Isolde and her father. It was not general, it was not ordinary preaching. He spoke of Isolde, he spoke of me. He knew things he could not know except by a genuine revelation.'

'He is inspiring,' Brother Peter conceded. 'Perhaps a visionary indeed. Certainly he has the gift of tongues – did you see how they listened to him?'

Luca made his way through the praying crowd to Isolde and found her on her knees with Ishraq standing over her. When she crossed herself, and looked up, he gave her his hand and helped her to her feet.

'I thought he was speaking of me,' he said tersely. 'And of the loss of my father.'

'I am sure he was speaking of me,' she agreed. 'Speaking *to* me. He said things that only one who had been at the castle, or who had been advised by God could know. He was inspired.'

'You believe him?'

She nodded. 'I do. I have to believe him. He could not have guessed at the things he said. He was too specific, it was too vivid a vision.'

He offered her his arm, and she put her hand in the crook of his elbow and they walked together down the narrow steps to the quayside inn. Freize and Ishraq followed them in sceptical silence, the little ginger kitten skipped along behind them, following Freize.

'I don't see you weeping?' Freize remarked to the young woman at his side.

'I don't cry easily,' she said.

'I cry like a baby,' Freize confessed. 'He was inspiring. But I don't know what to think.'

'He could have said that stuff anywhere,' Ishraq said roundly. 'Every port on the coast will have women who have lost a father. Most villages will have someone cheated of their inheritance.'

'You don't believe he is inspired by God?'

She gave a short laugh and risked the confession: 'I'm not even sure about God.'

He smiled. 'Are you a pagan indeed?'

'I was raised by my mother as a Muslim, but I have lived all my life in a Christian household,' she explained. 'I was educated by Isolde's father the Lord of Lucretili to be a scholar and to question everything. I don't know what I believe for sure.'

Ahead of them Luca and Isolde were talking quietly together.

'I have missed my father more than I would have believed,' Luca confided. 'And my mother . . .' He broke off. 'It was not knowing that has been so dreadful. I didn't know what happened when they were kidnapped and I still don't know if they are alive or dead.'

'They sent you to the monastery?' she asked.

'They were convinced that I was a boy of extraordinary abilities and that I had to be given a chance to be something more than a farmer. They had their own farm, and it gave us a good living, but if I had inherited it after them and stayed there, then I would have known nothing more than the hills around my home and the weather. I would have done nothing but keep the farm after their death and handed it on to my son. They wanted me to be able to study. They wanted me to rise in the Church. My mother was convinced that I was gifted by God. My father just saw that I could understand numbers quicker than the merchants, speak languages almost at the first hearing. He said that I must be educated. He said that they owed it to themselves to give me a chance.'

'But could you see them again? After they put you into your novitiate?'

'Yes. Bless them, they came to the abbey church most mornings, twice on Sundays. I would see them standing at the back and looking for me, when I was a choir boy too small to see over the choir stall. I had to stand on a kneeler so that I could see them in the congregation. My mother came to visit me every month and always brought me something from home, a sprig of lavender or a couple of eggs. I know how much she missed me. I was her only child. God Himself only knows how much I missed her.'

'Did she not want to keep you at home, despite your father's ambition?' Isolde asked, thinking of the delightful boy that Luca must have been.

He hesitated. 'There was something else,' he admitted. 'Another reason for them to send me away. You see – they were quite old when they had me. They had prayed for a son for years and God had not given them a child, so there were many people in the village who were surprised when I was born.'

'Surprised?' she queried. The cobblestones were slippery; she skidded for a moment and he caught her up. The two of them paused as if struck by the other's touch, then they walked together, in step, their long stride matching easily together.

'To tell you the truth, it was worse than that,' Luca said honestly. 'I don't like to speak of it. It was an awful time. The village said that I was a changeling, a child given to my parents, not made by them. People said that they had found me on their doorstep, or perhaps in the woods. People called me a f . . .' He could not bring himself to say the word. 'A f . . .'

'A faerie child?' she asked, her voice very low, conscious of his painful embarrassment.

He nodded as if he were confessing to a crime.

'There's no shame in that,' she said stoutly. 'People say the most ridiculous things, and ignorant people long to believe in magic rather than an ordinary explanation..'

'We were shamed,' he admitted. 'There was a wood near to our house, on our own land, that they called a faerie wood. They said that my mother had gone there, desperate to have a child, and that she had lain with a faerie lord. They said that she gave birth to me and passed me off to my father as a mortal boy. Then, when I grew up and could learn languages, and understand numbers in the blink of an eye, they all said that it proved that I had wisdom beyond the making of mortals.'

Isolde's face was filled with pity as she turned to the handsome young man. 'People can be so cruel. They thought you the child of a faerie lord?'

He turned his head away and nodded in silence.

'And so your parents sent you away? Just because you were such a clever boy? Because you were gifted? Because you were so good-looking?'

'I thought then that it was a curse and not a gift,' he admitted. 'I used to stand beside my father when he was seated by the fire and he would put his arm around me, and take coins from his pocket and ask me to calculate the value if he spent half of them, if he spent a third, if he put half out at interest and earned fifteen per cent but lost the other half. And always I was right – I could just see the answers as if written on the air, I could see the numbers as if they were shining with colours, and he would kiss my forehead and say "*my* boy, my clever boy", and my mother would say "he *is* your boy" as if it should be repeated, and he should be reassured.

'And then, one summer, strangers came to the village, a travelling troupe of Egyptians, and I went down to see them with the other village children and I heard them speaking amongst themselves. The children laughed at them, and someone threw a stone; but one of the gypsies saw me watching them and said something aside to me, and I answered him – I had their language in a moment, the very moment that I heard it. That was the end of it really. Next morning we found a thick ring of salt, all around the farm-house, and a horseshoe at north, south, east and west.'

'Salt?'

'A faerie can't cross iron and salt. They thought that they would imprison me. That decided it. My parents were afraid that they would trap me inside the house and then burn the house down.' He shrugged. 'It happens. People are afraid of what they cannot understand. It was not that they did not respect my father. But I did not have playmates among the village children, I was never quite like them, I could never talk easily with them. I could not fit with them. I was different and we couldn't deny it any more. My mother and father agreed that it was too dangerous for me to be in the outside world and they sent me to the monastery for safety.'

'Did you fit there?' she asked, thinking of her own experience in the nunnery where she had been isolated and alone but for Ishraq, another outsider.

He shook his head. 'Freize took a liking to me,' he smiled. 'He was the only one. He was the kitchen boy and he used to steal food to feed me up. And as soon as they taught me to read and calculate I started to ask questions.'

'Questions?'

He shrugged. 'I couldn't help it. But it turned out that most questions are heresies.'

'And then the Ottoman slaving galleys took your mother and father?' Isolde prompted him quietly.

Luca sighed, as if he still could not bear to think of it. 'You know, it's been four years now, but I think of them every day . . . I have to know if they survived the raid. If they are alive I should save them. They did everything for me. I want to see them again. And if I am too late and they are dead, then I should honour their deaths and see them properly buried. If Johann is right and they will rise again in

60

Jerusalem then I feel as if I have to go with him. It's like a calling; a sacred duty.'

Isolde flushed a warm rose colour. 'You're not thinking of going to Jerusalem?'

Reluctantly, Luca nodded. 'Part of me feels that I should go on with my quest. I have been commanded by Milord and licensed by the Pope, I have only just started ... but if I can get permission from the lord of our order, I feel that I should go. I feel as if Johann spoke to me and promised me that I would meet my parents in Jerusalem. What calling could be greater than to see them again, before the end of all the world? At the very moment of the end of the world?'

They arrived at the quayside and turned towards the inn, dawdling to prolong their time together.

'I'm going to go too,' Isolde said fervently. 'I won't go to Hungary, not now that I have heard this. I carry the death of my father like a wound. It is terrible to me. Every day I wake up and I think I am in my old bedroom at Lucretili and he is alive, and every day I have to remember that he is dead, and I have lost my home and I am half-lost myself. If I could only see him again! Just once. I would go anywhere for that chance.'

'You really think you will see him again in Jerusalem? You believe Johann?'

'While he was speaking I was certain of it – but now – when you ask me like that, of course I'm not so sure.'

She paused, and they stood together: her hand on his arm, the seagulls crying over their heads, and the boats beside them, bobbing at anchor. A pale moon started to lift in the twilight of the winter afternoon and lay a silver path across the sea.

'I know it sounds so incredible. And yet – you are here, commanded by the Pope because he believes that the end of days is coming. The Pope himself thinks it could be any day now. We all know that the dead will rise on Judgment Day . . .' She puzzled over it, then put her hand to the neck of the plain gown as if to feel the pace of her heart. It was as if the steady beat reassured her: 'Why should it not be true? I believe Johann has a vision. This must be a sign. It has to be a sign. I'm going to Jerusalem and I pray that I will meet my father there, among the risen dead, and that he will forgive me for failing him. And he will tell me how I can win back my home.'

Moved by her grief, Luca reached out his hand and touched her shoulder, and then, more daringly, put the back of his hand against the smooth line of her chin. As soon as she felt his gentle touch on her skin, he felt her tremble. For a moment she stood quite still and then, with an inarticulate murmur, she moved aside.

'Why do you say that you failed him?' he asked very quietly.

'When my father was dying my brother told me that he didn't want me to see him in pain and despair. I believed him, and I prayed in the chapel while my father died alone. When I discovered that my brother had lied to me and stolen my inheritance, I feared that he had lied to my father about me too. What if my father died asking for me, but my brother told him that I would not come? I cannot bear to think of that.'

Her voice was choked with tears. She cleared her throat.

'Why did you trust your brother?' Luca asked Isolde gently. 'Why did you not defy him at once?'

Her beautiful mouth twisted. 'I was raised to be a lady,' she said bitterly. 'A lady should be above lies and deceit, she is honourable and trustworthy. A lady plays her part in the world with honour, and trusts a man to play his. I believed my brother to be an honourable man, the son of a great lord, raised to be as good a man as my father. It has taken me a long long time to see him as a thief. It took me long enough to understand that I had to choose my own life, find my own road. I could not trust his honour. I could not wait to be rescued.'

They resumed their slow walk towards the inn, Isolde's hand tucked in the crook of Luca's arm, their steps matched. 'D'you really think your father will rise from the grave?' he asked her, curiously.

'I don't know how such a thing could be; but now I can't help but think it. How could Johann look at me, and describe my father? How could he speak of a cold bier in a chapel if he was not seeing, with the eyes of God, my own father's bier in our cold chapel? He must know the unknown things, see things that we are blind to.'

They paused before the open door of the inn, unable to prolong their walk any longer, and Luca took both of her hands in his. 'Odd that we should both be orphans,' he said.

Isolde looked up at him, her face warm. "It makes me want to comfort you,' she whispered.

He took a breath. 'And I, you.'

They stood handclasped. Ishraq and Freize hesitated on the quayside behind them, watching the young couple.

'Would you think of me as your friend?' Luca said very quietly to Isolde.

She did not hesitate for a moment. 'We're both alone in

the world,' she said. 'I would like to have a friend who could be constant as my father was, patient as he was, faithful as he was.'

'I'd want a friend that I could be proud of,' Luca said quietly. 'Perhaps I'll never be able to take you to meet my mother. Perhaps my mother has been dead for many years. But I would like to think that I could have taken you to meet my mother and she would have liked you ...'

He broke off, suddenly remembering his vows. She felt him almost snatch his hands away from their warm mutual hold.

'Of course, I cannot think of anything more than a friendship. I am in the early stages of the priesthood, I am going to be a priest, a celibate priest.'

'Only the early stages,' Isolde whispered. 'Not yet sworn.'

Luca looked at her as if she was tempting him. 'I am not yet sworn,' he confirmed. 'I am not bound by my word. It was my intention to join the priesthood ... before ...' He broke off before he could be tempted to say, 'before you.'

~

While the crowd before the church slowly dispersed, wondering at what they had heard and what it might mean, Brother Peter waited patiently for Johann to finish his whispered confession to Father Benito. After a little while the young man stood up, crossed himself, nodded respectfully to the priest and then walked across the church to kneel in silent prayer on the chancel steps, his head resting against the thickly carved rood screen which protected the mystery of the mass from the congregation. No-one but an ordained priest was allowed near to the altar.

Behind him, in the silent church, Brother Peter glanced around, and seeing that he was unobserved, crossed the church to kneel in confession. On the other side of the screen the parish priest waited in silence.

'Father Benito, I need your advice on this matter,' Brother Peter confided, folding his hands together but clearly not preparing to confess his sins.

The priest was bowed over his rosary, saying his prayers. His hands were shaking. He hardly lifted his head. 'I can tell you nothing.'

'This could not be more important.'

'I agree. This is the most important thing. I have never known anything of greater importance in this world.'

'I have to ask . . .'

The priest collected himself and sat back. 'Ah, you will want to know if he has a true vision,' he guessed.

'I *have* to know. This is not a matter of curiosity about a herdboy with a following of half a dozen. This is becoming a mighty crusade. If they get to the Holy Land it could change everything. I have to advise Milord who advises the Holy Father whether this is a true crusade. If this young man is a charlatan, I have to know at once, we have to be prepared. If he is a saint, it is even more important: we need to know all about him. He just confessed to you. Your opinion is most important.'

The parish priest looked through the carved wooden screen at the great man from Rome. 'My son, truly, I cannot help you.'

'It is a matter of the good of the Church itself. I command you to speak.'

Again the priest refused. 'I cannot help you.'

'Father Benito, I don't need details, you need not break the seal of the confessional. Just give me an idea. Just tell me: does he sin like a mortal boy? For if he confesses like a foolish ill-educated boy who has the knack of talking to a crowd, but nothing else, then he is a fraudster on a great mission, and we can treat him as such. We have dozens like him popping up every year and we manage them for the good of the church and the glory of God. Help me to know what we must do with this lad.'

The priest thought for a moment. 'No, you misunderstand me. I am not refusing to help you. I mean that I cannot tell you anything. He confessed nothing.'

'He refused to confess?' Brother Peter was surprised at the defiance.

'No! No! He confessed nothing.' The priest looked up and met Brother Peter's amazed face. 'Exactly. I am breaking no confessional secrets for there was no confession. I have nothing to hint at, nothing that I have to hold in silence, as a sinful secret. Johann came to me and made a full confession: and there was nothing. He lives a life without major sin. I set him no penance for he had no sins to atone.'

'No man is without sin,' Brother Peter said flatly.

The priest shrugged. 'I questioned him, and there was nothing.'

'Pride,' Brother Peter said, thinking of Johann's sermon and the hundreds of people listening, and how he himself would feel if he could preach like that and call people out of their homes to walk across Christendom. 'He sees himself as a vehicle of God,' he said, thinking that would be how the boy felt.

'He takes no pride in himself,' replied the priest. 'I tested him, and this is true. He takes no credit for himself. He has no pride, though he is a leader of hundreds. He says God leads them and he walks alongside.'

'Greed.' Brother Peter thought of the young man who ate a good breakfast.

'He fasts or eats as God commands him, it depends on whether God sends them food or not. Frequently he fasts because he believes that God wants him to hunger as the poor. Mostly he just goes hungry because there is little food to be had, and all that there is, they share. I am not surprised if he ate well at your table. He would believe that God had brought the food to him, and it was his duty to eat. Did he say grace?'

'Yes.'

'Did he thank you for your hospitality?'

'He did,' Brother Peter grudgingly allowed.

'Then what more do you ask of him?'

Brother Peter shrugged.

'If God commands him to eat, he does so. If God commands him to thirst, he does so. Then God releases him and he is free to do His work.'

'Does he take the children? Does he call them away from their parents when they should stay at home? Could we call him a thief? Does he covet followers?'

'He says he does the will of God. I asked him about the children. He says that since he was called by God his sins have emptied out of him so he is a vessel, not a man. He holds only God's will, not the sins of man. I asked him specifically, and he answered with conviction. He convinced me. I think that he may be a saint in the making. In all my years of hearing confessions I have never spoken to a young man who opened his life to me and it was a clean page. I never would have expected this. It is beyond the dreams of a priest.'

'Lust?' Brother Peter said thinking of the usual confessions of young men.

'He says he is a virgin and I believe him.'

Brother Peter's head was spinning. 'Can this be true? A pure young man? An innocent?'

'Brother – I believe in him. If he will allow me, if the bishop will give me leave, I am going with him.'

'You?'

'I know. I must seem ridiculous. I am a comfortable parish priest, grown plump and lazy in a good living. But this boy knows that the end of days is coming. He told me some of the signs. They are all as the Bible predicts them. He has not been taught what to say, it has been revealed to him. He says we must be in Jerusalem if we hope to be saved. I believe God has told Johann of the end of days. I will close up my house and go with the Children's Crusade to Jerusalem, if I am allowed. I want to go more than anything in this world.'

Brother Peter rose to his feet, his head whirling. 'I must send my report,' he said.

'Tell them,' the priest urged him. 'Tell them in Rome that a miracle is happening right here and now. A miracle in this little town, before us, worldly fools. God be praised that I am here to see it. God be praised that into this sinful house should come Johann the Good to lead me to Jerusalem.'

~

Brother Peter and Luca wrote the report together, while Freize found a stable lad willing to undertake the long ride to Avezzano.

'You'll take the old Roman road,' Freize explained to the lad who had been summoned into the dining room to take the precious letter. 'It's clear enough, you can't miss your way.'

'When you get there, you must go to the Church of St Paul and ask for the parish priest,' Brother Peter told him. 'He will tell you his name is Father Josef. You can give him this letter. He will send it on.'

Luca watched Brother Peter double-fold the letter, and light a taper at the dining room fire. From his little writing box, Brother Peter took a stick of sealing wax and held it to the flame, dripping the scarlet wax in three separate pools on the fold. While the wax was still warm and soft he took a sealing ring from a cord around his neck and pressed it into the hardening wax. It left the image that Luca had seen, tattooed on the arm of the man who had recruited him into the secret order. It was a drawing of a dragon eating its tail.

'You will wait,' Brother Peter told the round-eyed lad who looked at these preparations as a man might watch an alchemist make gold. 'You will wait that night, and the next day. You will stay in the church house and they will give you food and a bed. In the evening you will go to the church again, see Father Josef and he will give you a letter to bring to me. You will take it, keep it safely, bring it to me without reading it. Do you understand?'

'The boy can't read,' Freize said. 'So you're safe enough in that. Us servants know nothing. He won't read your secrets, he would not dream of breaking your seal. But he understands what you're saying. He's a bright enough boy.'

Reluctantly, Brother Peter handed the letter to Luca, who paused for only a moment to study the seals and then passed it to the boy, who knuckled his forehead in a sort of rough salute and went out.

'What does it mean?' Luca asked. 'That seal? I saw it on the arm of the man who recruited me to the order.'

'It is the symbol of the order that you know as the Order of Darkness,' Brother Peter replied quietly. He waited till the door had closed behind Freize and then he rolled up the sleeve of his robe to his shoulder and showed a faded version of the design, tattooed over his upper arm. He looked at Luca's shocked face.

'It's pale, because I have worn it for so long,' he said. 'I entered the Order when I was younger than you. I swore to it heart and soul when I was little more than a boy.'

'No-one has asked me to take the symbol on my body.' Luca said uneasily. 'I don't know if I would.'

'You're an apprentice,' Brother Peter replied. 'When you have held enough inquiries, and learned enough, when you are wise enough and thoughtful enough: then they may invite you to join the Order.'

'Who? Who will invite me?'

Brother Peter smiled. 'It's a secret order. Not even I know who serves in it. I report to Milord, and he reports to the Holy Father. I know you. I know two other inquirers that I have served with. I know no more than them. We look for the signs of God and Satan in the world and we warn of the end of days.'

'And do we only defend?' Luca asked shrewdly. 'Or do we also attack?'

'We do as we are commanded,' Brother Peter said smoothly. 'In defence or attack we are obedient to the Order.'

'And the one that you call Milord – it was him who took me from my monastery to Castle Sant' Angelo, who spoke to me, who gave me this mission and sent me to be trained?'

'Yes.'

'Is he the commander of the Order?'

'Yes.'

'Do you know his name?'

In reply Brother Peter showed Luca the blank reports in his writing box that were already addressed, ready for dispatch. They all read only:

Urgent

'No name?'

'No name.'

'He has no name but your letter will get to him? Just that? Just the seal of the dragon? It needs no name nor direction?'

'It will get to him, if the boy gets it to Father Josef in Avezzano.'

'This Father Josef – the parish priest of the Church of St Paul, Avezzano – he is of our Order?'

'He's not called Josef. And he's not the parish priest of Avezzano. But yes, if the boy gets the letter to him, he will open it, see the sign of the Order, and he will get it to Milord. Without fail. None of us would fail to pass on a report. We never know how important a report might be. It could be news of the end itself.'

'So if there is a man in a small town like Avezzano, whose name is not Josef, who knows the seal and knows where to take the letter, there may be many men, other men serving like him, all over Italy?'

'Yes,' Brother Peter admitted. 'There are.'

'All over France? All over Spain? All over Christendom?'

'I don't know how many,' Brother Peter said cautiously. 'I know of those I need to know, to get my reports to Milord, and to receive my orders from him. Every time I leave Rome on a new inquiry he tells me who I can rely on – in any direction. He tells me who to ask for at each church along the way.'

There was a tap on the door and Freize put his head inside. 'He's gone. I have sent him on my horse Rufino, who is a good horse, and he has promised to ride, take your letter, and wait for a reply, and then come back. It wasn't easy to persuade him to go. Half the town swears that they will go on this crusade and he wanted to go too.'

Brother Peter rose. 'He is sure of the church and who to ask for?'

'Yes, and he will wait there for the reply from Rome.'

'You have told him he must not fail?'

'He's a good lad. He'll do his best. And Rufino is a good horse and can be trusted to find the way.'

'Very well, you can go.' Brother Peter released him; but Freize leaned on the door to look in at Luca.

'In deep,' was all he observed. 'In very deep.' And then he picked up the kitten and went from the room.

Inspired by Johann the Good, the people who had come into the little town for the market went back to their villages and farms and spoke of him to their friends and neighbours. Next day, hundreds more people came into Piccolo bringing food and wine and money for the Children's Crusade, and to hear Johann preach. Once again he stood on the doorstep of the church and promised them all that if they would come with him to Jerusalem they would walk again with the people that they had loved and lost. These were people who had been orphaned young, who had lost their first-born children: when Johann spoke to them of the rising of the dead they wept as if for the first time. Isolde and Ishraq went to hear him preach, standing in the hot sun of the market square with the common people. Luca and Brother Peter stood inside the shadow of the door of the church with the priest and listened intently.

'Come home,' Johann said surprisingly to the crowd, who were all born and bred within about ten miles and whose homes were mostly unwelcoming hovels. 'Come home to your real home. Come home to Jerusalem. Come home to Bethlehem.' He seemed to look towards Ishraq who was dressed as modestly as a lady on a pilgrimage, her cape shielding her face, a gown down to her ankles, and strong riding boots hiding her brown feet with the silver rings on her toes. 'Come home to Acre, those of you who were born with the taste of milk and honey. Come back to where your mother first opened her eyes. Come to your motherland.'

Ishraq swallowed and turned to look at Isolde. 'Can he mean me?' she whispered. 'Does he really mean that Acre, the beautiful Arab city, is my true home?'

'I can hear your mother calling you,' he said simply. 'I can hear her calling you from across the sea.'

A woman from the crowd called out: 'I can hear her! I can hear Mama!'

'When we get to Jerusalem and the Lord puts out his hand for us, that will be the end of sorrow, that will be the end of grieving. Then shall the orphan find his mother and the girl know her father.' He glanced towards Ishraq. 'Then shall the girl who has lived all her life among strangers be with her people again. You will be warmed by the sun that you saw first, when your eyes first opened. You will taste the fruits of your homeland.'

'How can he know?' Ishraq whispered to Isolde. 'How can he know that I was born in Acre? How can he know that my mother promised me that one day we would go home? He *must* hear the voice of God. I have doubted him; but this must be a true revelation.'

74

Around the two young women, people were crying and pressing forward, asking the young man about their families; one woman begged him to tell her that her son, her lost son, was in heaven and she would see him again. He put out his hand so that they did not jostle him, and the people at the front of the crowd fell to their knees and linked arms before him as if he were an icon, to be carried through the crowd at shoulder height on a saint's day.

'Come with us,' he said simply. 'Come and see for yourself on that wonderful day of judgment when your children, your father and' – his bright blue gaze went to Ishraq – 'your mother takes your hand and welcomes you to your home.'

Ishraq stepped forwards as if she could not help herself, as if she were in a dream. 'My father?' she asked. 'My mother?'

'They are waiting for you,' Johann said, speaking only to her with a quiet certainty which was far more convincing than if he had shouted, as most preachers did. 'The ones that you loved and lost are waiting for you. The father whose name you don't know, the mother who died without telling you. She will be there, she will tell you then. You will see them together and they will smile at you, their daughter. We will all rise up together.

'Now,' he said quietly. 'I am going to confess and pray. God bless you.'

Without another word, he turned into the doorway of the church and Brother Peter and Luca stepped back for him, and the priest Father Benito went inside to kneel with this most surprising prophet. The priest unlocked the rood screen and took him inside, up to the very steps of the altar, where only those ordained by God might go, and they knelt down side by side, the village priest and the boy that he thought was a saint.

~

The girls found their way to Luca in the private dining room talking with Brother Peter. 'We've decided, for sure,' Isolde told him. 'Ishraq is as convinced as I am. The prophet Johann has spoken to her too. We're not going to Croatia. We're not going to Hungary.'

Luca was not even surprised. 'You're going to Jerusalem? You're certain? Both of you? You want to go with Johann?' He looked at Ishraq. 'You, of all people, want to join a Christian crusade?'

'I have to,' she said almost unwillingly. 'I am convinced. At first I thought it was some kind of trick. I thought he might talk to people, to work out what to say to convince them, take a bit of gossip and twist it into a prediction so that it sounds like a foretelling. I've seen fortune-tellers and palmists and all sorts of saltimbancos work a crowd like that. It's easy enough to do: you make a guess and when you strike lucky and someone cries, then you know that you're on to something and you say more. But this is something different. I believe he has a vision. I believe he knows. He has said things to Isolde, and today he said things to me that no-one in this town knows. He spoke of me in a way that I don't even acknowledge to myself. It's not possible that it could be a lucky guess. I think he must have a vision. I think he sees true.' She looked down, not meeting his questioning eyes, and cleared her throat.

'He spoke of my mother,' she said quietly. 'She died

76

without telling me the name of my father. She died speaking of Acre, her home, my birthplace. He knew that too.'

'We believe he has a true vision,' Luca confirmed. 'Brother Peter and I have reported it to Rome. We're waiting for the reply. And I have asked if we may go with him.'

'You have?' Isolde breathed.

'He spoke to me too,' Luca reminded her. 'He spoke of my father, of his kidnap by the Ottoman slavers. Nobody knows about that but the people I have told: Freize and yourself, but no one else. Freize spoke of it once to Brother Peter, but no-one in this village knows anything about us but that we are travelling together on a pilgrimage, and that I am authorised by the Holy Father. He can have learned nothing else from kitchen-door gossip. So he must have some way of knowing about us that is not of this world. I have to assume that it is as he says – that he is guided by God.'

'No questions?' Ishraq asked him with a little smile. 'Inquirer, I thought you always had questions. I thought you were a young man who could not help but question?'

'I have many,' Luca gave a little laugh. 'Dozens. But from all I have seen, for the moment, I believe Johann. I take him on trust.'

'I too,' Brother Peter said. 'The answer should come from Rome, the day after tomorrow. I think they will command us to go with the Children's Crusade, and help them on their way.'

Ishraq's eyes were shining. 'He said that I should go home,' she said. 'I have never thought of the Holy Land as my home. I was taught to call Lucretili my home; but now, suddenly, everything looks different.'

'You won't be different?' Isolde asked her, speaking almost shyly. 'You won't change with me? Even if you find your family in Acre?'

'Never,' Ishraq said simply. 'But to be in my mother's country and to hear her language! To feel the heat of the sun that she told me about! To look around and see people with skin the colour of mine wearing clothes like mine, to know that somewhere there is my family, my mother's family. Perhaps even my father is there.'

'He spoke to you as if you were a Christian and would see the Last Day like the rest of us,' Brother Peter observed.

'My mother would have said that we were all People of the Book,' she replied. 'We all worship the same god: Jews, Christians and Muslims. We all have the one god and we only have different prophets.'

'Your mother would be very wrong,' Brother Peter told her gently. 'And what you say is heresy.'

She smiled at him. 'My mother was a woman from Acre in a country where Jesus is honoured as a prophet but where they are certain he is not a god. She was with me in Granada, in a country of Christian, Jew and Muslim. I saw with my own eyes the synagogue next to the church next to the mosque, and the people working and reading and praying alongside each other. They called it the *Convivencia* – living alongside each other in harmony, whatever their beliefs. For the enemy is not another person who believes in a god, the enemy is ignorance and people who believe in nothing and care for nothing. You should know that by now, Brother Peter.'

Three days after they had sent the message to Rome, Freize, waiting outside the little church, saw his horse, Rufino, coming down the hill and through the main town gates. He called his name, and the horse put his head up and his ears forward at Freize's voice, whinnying with pleasure, and went towards him.

Freize took the reins and led the horse down the steep steps to the quayside inn. In the stable yard he helped the weary lad from the saddle, took the sealed letter from him and tucked it inside his jerkin. 'You've done well,' he said to the lad. 'And you've missed nothing here. There's been a lot of praying and promising and some planning, but the Children's Crusade is still in town and if your Ma will let you – and I would have thought she would forbid you – you can still march out with them. So go and get your dinner now, you've been a good boy.' He dismissed the lad and turned to the horse.

'Now, let's settle you,' he said tenderly to his horse, taking the reins and leading the tired animal into the stall himself. He took off the saddle and the bridle and rubbed the horse all over with a handful of straw, talking to him all the time, congratulating him on a long journey and promising a good rest. Gently, he slapped the horse's tired muscles, and then brushed the patterned white, black and brown coat till it shone. When he had made sure that the animal had a small feed, with hay and water for the night, he lifted the ginger kitten from where she was sleeping in the manger, and went to the inn.

'Here's your reply,' he said, handing the sealed letter to Luca, who was sitting in the dining room with Brother Peter. The two men had been studying prophecies together, from the manuscripts that they had brought with them in carefully rolled scrolls and a bound Bible spread out on the dining room table before them. In the seat by the window, catching the last of the evening light, the two girls were bent over their sewing, working in silence.

Luca broke the seals and spread out the letter on the table so that he and Brother Peter could read it together. Freize and the girls waited.

'He says we can go,' Luca announced breathlessly. 'Milord says that we can go to Jerusalem with Johann.'

The two girls gripped each other's hands.

'He says that I must observe Johann's preaching, and . . .' He broke off, the excitement draining from his face. 'He says I must watch him for heresy or crime, examine everything he says, and report it to the bishop, wherever we are, if I think he says something which is outside the Church's teachings. I must question him for signs that he has made a pact with the Devil, and watch him for any ungodly acts. If I see anything suspicious, I must report him at once to the Church authorities and they will arrest him.' He turned to Brother Peter. 'That's not an inquiry, that's spying.'

'No, see what Milord says.' Brother Peter pointed to the letter. 'It is part of our usual inquiry. We are to travel with him and look for the light of God in all that he does, ensure that his mission is a true one, watch him for any signs that he is a true prophet of the end of days. If we see any trickery or falsehood we are to observe it, and report it; but if we think he is hearing the voice of God and doing His bidding, we are to help him and guide him.

'The Holy Father himself will send money and arms to help the children get to the Holy Land. He says that we are to guide them to Bari where he himself will see that there will be enough ships to take us to Rhodes. The Hospitallers will guide and guard us from there. It is their duty to guide pilgrims to the Holy Land. The Holy Father will warn them that greater numbers than they have ever seen before are coming – and then – who knows what the Hospitallers will do to guard this army of children?'

'Does your lord not expect the sea to part for the children?' Freize asked. 'Surely that's the plan? Why would you need ships? Why would you need the Hospitallers? Isn't God going to part the oceans?'

Brother Peter looked up, irritated by the interruption and by Freize's sarcastic tone. 'God is providing for the children,' he said. 'If a miracle takes place we are to report it, of course.'

'I won't spy on him and I won't entrap him,' Luca stipulated.

Brother Peter shrugged. 'You are to inquire,' he said simply. 'Look for God, look for Satan. What else have you been appointed to do?'

It was true that Luca had agreed to inquire into anything and everything. 'Very well,' he said. 'We will look clear-sighted at whatever happens. I won't entrap him, but I will watch him closely. I'll tell Johann we will travel with him and pay for the ships.'

'Does your lord send money for feeding the children?' Freize asked dulcetly.

'A letter for the priest, and for other religious houses along the way,' Brother Peter answered, showing him the messages. 'To tell them to prepare food and distribute it. His Holiness will see that they are reimbursed.'

'I'll take that to the church then,' Freize said. 'That's probably more important than the protection of the Hospitallers, who are, if I hear truly, an odd bunch of men.'

'They are knights devoted to the service of God and the guarding of pilgrims on their way to Jerusalem,' Brother Peter said firmly. 'Whatever they do, they do it for the great cause of Christian victory in the Holy Land.'

'Murderers, who have found a good excuse to wage war in the name of God,' Freize said quietly, as he went out and closed the door on his own insubordination.

~

Luca found Johann sitting on a wooden mooring post on the quayside looking out to sea. 'May I speak with you?' he asked.

'Of course.' Johann smiled his sweet smile. 'I was

82

listening to the waves and wondering if I could hear God. But He will speak to me in His own time, not mine.'

'I have written of you to Milord, the commander of our order, and he has spoken of you to the Holy Father.'

Johann nodded but did not seem particularly excited by the attention of the great men.

'The Holy Father says that I am to guide you to Bari, further down the coast, where he will arrange for ships to take you and the children to Rhodes. From there, the Hospitallers will help you to Jerusalem.'

'The Hospitallers? Who are they?'

Luca smiled at the boy's ignorance. 'Perhaps you won't have heard of them in Switzerland? They're an order of knights who help pilgrims to and from the Holy Land. They nurse people who fall sick, and support people on their way. They are soldiers too, they guard pilgrims against attack from the infidels. They are a powerful and mighty order and if you are under their protection you will be safe. They can protect you from attack, and can help you with food and medicine if it is needed. The Holy Land has been conquered by the infidels and sometimes they attack pilgrims. You will need a friend on the way. The Hospitallers will be your guardians.'

The boy took in the information but did not seem very impressed. 'God will provide for us,' he said. 'He always has done. We need no help but His. And He is our friend. He is the only guardian we need.'

'Yes,' Luca agreed. 'And perhaps this is His way to help you, with His Holy Order of Hospitallers. Will you let me guide you to Bari and we can all go on the ships that the Holy Father will send for us? It's a long way to the Holy

Land, and better for us all if there are good ships waiting for us and the Hospitallers to guard us.'

Johann looked surprised. 'We are not to walk all the way? We are not to wait for the seas to part?'

'Milord says that the Holy Father suggests this way. And he has sent me letters that we can show at holy houses, abbeys and monasteries all along the way, and at pilgrims' houses, and they will feed the children.'

'And so God provides,' Johann observed. 'As He promised He would. Are you coming with us all the way to Jerusalem, Luca Vero?'

'I would like to do so, if you will allow it. I am travelling with a lady and her servant, and they would like to come too. I will bring my servant Freize and my clerk Brother Peter.'

'Of course you can all come,' Johann said. 'If God has called you, you have to obey. Do you think He has called you? Or are you following the commands of man?'

'I felt sure that you were speaking of me when you spoke of a fatherless boy,' Luca said. He was shy, telling this youth of his deepest sorrow. 'I am a man who lost both his father and mother when he was only a boy and I have never known where they are, nor even if they are alive or dead. I believed you when you said that I should see them in Jerusalem. Do you really think it is so?'

'I know it is so,' the boy said with quiet conviction.

'Then I hope I can help you on the journey, for I am certain that it is my duty as their son that I should come with you.'

'As you wish, Brother.'

'And if you have any doubts about your calling,' Luca

said, feeling like a Judas, tempting the boy to betray himself. 'Then you can tell me. I am not yet a priest – I was a novice when I was called from the monastery to serve in this way – but I can talk with you and advise you.'

'I have no doubts,' Johann said, gently smiling at him. 'The doubts are all yours, Brother Luca. You doubted your calling to the monastery, and now you doubt your mission. You doubt your instructions, you doubt the lord of your order, and you doubt even the words you speak to me now. Don't you think I can hear the lies on your tongue and see the doubts in your mind?'

Luca flushed at the boy's insight. 'I had no doubts when I heard you speak. I had no doubts then. My father was taken by the slavers when I was only fourteen. I long to see him again. My mother was taken too. Sometimes I dream of them and the childhood that I had with them. Sometimes even now I cannot bear that they are lost to me, cannot bear to think that they may be suffering. I was helpless to save them then, I am helpless now.'

Johann was silent for a moment, his brilliant blue eyes searching Luca's face. 'You will see them,' he said gently. 'You will see them again. I know it.'

Luca put his hand on his heart, as if to hold down his grief. 'I pray for it,' he said.

'And I will pray for you,' Johann said. 'And tomorrow morning at dawn, we will walk on.'

'To Bari?' Luca confirmed. 'You will allow me to guide you and help you to Bari?'

'As God wills,' Johann said cheerfully.

∼

In the top bedroom of the inn Ishraq and Isolde were packing their few clothes in a saddlebag, for the journey on the next day. Isolde twisted back her plait of fair hair. 'D'you think the landlady would send up a bath and hot water?'

Ishraq shook her head. 'I already asked. She is boiling our linen in her washday copper and she was displeased at having to get that out for us. She washes her own things once a month. They bathe only once a year, and that on Good Friday. She was scandalised when I said we wanted more than a jug of water for washing.'

Isolde laughed out loud. 'No! So what are we to do?'

'There's a little lake in the woods outside the west gate – the stable boy told me that the lads go there to swim in summer. Could you bear to wash in cold water?'

'Better than nothing,' Isolde agreed. 'Shall we go now?'

'Before the sun goes down,' Ishraq agreed with a shiver. 'And whether she likes it or not I shall have some linen towels from the landlady to dry us off, and our clean clothes to wear.'

~

Discreetly, the two girls watched Luca talking to Johann on the quayside, checked that Freize was helping in the kitchen and Brother Peter studying in the dining room and then went up the cobbled steps to the market square, and out through the west gate. The porter watched them go. 'Gate closes at dusk!' he shouted.

'We'll be back before then,' Ishraq called back. 'We're just going for a walk.'

He shook his head at the peculiarities of ladies and let

them go, distracted by the stable boy from the inn. 'Shouldn't you be at work?' the gatekeeper demanded.

'Afternoon off,' the lad replied.

'Well the gate closes . . .'

'At sunset!' the boy finished cheekily. 'I know. We all know.'

~

The swimming lake was as round as the bowl of a fountain, tucked in the deep green of the forest, completely secluded with a guarding circle of trees, grass down to the soft sand edge, and clean clear water down to twenty feet.

'It's beautiful,' Isolde said.

'It'll be cold,' Ishraq predicted, looking at the darker depths.

'Better jump in then!' Isolde laughed, and shed her gown and her linen petticoat and, wearing only a little linen chemise, took a bare-legged run and a great joyful leap into the water. She screamed as she went under and then came up laughing, her golden hair floating around her shoulders. 'Come on! Come on! It's lovely!'

Ishraq was naked in a moment and waded into the water, shivering and hugging herself. Isolde swam up to her and then turned on her back and kicked a little spray into Ishraq's protesting face.

'Oh! Cold! Cold!'

'It's fine when you're in,' Isolde insisted. 'Come on.' She took her friend's hands and pulled her in deeper. Ishraq gave a little scream at the cold and then plunged in, swimming swiftly after Isolde who turned and splashed away as fast as she could.

They played like a pair of dolphins, twisting and turning in the water until they were breathless and laughing, and then Ishraq went to the side of the pool where they had left their clothes and gave Isolde a bar of coarse lye soap.

'I know,' she said at Isolde's little disappointed sniff. 'But it's all they had. And I have some oil for our hair.'

Isolde stood knee deep in the water and lathered herself all over, and then passing the soap to Ishraq, lowered herself into the clean water, and stepped out of the pool. She stripped off her wet chemise and wrapped herself in the linen towel, then held a towel for Ishraq who, washed and rinsed, came out too, teeth chattering.

Warmly wrapped, they combed their wet hair and smoothed the rose-perfumed oil from scalp to tip, and then Isolde turned her back to Ishraq, who twisted her golden locks into a plait and then turned her own back as Isolde plaited Ishraq's dark hair into a coil at the nape of her neck.

'Elegant,' Isolde said with pleasure in her own handiwork.

'Wasted,' Ishraq pointed out as she threw on her dress and pulled the hood of her cape over her head. 'Who ever sees me?'

'Yes, but at least we know we are clean and our hair plaited,' Isolde said. 'And we are making a long journey tomorrow, and who knows when we will be able to wash again?'

'I hope it's hot water next time,' Ishraq remarked as they took up their little bundles and set off down the road. 'Do you remember in Granada, the Moorish baths with hot steam and hot water and heated towels?

Isolde sighed. 'And in the women's bathhouses the old

lady who scrubs you with soap, and rinses you with rose-water, and then washes your hair and oils it and combs it out?'

Ishraq smiled. 'Now *that* is civilised.'

'Perhaps in Acre?' Isolde asked.

'In Acre for sure.' Ishraq smiled. 'Perhaps our next bath will be a proper Moorish bath in the Acre bathhouse!'

~

The girls got back to the inn unnoticed, and were on time for dinner that evening, ready to plan for their departure with the pilgrimage on the next day. Luca was clear that he could not ride while children walked, could not bring himself to be mounted high on an expensive horse while Johann led everyone else on foot. He was going to walk alongside them to Bari. Ishraq and Isolde said that he was right, and they would walk also; Brother Peter agreed. Only Freize pointed out that it was too far for the young women to walk without exhaustion and discomfort, that if they travelled alongside the pilgrimage they would have to stop and eat where the children ate, and that would mean that food would be scarce and poor. Were they to eat nothing but rye bread and drink water from streams? Were the ladies to sleep in barns and in fields? he demanded irritably. And how were they to carry the tools of the inquirer's trade: Brother Peter's little writing desk, the manuscripts for reference, the Bible, the money bag? How were they to carry their luggage: the ladies' clothes and shoes, their combs, their hand mirrors, their little pots of scented oils? Would it satisfy their desire to appear more humble if they walked like poor people, but Freize followed behind them riding one horse, leading four others, and the donkey with the baggage tied at the end of the string? Would they not be play-acting a pilgrimage and pretending to poverty? And how was that more holy?

'Surely we can walk with them during the day, and stay in pilgrim houses or inns for the night?' Isolde asked.

'Walk away and leave them sleeping in a bare field?' Freize suggested. 'Join them in the morning after you've had a good sleep and a hearty breakfast? And then there's illness. One of you is almost certain to take a fever, and then either you'll be left behind or we'll all have to stay with you, and nobody going anywhere.'

'He's right. This is ridiculous. And you can't walk all that way,' Luca said to Isolde.

'I could not allow it,' Freize said pompously.

'I can walk!' Isolde said indignantly. 'I can walk with the children. I'm not afraid of discomfort.'

'You'll get headlice,' Freize warned her. 'And fleas. It's not a beautiful mortification of the flesh that you'll look back on with secret pride: it's dirt and bites and rats and disease. And long tedious days of trudging along while your boots rub your feet raw and you hobble like an old lady with aching bones.'

'Freize,' she said. 'I am determined to go to the Holy Land.'

'You'll get corns on your feet,' he warned her. 'And you'll never be able to wear a pretty shoe again.'

It was inarguable, and he knew it. Despite her serious intentions she was silenced.

'You'll smell,' he said, clinching the argument with a mighty blow. 'And you'll get spots.'

'Freize,' she said. 'This is not a whim, it is a vision. I am sure that my father would want me to go. Ishraq is determined to go. We are going. Nothing will stop us.'

'What about a nice boat to Bari?' Freize suggested.

'What?'

'Go by boat,' Freize repeated. 'We can ship the horses and the baggage and the ladies by boat, we three men can walk with the children and help as we are required to do. The ladies can get there without walking, get there before us, find themselves an inn and wait in comfort till we arrive.'

He looked at Isolde's mutinous face. 'My lady, dearest lady, you will have to travel in heat and dirt when you get to the Holy Land. Don't think you are taking the easy way. Discomfort will come. If you want to trudge along in burning heat and miserable dirt, attacked half the time by madmen in turbans, scratching yourself raw with flea-bites, sleeping in sand with cobras under your pillow, your ambition will be satisfied. But do it when you get to the Holy Land. There's no particular merit in walking on rough ground in Italy.'

'Actually,' Brother Peter intervened. 'If the ladies were to be at Bari first then they could make sure that the ships were waiting for us. We'll be – what? – three days on the road? Perhaps four?' He turned to the two of them. 'If you were willing to go ahead, I could give you the papal letters of authorisation, and you could get the food ready for the children, and make sure there were enough ships. It would be very helpful.'

'You would be helping the pilgrimage, not escaping the walk,' Luca said to Isolde. 'This is important.'

'I don't know . . .' She hesitated.

'Perhaps they can't do it alone,' Freize said. 'I could go too. Perhaps I had better accompany them.'

Luca gave him a long narrow gaze from his hazel eyes. 'You go by boat as well?'

'Just to help,' Freize said. 'And guard them.'

'And so you go by comfort in the ship and escape a long and uncomfortable walk,' Luca accused.

'Why not?' Freize asked him. 'If my faithless heart is not in it? If I would only blunt your resolve with my sinful doubts? Better keep me out of it. Better by far that only those who have the vision should take the walk.'

'Oh very well,' Luca ruled. 'Isolde, you and Ishraq and Freize will go by boat to Bari, take all the horses, and we will join you there within three days. Freize, you will keep the girls safe, and you will find ships that will take the children to Rhodes, agree a price, and take the papal letter of credit to the priest and to the moneylenders.'

'I want to walk,' Isolde demurred.

'I don't,' Ishraq said frankly. 'Freize is right, we'll walk enough when we get there.'

'So we are agreed,' Brother Peter said. He opened his little writing desk and took out the papal letters. 'These will draw on credit with the goldsmiths of Bari,' he said. 'They will no doubt be Jews, but they will recognise the authority; do the best you can to get a good price. They are a wicked people. They have a guilt of blood on their heads and will carry it forever.'

Ishraq took the paper and tucked it in her sleeve. 'And yet you are depending on their honesty and their trustworthiness,' she observed tartly. 'You are sending them a letter and expecting them to give you credit on that alone. You know that they will understand the authorisation and they will lend you money. That's hardly wicked. I would have thought it was very obliging. The Pope himself is trusting them, they are doing the work that you allow them to do, they are doing it with care and good stewardship. I don't see why you would call them wicked.'

'They are heathens and infidels,' Brother Peter said firmly.

'Like me,' she reminded him.

'You are in service to a Christian lady,' Peter avoided her challenge. 'And anyway, I have seen that you are a good and loyal companion.'

'Like the women of my race,' she pressed. 'Like the other infidels.'

'Perhaps,' he said. 'We'll know more when we have landed in the Holy Land.'

Isolde gave a little shiver of joy. 'I can't imagine it.'

Ishraq smiled at her. 'Me neither.'

In the morning, after breakfast, the two girls, with the hoods of their capes pulled forward for modesty, came out of the inn door and walked along the quayside where Freize was loading the horses onto the ship which would take them south down the coast to Bari. Luca and Brother Peter went with them, Brother Peter carrying the precious manuscripts stitched into packages of oiled sheepskin against the damp, his writing box strapped on his back. On the quayside, amid the ships returning from their dawn fishing voyages, Freize was loading the donkey and the five horses.

The gangplank was wide and strong from the quayside onto the deck of the boat, and the first three horses went easily across the little bridge and into their stalls for the journey. Ishraq watched as the last horse, Brother Peter's mount, jibbed at the gangplank and tried to back away. Freize put a hand on its neck and whispered to it, a few quiet words, and then unclipped the halter so the horse was quite free. Brother Peter exclaimed and looked around, ready to summon help to catch a loose horse, but Luca shook his head. 'Wait,' he said. 'He knows what he's doing.'

For a moment the horse stood still, realising that it had been loosed, and then Freize touched its neck once more and turned his back on it, walking across the gangplank on his own. The horse pricked its ears forwards as it watched him, and then delicately followed, its hooves echoing on the wooden bridge. When it came freely onto the deck, Freize patted it with a few words of quiet praise, and then clipped the rope on again and led it into the stalls in the ship.

'They love him,' Luca remarked, coming beside the two young women. 'They really do. All animals trust him. It's a gift. It's like St Francis of Assisi.'

'Does he have a kitten in his pocket?' Ishraq asked, making Luca laugh.

'I don't know. I wouldn't be surprised.'

'I think he has been feeding a stray kitten and carrying it around,' she said. 'I moved his jacket from the dining room chair last night, and it squeaked.'

Isolde laughed. 'It's a ginger kitten – he found it days ago. I didn't know he still had it.'

Freize came back off the boat. 'There's a little cabin and a cooking brazier,' he told the girls. 'You should be comfortable enough. And the weather is supposed to be good, and we will be there in a few hours. We should get into port at about dinner time.'

'Shall we go aboard?' Isolde asked Luca. The master was on the ship, shouting orders, the sailors ready to let go the ropes. The children of the crusade idly watched the preparations.

'God bless them,' Isolde said earnestly, one foot on the gangplank, her hand in Luca's grasp. 'And God bless you too, Luca. I will see you in Bari.'

'In just a few days' time,' he said quietly to her. 'It's better that you travel like this, although I will miss you on the road. I won't fail you. I shall see you there soon.'

'Cast off!' the master shouted. 'All aboard!'

Brother Peter handed his box of manuscripts and his precious writing case to Freize to take into the little cabin. Isolde turned to go up the gangplank when she felt the quayside suddenly shake beneath her feet. For a moment she thought that a ship had knocked against the quay and shaken the great slabs of stone, and she put out her hand and grasped the gangplank's end beam. But then the shake came again and a deep low rumble, a noise so massive and yet hushed that she snatched Ishraq's hand for fear and looked around. At once there was an anxious slapping on the side of the quay as a thousand little waves rippled in, as if blown by a sudden gale, though the sea was flat calm.

The children on the quayside jumped to their feet, as the ground shook beneath them, the younger ones cried out in fear. 'Help me! Help me!'

'What was that?' Isolde asked. 'Did you hear it? That terrible noise?'

Ishraq shook her head. 'I don't know. Something strange.'

'I know that my Redeemer lives!' Johann called out. Everyone turned to look at him. He was quite undisturbed. He

97

spread his arms and smiled. 'Do you hear the voice of God? Do you feel the touch of His holy hand?'

Luca stepped forwards to the girls. 'Better go back to the inn ...' he started. 'Something is wrong ...'

The great noise came again, like a groan, so deep and so close that they looked up at the clear sky though there were no thunderclouds, and down again to the sea which was stirred with quick little waves.

'God is speaking to us!' Johann called to his followers, his voice clear over their questions. 'Can you hear Him? Can you hear Him speaking through earthquake, wind and fire? Blessed be His Name. He is calling us to His service! I can hear Him. I can hear Him!'

'Hear Him!' the children repeated, the volume of their voices swelling like a chorus. 'Hear Him!'

'Earthquake?' Isolde asked. 'He said: earthquake, wind and fire?'

'We'd better wait at the inn,' Ishraq said uneasily. 'We'd better not get on the boat. We'd better get under cover. If a storm is coming ...'

Isolde turned with her, to go to the inn, when one of the children shouted, 'Look! Look at that!'

Everyone looked where the child was pointing, to the steps of the quay where the water was splashing over the lower steps in an anxious rapid rhythm. As they watched, they saw an extraordinary thing. The tide was going out, ebbing at extraordinary speed, rushing like a river in spate, faster than any tide could go. The wet step dried in the bright sunshine as the next step was laid bare. Then, as the water receded, the green weed of the step beneath came into view, and the step below that, all the way down to the floor of the harbour.

Water was pouring off the steps like a sudden waterfall, steps that no-one had seen since they were built in ancient times were now suddenly dry and in the open air, and in the harbour bed the sea was flowing backwards, running away from the land, falling away from the walls so that the depths were revealing all the secrets and becoming dry land once more.

It was a strange and hypnotic sight. Brother Peter joined the others as they crowded to the edge of the quay and gazed down as the water seeped away. The sea revealed more and more land as it crept further and further out. The horses on the deck neighed in terror as their boat grounded heavily on the harbour floor, other boats nearby hung on their ropes at the quayside wall or, further out in what had been deeper water, dropped and then rolled sideways as the sea fled away from them, leaving them abandoned and their anchors helplessly exposed, thrust naked into the silt – huge and heavy and useless.

'And Moses stretched out his hand over the sea; and the Lord caused the sea to go back by a strong east wind all that night, and made the sea dry land, and the waters were divided!' Johann cried from the back of the crowd. There were screams of joy, and children crying with fear, as he walked through them all to stand on the brink of the quayside and look down into the harbour, where crabs were scuttling across the silt of the harbour floor and fish were slapping their tails in trapped pools of water. 'And Moses stretched out his hand over the sea; and the Lord caused the sea to go back by a strong east wind all that night, and made the sea dry land, and the waters were divided!' he said again. 'See – God has made the sea into dry land – just for us. This is the way to Jerusalem!'

Isolde's cold hand crept into Luca's. 'I'm afraid.'

Luca was breathless with excitement. 'I've never seen anything like it. I didn't dream it could happen! He said it would happen but I couldn't believe it.'

Ishraq exchanged one frightened glance with Isolde. 'Is this a miracle of your God?' she demanded. 'Is He doing it? Right now?'

On board the grounded ship, the tethered horses and the donkey were rearing against their ropes. Freize walked among them, trying to calm them down as they pulled their heads away from their halters, their hooves clattering against the wooden stalls. The wooden gangplank had sunk down at one end with the ship. Now it splintered and broke, falling down into the silt of the harbour.

'Hush, my lovelies, be calm! Be calm!' Freize called to the horses. 'We're all settled here now. High and dry, nothing to fear, I am sure. Be calm and in a moment I'll have you out of here.'

'Follow me! Follow me!' Johann cried, and started down the stone steps of the quay. 'This is the way, this is the way to Jerusalem! This is the way made straight!'

The children followed him at once, filled with excitement at the adventure. At the back someone started to sing the Canticle of Simeon: 'Lord, now lettest thou thy servant depart in peace, according to thy word: For mine eyes have seen thy salvation, Which thou has prepared before the face of all people . . .'

'God shows us the way!' Johann cried out. 'God leads us to the Promised Land. He makes the wet places dry and we shall walk to the Holy Land!'

'Should we go with him?' Isolde asked Luca, trembling with hope and fear. 'Is this truly a miracle?'

Luca's face was alight. 'I can't believe it! But it must be. Johann said that there would be dry land to Jerusalem, and here is the sea pouring away from the land!'

The children were singing like a thousand-strong choir, spilling down the steps of the harbour, some of them jumping off the wet steps and laughing as they went ankle deep into the silt, picking their way through the thick wet weeds where the shells crunched under their feet, walking hand in hand, scores of them, hundreds of them, side by side, winding their way around the grounded ships and old wrecks, to the mouth of the harbour where the sea still retreated before them, further and further out towards the horizon, far quicker than they could walk, as it built a bridge of land for them, just for them, all the way to Palestine.

'I think we should go,' Luca decided, his heart racing. 'Go with them now. I think it's a true miracle. Johann said that the sea would part for us and it has done so.'

Luca went to the head of the harbour steps, Brother Peter beside him. 'D'you think this is true?' Luca shouted, his brown eyes bright with excitement.

'A miracle,' the older man confirmed. 'A miracle, and that I should see it! Praise be to God!'

'What are you doing?' Ishraq demanded, alarmed. 'What d'you think you're doing?'

'I have to see,' Luca spoke over his shoulder, his eyes fixed on the disappearing sea. 'I have to see the new land. Johann is leading the children to Jerusalem. I have to see this.'

Freize, on the grounded boat, trying to steady the horses, suddenly let out a sharp yelp of pain. The pocket of his jacket was jumping and squirming. His fingers were bloody from where he had reached inside. He tried again and pulled out the small ginger kitten. She was a little ball of spitting terror, her fur on end, her eyes madly green. She struggled wildly in his grip, he let her drop to the deck and she bounded away, agile as a monkey, up the straining mooring rope to the quayside, racing for the inn. But she didn't go in the open door, she swarmed up the vine that grew by the door and scrambled onto the tiled roof. She did not stop there but went higher, up to the very smoke vent, and balanced on top of the highest point on the quayside, her claws scrabbling on the terracotta tiles, as she clung to the roof, yowling with terror.

'No!' Freize suddenly shouted, his voice loud and frightened over the singing of the children. He vaulted over the side of the boat, dropping heavily into the sludge of the harbour floor. He struggled round the grounded boat to the lowest of the wet harbour steps, slipping on the seaweed and grabbing a mooring ring to stop himself from falling. He crawled, his feet slipping and sliding, to the top of the steps where Luca, almost in a trance, was starting to walk down, his face radiant. Freize barrelled into him, grabbed him round the waist pushing him back to the quayside, and thrust him bodily towards the inn.

'I want to see . . .' Luca struggled against him. 'Freize – let me go! I'm going! I'm walking!'

'It's not safe! It's not safe!' Freize babbled. 'The kitten knows. The horses know. God help us all. Something terrible is going to happen. Get into the inn, get into the attic, get onto the roof if you can. Like the kitten! See the kitten! The sea is going to turn on us.'

'It's parting,' Brother Peter argued, standing his ground.

'You can see. Johann said that it would part for him and he would walk to Jerusalem. He's going, the children are going; we're going with him.'

'No, you're not!' Freize pushed Luca roughly towards the inn, slapping him on his shoulders in frustration. 'Take Isolde!' he shouted into Luca's bright face, shaking his shoulders. 'Take Ishraq! Or they'll drown before your eyes. You don't want that, do you? You don't want to see the waters come back and sweep Isolde away?'

Luca woke as if from a dream. 'What? You think the sea will come back?'

'I'm sure of it!' Freize shouted. 'Get them to safety. Get them out of here! Save the girls! Look at the kitten!'

Luca shot one horrified look at the kitten which was still clinging to the topmost point of the roof, spitting with fear, and then grabbed Isolde's hand and Ishraq's arm and hurried them both into the inn. Isolde would have held back but Ishraq was as frightened as Freize, and dragged her onwards. 'Come on!' she said. 'If it's a miracle, then the sea will stay dry. We can follow later. Let's get inside, let's get up to our bedroom. We can look from the window. Come on, Isolde!'

Freize saw they were on their way to safety and turned back and ran down the stone steps to the damp floor of the harbour, his boots churning in the deep mud. 'Come back!' he shouted to the children. 'Come back. The sea will turn! That's not the way!'

They were singing so loudly, in such happy triumph, that they did not even hear him. 'Come back!' Freize yelled. He started to run after them, slipping on the silt and the weeds, splashing doggedly through the puddles of seawater in his big boots. The slowest children at the back turned when they heard him and paused when they saw him coming, waving his arms and shouting.

'Go back!' Freize commanded them. 'Go back to the village!'

They hesitated, uncertain what they should do.

'Go back, go back,' Freize said urgently. 'The sea will turn, it will wash into the harbour again.'

Their blank faces showed that they could not understand him, their whole conviction, their whole crusade, was pressing them onwards. Johann had promised them this miracle and they believed that it was happening then and there. All their friends, all their fellow pilgrims were convinced, they were singing as they walked, further and further towards the harbour mouth where the receding sea shone white as it rushed away southwards. They all wanted to go together. They could see their road unfolding before them.

'Sweetmeats,' Freize said desperately. 'Go to the inn, they are giving away free sweets.'

Half a dozen children turned, and started to go back to the quayside.

'Hurry!' Freize shouted. 'Hurry or they'll be all gone. Run as fast as you can!'

He caught another half-dozen children and told them the same thing. They turned to go back and so did their friends who were a little before them.

Freize battled his way, pushing through the children to the front of the crowd. 'Johann!' he shouted. 'You are mistaken!'

The boy's face was bright with conviction, his eyes fixed on the sea that still receded steadily, invitingly, before him.

The harbour mouth was dry, and yet still the sea drained away and the tawny mud unrolled before them like a Berber rug, like a dry smooth road all the way to his destination. 'God has made the way dry for me,' he said simply. 'You can walk with me. Tomorrow morning we will walk into Palestine and dine on milk and honey. I see it, though you do not see it yet. I am walking dry-shod, as I said we would.'

'Please,' Freize shouted. 'Walk tomorrow. When it has had time to dry out properly. Don't go now. I'm afraid the waters will come . . .'

'You are afraid,' Johann said gently. 'You doubted from the beginning, and now you are afraid, as you will always be afraid. You go back. I shall go on.'

Freize looked back to the quayside. A scuffle caught his eye. The little girl that he had first met with the bleeding feet was trying to get back to the quayside. Two boys had hold of her and were dragging her onward, trying to catch up with Johann. 'You let her go!' Freize called to them.

They held her tightly, pulling her onwards. Freize turned and ran back for her, burst through the two of them, pulled her away. 'I want to go back to shore!' she gasped. 'I'm frightened of the sea.'

'I'll take you,' he said.

Mutely, she lifted up her arms to him. Freize bent down and swung her up onto his shoulders, and turned to run clumsily back to the quayside, ploughing through the mud which sucked wetly at his feet, calling to the children to follow him as he ran.

He could hear the church bell of Piccolo starting to toll loudly, as the villagers poured out of their homes down to the quayside, the fishermen aghast at the state of the harbour and the loss of their ships. People were staring in wonderment at the anchors and chains lying alongside the beached craft, at the lobsters, dry in their pots, at the sudden extraordinary revelation of the floor of the harbour which was usually sixty feet under water.

Freize flung the little girl up the green steps and shouted at the people gathered there, starting to come down the steps to see the floor of the sea. 'Go back! Go to your homes! Go to the hills! Get as high as you can. The waters will come back! There's going to be a flood!'

Freize ploughed his way across the harbour mud to the grounded ship where the horses were rearing and kicking in the stalls on the boat. 'Be still my dears!' he called breathlessly. 'I'm coming for you!'

A few people, remembering stories of inexplicable great waves in fairy tales and folk stories, felt the chill of old fears at their backs, and turned and started to run. Their panic was infectious, and in moments the quayside was empty, people banging into their houses and bolting the doors, climbing to the upper windows to look out towards the sea, other people running past them, up the steep streets to the highest point of the village, to the walls around the landward side of the town, some taking shelter in the church and climbing up the stone steps of the bell tower to look out to sea. A few women ran against the terrified crowd, down to the quayside, shading their eyes against the dazzle of bright sunshine on wet mud, calling their children's names, begging them to come away from the crusade, to come home.

What they saw made them moan with horror. On the dry bed of the harbour, advancing in a ragged half-circle, as if going to dance hand-in-hand, were the children, singing as they went, certain of salvation. And, beyond them, far away towards the horizon, but coming closer with incredible speed, was the white crest of a great wave, higher than a tree, higher than a house, high as the church tower itself, coming at the speed of a galloping horse. The children, looking to Johann, or with their eyes on heaven, did not see it, did not see anything. They only understood their danger when they started to feel it. The water which had been sucking away from under their feet so they were triumphantly dry-shod on the sea bed, started to gurgle and flow forwards again. The smaller children were knee deep in moments; they looked down, and cried out, but their voices were drowned in the singing.

They pulled on the hands of the bigger children beside them, trying to get their attention, but the children swung hands gladly, and went on. Then they all heard it. Over the sound of their own Canticle they heard the deep terrible roar of the sea.

When they looked up, they saw the wave coming towards them, heard its full-throated rage, and knew that the water that had flowed away so quickly, emptying the harbour in mere moments, had turned on them and was coming back as one wave, as one great surge. At once, some of them cried out and spun around, broke the line and tried to run, thigh deep in water, as if they dreamed that they could outrun the sea. But most of them stood stock still, holding each other's little hands and watching, open-mouthed, as the wall of the wave powered up to them and then fell down upon them and buried them in full fathoms in a second.

Moments later it hit the town. Boats that had been

beached on the floor of the harbour were now thrown roof-high, tossed up and dropped down again. The first wave hit the quayside wall and crashed upwards like an eruption, and then, terrifyingly, beyond reason, flowed on, out of its bounds, rushing past houses, up alleyways, towards the market square where no sea had ever been. The quayside disappeared at once underwater, the panes of the windows of the inn smashing in a fusilade, as the waves breached the walls and poured inside the inn and into all the quayside houses. In Ishraq and Isolde's bedroom the two girls flinched back as the windows popped like paper and the water poured in; they were waist deep in seconds and yet the wave still came on, the water still rose.

'This way,' Luca yelled beside them. He kicked out the frame of the window. Wood and the remaining horn panes of the window whirled away as the sea thrust him backwards. Soon the water in the room was up to their shoulders, Ishraq and Isolde off their feet, and flailing in the icy seawater as they gripped each other's hands, bobbing in the turbulence as the waves crashed into the little room and washed out again.

Luca swam towards Isolde, the current pushing them deeper into the room and away from the safety of the open window. 'Take a breath!' he shouted, and with his arm around her shoulders, he dragged her under the water as if he would drown her. She slipped from his grip and went like an eel through the broken aperture to the raging water outside. He bobbed up and saw Brother Peter supporting Ishraq, both of them, faces raised to the ceiling of the room, mouths upturned, snatching at the last inches of air.

'We have to get out of the window!' he shouted. He

gulped air, grabbed at Ishraq and thrust her deep down into the water of the room. He felt her struggle and then turn towards him and he pushed her clumsily towards the open window and swam behind her, forcing her on. A hand on his foot told him that Peter was following them.

Luca had his eyes open underwater, though all he could see was a swirl of grey and all he could hear was the terrible roar of the wave as it reclaimed the land. But then he saw that the faint square of the window was blocked, and he realised that Ishraq was not through, she was caught.

Her gown had snagged on one of the broken spars of the window; she was trapped inside the broken window frame deep below the water. Luca shot up for the ceiling of the room again, snatched a breath and dived down. He could see air pouring from her mouth in a stream of silver, as her hands struggled with the gown. Luca swam towards her, grabbed hold of her shoulders, and when she turned her face to him, pressed his mouth to hers, desperately giving her air from his mouth to hers. For a moment they were locked together, gripping like lovers as he breathed into her lungs and then he kicked up to the ceiling again, snatched at a breath, his lips against the roof beams, then he dived down again. He was afraid she was still caught. Then he saw her shrug, like a snake sloughing a skin, like a beautiful mermaid, and she was out of her gown and her chemise was a flash of white and she escaped through the hole of the window and was outside, leaving her gown waving in the flood like a drowned ghost.

Ishraq, Luca, and Brother Peter burst, choking and desperately heaving for air, into a terrifying open sea, an ocean where the village had been, with nothing around them but little islands of roofs and chimneys, the current snatching them at once and dragging them inland.

'Take my cloak!' came a scream from above.

Ishraq looked up, choking, fighting against the rush of water which was peeling her away from the roof of the inn and rushing her inland, and saw Isolde, clinging to the chimney of the inn with one hand and reaching down with the other. She was holding out her cloak twisted like a rope towards them. Ishraq grabbed it and pulled herself towards the roof, fighting the current that threatened to tear her away. She could feel the overlapping tiles like slippery steps under her scrabbling feet and hands. Clinging like a monkey, Ishraq gripped the twisted cape and swarmed up the steep slope of the roof, buffeted by the waves, crawling through the rough water, getting higher and higher until she made it into the dry on the very apex of the roof, followed by Brother Peter, and then Luca. All four of them sat astride the roof, as if they were riding it, while the crash of the water below made the building sway, and the terrifying swiftness of the surge flung loose ships at the height of chimneys towards them. They clung together in the boil and terrible noise of the flood and prayed to their own gods.

'If the building goes ...' Brother Peter shouted in Luca's ear.

'We should rope together,' Luca said. He took their capes and knotted them in a line. The girls wrapped their arms around the middle section. They all knew that they were preparing for little more than drowning together.

'See if we can catch some driftwood,' Luca shouted at Brother Peter.

Brother Peter said no more. They watched in horror as

lumber and wreckage, uprooted trees and an overturned market stall thudded into the wall of the inn, and the roof below them. They heard the roof shed its tiles into the water and the roof beams shift. An old wooden chest bobbed up from out of the attic below them and Luca reached out and grabbed hold of it, struggling to hold it against the current. 'If you fall in the water, you must hang on to this!' he shouted at the two girls, who were clinging to each other as they realised that if the building collapsed the old chest would not save them, they would go down, tumbled among roof beams and tiles, almost certain to drown.

Isolde leaned down and put her face against the ridge tiles of the inn, closing her eyes against the terror of the boiling flood around her, whispering her prayers over and over by rote, the words of her childhood, though she was too frightened to think. Ishraq stared wide-eyed as the sea boiled around them, watched the waters thrust and break on the roof, as they rose steadily higher. She looked at Luca and at Brother Peter, watched Luca struggling to hold the wooden chest balanced on the roof and saw that it might support her and Isolde but that the men would be lost. She gritted her teeth, and watched the rising water, trying to measure its height, as it broke against the roof, each time coming a little closer to them. A sudden eddy would make a high wave break over her feet and she could see Isolde flinch as the cold water snatched at her foot, but then the dip between the waves would make it seem as if it was ebbing. Ishraq held her foot very still and counted the unsteady roof tiles between her foot and the water. She glanced over at Luca and saw that he was doing the same thing. Both of them were desperately hoping that the wave was at its full height, that the flood had run inland and was now steadying, both of them trying to calculate the rise of the waters to know how long before they would be hopelessly engulfed.

Luca met her eyes. 'It's still rising,' he said flatly.

She nodded in agreement and pointed. 'It's two tiles below me now, and before it was three.'

'It will be over the roof in an hour,' Luca calculated. 'We'll have to be ready to swim.'

She nodded, knowing that it was a death sentence, and crept a little closer to Isolde. And then, slowly, after what felt like long, long hours, the waters started to become still. The sea coiling and recoiling like a wild river around the town flowed through ancient streets, spat out of hearths, swirled through windows, gurgled in chimneys; but the incoming roar of the wave fell silent, the groan of the earth was finished, and the water steadied, one tile below Ishraq's bare foot.

Somewhere, all alone, a bird started to sing, calling for its lost mate.

'Where's Freize?' Luca suddenly asked.

The group's slowly dawning relief at their own escape suddenly turned into nauseous fear. Luca, still clenching his knees on the sides of the roof, raised himself up and shaded his eyes against the bright sunshine. He looked out to sea, and then down to the quayside. 'I saw him running out towards the children,' he said.

'He turned some of them back. They got into the inn yard,' Isolde replied in a small voice. 'I saw that.'

'He turned around,' Brother Peter said. 'He was coming back in, carrying a little girl.'

Isolde let out a shuddering sob. 'What happened?' she asked. 'What just happened?'

Nobody answered her. Nobody knew. Luca tied his cloak to the chimney, and using it to steady himself like a rope, climbed down the steeply sloping roof, kicking his booted feet in between the displaced tiles. He looked down. The water level was falling now, as the sea flowed away. It was below the window of the girls' room. He held on to the end of the cloak and got his feet onto the sill of their smashed window.

'Climb down to me,' he said. 'I'll help you in.'

Brother Peter gripped Isolde's hands and lowered her down the rope of capes towards Luca, who held tight to her legs, her waist and her shoulders as she scrabbled over him and dropped into the room, knee deep in flood water. Ishraq followed, naked but for her linen chemise. Brother Peter came last.

The girls' bedroom was draining fast, the water sluicing through the gaps in the floorboards to the room below, as the water level all over the village dropped and the sea drained out of houses, down the higher streets and gurgled in drains and watercourses.

'You'd better stay here,' Luca said to Ishraq and Isolde. 'It may be bad downstairs.'

'We'll come,' Isolde decided. 'I don't want to be trapped in here again.'

Ishraq shuddered at the wet chaos that had been their room. 'This is unbearable.'

They had to force the door; Luca kicked it open. It was crooked in its frame as the whole house had shifted under the impact of the wave. They went down the stairs that were awash with dirt and weed and debris, and dangerously slippery underfoot. The whole house which had smelled so comfortingly of cooking and woodsmoke and old wine only a few hours ago, was dank and wet, and filled with the noise of water rushing away, and of loud dripping, as if it were an underwater cave and not an inn at all. Ishraq shuddered and reached for Isolde. 'Can you hear it? Is it coming again? Let's get outside.'

Downstairs was even worse, the ground floor chest deep in water. They held hands to wade through the kitchen and out into the yard. Isolde had a sudden horror that she would step on a drowned man, or that a dead hand would clasp round her foot. She shuddered and Luca looked around at her. 'Are you sure that you wouldn't rather wait upstairs?'

'I want to be outside,' she said. 'I can't bear the smell.'

Outside in the stable yard was the terrible sight of drowned horses in their stalls, their heads lolling over the stable doors where they had gasped for air; but the innkeeper was there, miraculously alive. 'I was on the top of the haystack,' he said, almost crying with relief. 'On the very top, chucking down some hay, when the sea came over my yard wall, higher than my house, and just dropped down on me like an avalanche. Knocked me flat but knocked me down on the hay. I breathed in hay while it battered down on me and then it tore me to the stable roof, and when I stopped swimming and put down my feet, I was on an island! God be praised, I saw fishing ships sail over my stable yard, and I am here to say it.'

'We were on the roof,' Ishraq volunteered. 'The sea came rushing in.'

'God help us all! And the little children?'

'They were walking out to sea,' Isolde said quietly. 'God bless and keep them.'

He did not understand. 'Walking on the quayside?'

'Walking on the harbour floor. They thought the sea had parted for them. They walked out towards the wave as it came in.'

'The sea went out as Johann said it would?'

'And then came in again,' Luca said grimly.

They were all silent for a moment with the horror of it.

'They swam?'

'I don't think so,' Luca said.

'Some of them came back,' Ishraq said. 'Freize sent some of them back. Did you see them?'

The innkeeper was stunned. 'I thought they were playing a game, they ran through the yard. I shouted at them for disturbing the horses, they were kicking and rearing in their stalls. I didn't know. Dear God, I didn't know. I didn't understand what they were shouting, or why the horses were so upset.'

'Nobody knew,' Isolde said. 'How could we?'

'Did Freize come in with the children?' Luca demanded.

'Not that I saw. Have you seen my wife?' the man asked.

They shook their heads.

'Everyone will be at the church,' the innkeeper said. 'People will be looking for each other there. Let's go up the hill to the church. Pray God that it has been spared and we find our loved ones there.'

~

They came out of the yard of the inn and paused at the quayside. The harbour was ruined. Every house that stood on the quayside was battered as if it had been bombarded, with windows torn away, doors flung open and some roofs missing, water draining from their gaping windows and doors. The ships which had been anchored in the port had been flung up and down on the wave, some washed out to sea, some thrown inland to cause more damage. The iron ring on the quay where their ship had been tied was empty, its ropes dangling down into the murky water. The gang-plank had been washed far away, and their ship and the horses and Freize were gone. Where it had grounded on the harbour floor was now an angry swirl of deep water – it was unbelievable that this had ever been dry, even for a moment.

'Freize!' Luca cupped his hands to his mouth and yelled despairingly into the harbour, towards the town, and back over the sea again.

There was no answering shout, only the terrible agitated slapping of the sea, washing too high, against the harbour wall, like a familiar dog which has risen up and savaged ter-ribly and now settles back down again.

~

The church was a scene of families greeting each other, others crying and calling over the heads of the crowd for missing children. Some of the fishing ships had been at sea when the wave had risen and some people thought that they might have been able to ride out the storm; the older men, who had heard of stories of a monster wave, shook their heads and said that such a wall of water was too steep for a little boat to climb. Many people were sitting silently on the benches which ran all round the side of the church, their heads bowed over their hands in fervent prayer while their clothes streamed water onto the stone floor.

When the wave had hit the town some people had got to the higher ground in time – the church was safe, the water had rushed through it at knee height, and anything west and north of the market square was untouched by the flood. Many people had clung to something and had the wave wash over them, half-drown them but rush on, leaving them choking and terrified but safe. Some had been torn away by the force of the water, turning over and over in the flood that took them as if they were twigs in a river in spate, and their families put wet candles in the drenched candle stands for them. Nobody could light candles. The candle which had burned on the altar to show the presence of God had blown out in the blast of air that came before the wave. The church felt desolate and cold without it, godforsaken.

Luca, desperate for something to do to help restore the village to normal life, went to the priest's house and took a flint and, finding some dry stuff in a high cupboard, lit a fire in the kitchen grate so that people could come and take a candle flame or taper and spread the warmth throughout the shaken village. He took a burning taper into the church and went behind the rood screen to the altar to light the candle.

'Send Freize back to me,' he whispered as the little flame flickered into life. 'Spare all Your children. Show mercy to us all. Forgive us for our sins and let the waters go back to the deep. But save Freize. Send my beloved Freize back to me.'

Brother Peter seated himself in the church before the damp church register and started a list of missing persons, to post on the church door. Every now and then a bedraggled child would come to the door and his mother would fall on him and snatch him up and bless him and scold him in the same breath. But the list of missing people grew in Brother Peter's careful script, and no-one even knew the names of the children on their crusade. No-one knew how many of them had walked dry-shod in the harbour, no-one knew how many had turned back, nor how many of them were missing, nor even where their homes had been.

Ishraq borrowed a cape from the priest's housekeeper and then the five of them – Isolde and Ishraq, Luca, Brother Peter and the innkeeper – went back to the inn, looking out to sea as if Freize might be swimming home. 'I can't believe it,' Luca said. 'I can't believe he didn't come with us.'

'He went out in the harbour to try to get the children to come back to land,' Ishraq said. 'It was the bravest thing I'll ever see in my life. He pushed us towards the inn and then he went out towards the sea.'

'But he always comes with me. He's always just behind me.'

'He made sure we were safe,' Isolde said. 'As soon as we were running for the inn he went back for the children in the harbour.'

'I can't think how I let him go. I can't think what I was doing. I really thought that the sea was going out, and I would walk with them, and then everything happened so fast. But why would he not come with me? He always comes with me.'

'God forgive me that I did not value him,' Brother Peter

said quietly to himself. 'He did the work of a great man today.'

'Don't talk of him as if he's drowned!' Isolde said sharply. 'He could have climbed up high like we did. He could be on his way back to us right now.'

Luca put his hand over his eyes. 'I can't believe it,' he said. 'He's always with me. I can't get rid of him! – that's what I always said.'

They stood for a moment on the quayside, looking at the empty sea. 'You go on,' Luca said. 'I'll come in a moment.'

At the inn they found the innkeeper's wife in the kitchen, furiously throwing buckets of muddy water from the stone-flagged kitchen into the wet stable yard outside.

'Where the hell have you been?' the innkeeper demanded of her, instantly angry.

'In my laundry room,' she shouted back. 'Where else would I be? Where else do I ever go when there is trouble? Why didn't you look for me? The door was jammed and I was locked in. I'd still be in there if I hadn't broken it down. And anyway, I come out here and the yard is empty and the kitchen filled with water! Where have *you* been? Jaunting off when I could have been drowned?'

Her husband shouted with laughter and clasped her round her broad waist. 'Her laundry room!' he exclaimed to the girls. 'I should have looked there first. It's a room without windows, backs onto the chimney breast – whenever there is trouble or a quarrel she goes there and tidies the sheets. But what woman would go to a laundry room when the greatest wave that has ever been seen in the world is rushing towards her house?'

'A woman who wants to die with her sheets tidy,' his wife

answered him crossly. 'If it was the last thing in the world, I'd want to be sure that my sheets were tidy. I heard the most terrible groaning noise and I thought straight away that the best place I could be was in my laundry room. I was tucked in there, heart beating pit-a-pat, when I heard the water banging into the house. I sorted my linen and I felt the cold water seeping under the door like an enemy. But I just kept arranging the linen, and sang a little song. Is it very bad in the village?'

'As bad as a plague year, but come all at once,' the innkeeper said. 'Your friend Isabella is missing and her little girl. Like a plague year, a terrible year, but all the deaths done in an afternoon, in a moment, in a cruel wave.'

The woman glanced out into the yard where the horses were drowned in their stalls, and the dog limp and wet like a black rag at the end of his chain, and then she turned her face from the window as if she did not want to see.

'Hard times,' she said. 'Terrible times. What do they think it means, the sea rushing onto the land like this? Did Father Benito say anything?'

Everyone turned to Brother Peter. He shook his head. 'I don't know what it means,' he said. 'I thought I was witnessing a miracle, the parting of the waters – now I think I saw the work of Satan. Satan in his terrible power, standing like a wall of water between the children of God and Jerusalem.'

'Perhaps,' Luca said coming in the kitchen door. 'Or perhaps it was neither good nor evil. Perhaps it was just another thing that we don't understand. It feels like our punishment for sin is to live in a world that is filled with things that we don't understand, and ruled by an unseen

God. I know nothing. I can't answer you. I am a fool in a disaster, and I have lost my dearest friend in the world.'

Quietly, Isolde reached out and took his hand. 'I'm sure everything will be all right,' she said helplessly.

'But how could a loving God ever take Freize?' he asked her. 'How could such a thing happen? And in only a moment? When he saved us and was going to help others? And how shall I live without him?'

~

As darkness fell they got the fire lit in the kitchen and they took off some of their wet clothes to be dried before it. Most of their goods, their clothes, the precious manuscripts and the writing desk had gone down with the ship. The innkeeper's wife found an old gown for Ishraq and belted it around her narrow waist with a rope.

'I have your mother's jewels safely sewn into my chemise,' Ishraq whispered to Isolde.

She shook her head. 'Rich in a flood is not rich at all. But thank you for keeping them safe.'

Ishraq shrugged. 'You're right. We can't hire another Freize, not if I had the jewels of Solomon.'

People from the village who had been washed out of their homes came to the inn and ate their dinners at the kitchen table. There was a cheese that someone had been storing in a high loft, and some sea-washed ham from the chimney. Someone had brought some bread from the only baker in the village whose shop stood higher up the hill, beyond the market square and whose oven was still lit. They drank some wine from bottles which were bobbing around the cellar, and then the villagers went back to their comfortless homes and Brother Peter, Luca, Isolde and Ishraq wrapped themselves up in their damp clothes and slept on the kitchen floor, with the innkeeper and his wife, while the rest of the house dripped mournfully all around them. Luca listened to the water falling from the timbers to the puddles on the stone floor all night, and woke at dawn to go out and look for Freize in the calm waters of the grey sea.

All morning Luca waited on the quayside, continually starting up when a keg or a bit of driftwood bobbed on the water
and made him think it was Freize's wet head, swimming
towards home. Now and then someone asked him for a
hand with heaving some lumber, or pushing open a locked
door, but mostly people left him alone and Luca realised
that there were others alongside him, walking up and down
the quayside, looking out to sea as if they too hoped that a
friend or a husband or a lover might miraculously come
home, even now, swimming through the sea that now
lapped so quietly at the harbour steps that it was impossible
to believe that it had ever raged through the town.

Brother Peter came down to see him at noon as the church

bells rang for Sext, the midday prayers, carrying some paper in his hand. 'I have written my report, but I can't explain the cause of the wave,' he said. 'I don't know if you want to add anything. I have said that Johann was following his calling, that the sea had parted as he said it would, when he was swallowed up by a flood. I don't attempt to explain what it means. I don't even comment on whether it was the work of God to try us, or the work of the devil to defeat Johann.'

Luca shook his head. 'Me neither. I don't know. I don't know anything.'

'Would you want to add anything?'

Again, wearily, Luca shook his head. 'It might just be something of Nature,' he suggested. 'Like rain.'

The older man looked towards the sea where the great wave had come from nowhere and then lain flat again. 'Like rain?' he repeated incredulously.

'There are many, many things that happen in this world and we really don't know how,' Luca said wearily. 'We don't even understand why it rains somewhere and not elsewhere. We don't understand where clouds come from. You and I are scratching about like hens in the dirt trying to understand the nature of grit. Not seeing the mountains that overhang us, not knowing the wind that ruffles our stupid feathers. We don't understand the wave, we don't understand a rainbow. We don't know why the winds blow, nor why the tides rise. We know nothing.'

'We can't blame ourselves for not understanding the wave. Nobody has seen anything like this in their lifetime!'

'But they have! It has happened before,' Luca exclaimed. 'Last night the fishermen around the fire had all heard of great waves. Someone said they thought that the pestilence –

the great plague – was first started by a wave a hundred years ago. What I am saying is that it might be caused by something other than the will of God; something which works in a way we don't yet understand but which we might come to know. If we had known more, we might have known that it would happen. When the water went out we would have known it was gathering itself to return. We could have guarded the children. And Freize ... and Freize ...' he broke off.

The older man nodded, seeing that Luca was close to breaking down. 'I'll send this off as it is,' he said. 'And we'll go on looking for him.'

'You think it's hopeless,' Luca said flatly.

Brother Peter crossed himself. 'I'll pray for him,' he said. 'Nothing is hopeless if God will hear our prayers.'

'He didn't hear the children singing hymns,' Luca said flatly, and turned and stared out to sea. 'Why should He hear us?'

~

At dinner time, Isolde went down to the quayside to find Luca, wrapped in his cloak, looking at the darkening horizon. 'Will you come in for dinner?' she asked. 'They have dried out the dining room and stewed a chicken.'

He looked at her without seeing her heart-shaped face and grave eyes. 'I'll come in a moment,' he said, indifferently. 'Start without me.'

She put a hand on his arm. 'Come now, Luca,' she whispered.

'In a moment.'

She took a few steps back and waited for him to turn around. He did not move. She hesitated. 'Luca, come with me to dinner,' she commanded sweetly. 'You can't stay here,

you do no good mourning alone. Come and have something to eat and we'll come out together, afterwards.'

He did not even hear her. She waited for a little longer
and then understood that he was deaf to her and could
hardly see her. He was looking for his friend, and could see
nothing else. She went back to the inn alone.

~

The darkness of early autumn found Luca still seated on
the quayside, still looking out at the darkening sea. A
few of the mothers whose children had been lost on the
crusade had come down and thrown a flower or a cross
made from tied twigs into the gently washing water of
the harbour, but they too were gone by nightfall. Only
Luca stood waiting, looking out to the paler line of the
horizon, as if the act of staring would make Freize visible,
as if he gazed for long enough he would be bound to see
the wet head of Freize, and his indomitable beaming smile,
swimming for home.

The church clock chimed for Matins: it was midnight.

'You fear you have lost him, as you lost your mother and
father,' a cool voice said behind him, making him swing
around. Ishraq was standing in the shadows, her head
uncovered, her dark hair in a plait down her back. 'You
believe that you failed them, that you failed even to look for
them. So you are looking for Freize, hoping that you will
not fail him.'

'I was not even there when they were taken,' he said bitterly. 'I was in the monastery. I heard the bell started to toll,
the warning tocsin that rang in the village when they saw
the galleys of the slaving ships approaching. We hid the holy

things in the monastery and we locked ourselves into our cells and prayed. We spent the night in prayer. When we were allowed to go out, the Abbot called me from the chapel and told me that he was afraid that the village had been attacked. I ran down to the village and across the fields to our farmhouse, which was a little way out towards the river. But I could see from a long way off that the front door was banging open, the house was empty, all the things of value were gone, and my mother and father disappeared.'

'They came like a wave from the sea,' Ishraq observed. 'And you did not see them take your parents nor do you know where they are now.'

'Everyone says they are dead,' Luca said blankly. 'Just as everyone thinks Freize is dead. Everyone I love is taken from me, I have no one. And I never do anything to save them. I lock myself into safety or I run like a coward, I save myself, I save my own life, and then I realise that my life is nothing without them.'

Ishraq raised a finger, as if she would scold him. 'Don't pity yourself,' she said. 'You will lose all your courage if you wallow in sympathy for yourself.'

He flushed. 'I am an orphan,' he said bitterly. 'I had no friend in the world but Freize. He was the only person in my life who loved me, and now I have lost him to the sea.'

'And what do you think he would say?' she demanded. 'If he saw you here like this?'

Luca's mask of sorrow suddenly melted and he found he was smiling at the thought of his lost friend. Colour rushed into his cheeks and his voice choked. 'He would say, "There's a good inn and a good dinner, let's go and eat. Time enough for all this in the morning."'

Ishraq stood waiting, knowing that Luca's heart was racing with grief.

A cry broke from him and he turned to her and she opened her arms to him. He stepped towards her and she held him tightly, her arms wrapped around him as he wept with great heaving sobs, on her shoulder. She said nothing at all but just held him, her arms wrapped around him in a hug as strong as a man's, rocking him gently as he wept broken-hearted for the loss of his friend.

'I never told him,' he finally gasped, as the truth was wrenched out of him. 'I never told him that I loved him as if he were my own brother.'

'Oh he knew,' she assured him, quietly and steadily in his ear. 'His love for you was one of his greatest joys. His pride in you, his admiration for you, his pleasure in your company was well known to him and to us all. You did not need to speak of it. You both knew. We all knew. He loved you and he knew you loved him.'

The storm of his weeping subsided and he pulled back from her, wiped his face roughly on his damp cloak. 'You will think me a fool,' he said. 'A woman weeping. As soft as a girl.'

She let him go at once, and stepped back to perch on one of the capstans, the mooring posts where they tied up the ships, as if she were settling down to talk all night. She shook her head. 'No, I don't think you a fool to mourn for one you love.'

'You think me a weakling?'

'Only when you were writing your life into a ballad of self-pity. I thought that you were too strong in your grief. You can't bring him back to life by your determination.

Alas, if he is lost to us then you cannot bring him back again by wishing. You have to know that there are things you cannot do. You have to let him go. Perhaps you will have to let your parents go too.'

'I can't bear to think that I will never see any of them again!'

'Perhaps the task of your life is to think the unthinkable,' she suggested. 'Certainly, your mission is to look at the unknown and try to understand it. Perhaps you are called to understand things that most people never consider. Perhaps you have to find the courage to think terrible things. The disappearance of your parents, like the loss of Freize, is a mystery. Perhaps you have to let yourself know that the very worst thing that could have happened, has indeed taken place. Your task is to start to think about it, to ask why such things happen? Perhaps this is why you are an inquirer.'

'You think my grief prepares me for my work?'

She nodded. 'I am certain of it. You will have to look at the worst things in the world. How can you do that if you have not faced them in your own life, already?'

He was quiet, turning over her words in his mind. 'You're a very wise woman,' he said as if seeing her for the first time. 'It was good of you to come down here for me.'

'Of course I would come for you,' she replied.

He was thinking of something else. 'Did Isolde come earlier?'

'Yes. She came to fetch you for dinner. But you were deaf and blind to her.'

'That was some time ago?'

'Hours.'

'It's very late now, isn't it?'

'Past midnight,' she said. She rose and came close to him as if she would touch him again. 'Luca,' she said his name very quietly.

'Did Isolde ask you to come for me?' he asked. 'Did she send you to me?'

A rueful smile flickered across her face and she took a careful step back from him. 'Is that what you would wish?'

He made a little gesture. 'I dare not hope that she is thinking of me. And today she has seen me act like a fool and yesterday like a coward. If she thought of me at all before now, she will not think of me again.'

'But she is thinking of you, and of Freize,' Ishraq claimed. 'She and Brother Peter are at church now, praying for him and for you.' She considered him. 'You know that you will serve your love of him best if you come back to the inn now and take your grief like a man, and live your life in such a way that he might be proud of you?'

She could see him square his shoulders and knew she had brought him to himself.

'Yes,' he said. 'You are right. I should be worthy of him.'

Together they turned for the inn. At the doorway, where a torch burned, set in the wall beside the door, its yellow flickering light reflected in the wet cobbles beneath their feet, he stopped and turned to her. He took her face in both his hands and looked into her dark eyes. Without fear or coquetry she stood still and let him hold her, slowly closing her eyes as she turned her face up to him. She felt a sense of belonging to him, as if it were natural to stand, face to face, all-but embracing.

Luca breathed in the scent of her hair and her skin and

put a kiss between her eyebrows, where a child would be signed with the sign of the cross at baptism. Ishraq felt his kiss where her mother used to kiss her – on the third eye, where a woman sees the unseen world – and she opened her dark eyes and smiled at him as if they understood each other; then they went quietly into the inn together.

The next day was a Sunday but nobody thought that they should rest for the Sabbath. The lower half of the town was a mess of wreckage and filth. Luca helped in clearing up the village, his teeth gritted as he shifted piles of wood and rubble and found, among the roof beams and broken spars the bodies of some of the drowned children.

Reverently, Luca and the other men used an old door as a stretcher and carried the little corpses two at a time up to the church and laid them down in a side chapel. The light was burning on the altar as the midwives of the village washed the bodies and prepared small shrouds. Luca prayed over the lost children and then went up to the cliff just outside the village walls where they were making a new graveyard for the drowned, as there was not enough space for them to be laid all together in the old churchyard.

Luca helped the men digging the graves in the hard soil, swinging a pick, and felt a sense of relief when he stripped off his shirt and worked in his breeches, sweating with the hard labour against the unyielding earth under the bright unforgiving sun.

Ishraq brought him some ale and some bread at midday and saw the grimness of his face and the tension in his broad shoulders. 'Here,' she said shortly. 'Rest for a moment. Eat, drink.'

He ate and drank without seeing the food. 'How could I be so stupid as to let him go?' he demanded. 'Why didn't I make sure that he was behind us? I just assumed he was there, I didn't think twice.'

Just then a little girl limped up to the makeshift wall that they had built around the little graveyard. 'Where's the other man?' she demanded.

The two of them started as if they had seen a ghost. It was the little girl with the bleeding feet that they had seen on the very first day. The little girl that Freize had carried back, through the mud of the harbour, just before the wave had struck.

'He told me to run back to the inn for sweetmeats,' she said accusingly. 'I'm here to tell him he's a liar. There were no sweets. The kitchen was empty, and there was a terrible noise. It frightened me so much that I ran up the hill and when I looked behind the sea was chasing me. I ran and ran. Where's the man? And where's Johann the Good and the other children?'

'I don't know where the man is right now,' Luca said, his voice a little shaky. 'We haven't seen him. He went out in the harbour to try to get all you children back to high ground, away from the sea. That's why he lied to you about sweets. He wanted you to get to safety. Then the great wave came ... but he can swim. Perhaps he is swimming now. Perhaps your companions and Johann have been washed in somewhere, and are walking back right now. We're all hoping for them all.'

Her little face trembled. 'They're both gone?' she asked. 'They're all gone? The sea took them? What am I to do now?'

Luca and Ishraq were silent for a moment. Neither of them had any idea what this little girl should do.

'Well anyway, come with me to the inn and we'll get you some food and something to wear and some shoes,' Ishraq said. 'Then we'll think what would be the best for you.'

'He saved you,' Luca said, looking at her little white face trembling on the edge of tears. 'We'll care for you for his sake, as well as for your own.'

'He lied to me,' she complained. 'He said there were sweets and there was a great wave and I could have drowned!'

Luca nodded. 'He did it to save you,' he repeated. 'And I am afraid that it is he who is drowned.'

She nodded, hardly understanding, and then took Ishraq's proffered hand and walked down the hill to the village with her.

~

Luca's day had started at dawn on the quayside looking out to sea, and dusk found him there too. But when it grew dark he came in and ate his dinner as a man who has set himself a dreary task to do. After dinner he prayed with Brother Peter and the little party listened as Brother Peter read the story of Noah, of men and women and the animals saved from a Flood. The little girl, whose name was Rosa but who answered to the name of Ree, had never heard the story before and went to bed with her head full of the rainbow at the end of the story.

The rooms had been dried out and the landlady had borrowed dry bedding. She offered Ree a truckle bed in the warm kitchen. The four travellers, so conscious that they were missing one, that they should be five, went to their beds early. The inn was filled with people who had come in from villages to the north of Piccolo who had lost their children to the Crusade, but hoped that they had been saved from the wave. The murmur of their quiet talking, and some of the mothers crying, went on all night. Brother Peter and Luca took a share in the big bed of the men's room but Luca spent the night gazing blankly at the ceiling, not sleeping at all.

Isolde and Ishraq went to their bedroom and plaited each other's hair in unhappy silence.

'I keep thinking about him,' Isolde started, 'and how sweet and funny he was.'

'I know.'

They had no night gowns, so they hung their robes on the post of the bed and prepared to sleep in their linen shifts. Isolde knelt in prayer and mentioned Freize by name. When she rose up, Ishraq saw that her eyes were red.

'He ran back for the horses,' Ishraq said. 'When he heard them crying and neighing. He knew that something bad was happening. He wouldn't leave them on board. He called the children to shore, he saw that we were safe, and then he went to the horses.'

Isolde climbed into the bed. 'I've never met a man more steady,' she said. 'He was always cheerful and he was always brave.'

'I was unkind to him,' Ishraq confessed. 'He asked me for a kiss and I threw him down in the stable yard at Vittorito. I regret it now, I regret it so much.'

'I know he said that he was offended at the time, but I think he found it funny,' Isolde volunteered. 'I think he liked you for your pride. He spoke of it and laughed, as if he were offended and admiring, both at once.'

'Right now, I wish I had given him a kiss,' she said. 'I liked him more than I told him. Now I wish I had been kinder.'

'Of course you could not kiss him,' Isolde said sorrowfully. 'But it was so like him to ask! I wish we had all been kinder to him. We never tell people that we love them for we think, like fools, that they are going to be with us forever. We all act as if we are going to live forever, but we should act as if we would die tomorrow, and tell each other the best things.'

Ishraq nodded, she got into bed beside her friend. 'I love you,' she said sadly. 'And at least we have always said goodnight like sisters.'

'I love you too,' Isolde replied. 'D'you think you can sleep?'

'I just keep thinking of the wave, that terrible wave. I keep thinking of him out in the water, under the water. I just keep thinking that if he is drowned – what difference does it matter if I sleep or not? If he is drowned, what would it have mattered if I had kissed him or not?'

They lay in silence until Isolde's quiet breathing told

Ishraq that she had fallen asleep. She turned in the bed and closed her eyes, willing herself to sleep too. But then her dark eyes suddenly snapped open and she said aloud: 'The kitten!'

'What?' Isolde murmured sleepily but Ishraq was already out of bed pulling her cape over her shift, stepping into her slippers.

'I have to get the kitten.'

'Go to sleep,' Isolde said. 'It's probably tucked up warm in the hay loft. You can get it in the morning.'

'It's not in the hay loft. I'm going now.'

'Why?' Isolde asked, sitting up in bed. 'You can't go now, it's dark.'

'There's a ladder in the men's room,' she said. 'They were mending the roof beams today. There's a ladder from their room that goes through the beams and up to the roof.'

'Why?'

'Because the kitten's still up there.'

'It's almost certainly gone. It'll have got itself down when the roofer was up there.'

'What if it hasn't?' Ishraq rounded on her friend. 'Almost the last thing I saw Freize do was lift that kitten out of his pocket, and it was when it ran for the roof that he knew of the danger. It warned us. We should make sure it's safe.'

'It didn't know what it was doing.'

'But Freize did. He was kind to it, just as he was kind to everyone, to every animal. I'm going to get the kitten down. *He* wouldn't leave it there till morning.'

'Ishraq!' Isolde cried out, but the girl was already pulling on her cape, opening the ill-fitting bedroom door, crossing the little landing, and opening the door of the men's room.

Ishraq heard the snoring of several men, and grimaced at her own embarrassment. 'I am sorry,' she said clearly into the darkened room. 'But I am going to walk through this room and go up that ladder.'

'Is that a lass?' came a hopeful, sleepy inquiry. 'Wanting some company? Want a little kiss and a cuddle, bonnie lass? Want a little company?'

'If anyone touches me,' Ishraq went on in the same courteous tone, closing the door behind her and stepping carefully into the dark room. 'I will break his hand. If two of you try it together, I will kill you both. Just so you know.'

'Ishraq?' said Luca, shocked from sleep. 'What the hell are you doing?' He rose up out of the darkness, naked but for his breeches, and they met at the foot of the ladder.

'Fetching the kitten,' she said. 'Leave me alone.'

'Are you mad? What kitten?'

'Freize's kitten,' she said. 'The one he had in his pocket.'

'It'll have got itself down.'

'I'm going to see.'

'In the middle of the night?'

'I only just remembered it,' she confessed.

'Oh for God's sake!' Luca was suddenly furious with her, worrying about a kitten in a town filled with parents who had lost their children. 'What does a kitten matter? In the middle of all this? In the middle of the night when half these people have cried themselves to sleep and everyone is missing someone?'

Ishraq did not answer him but turned and put her foot on the first rung of the ladder. 'It's pitch black,' Luca cautioned. 'You'll fall and break your neck.'

He made a gesture to stop her, but she slapped his hand

away and went up the little ladder to the roof. A ridged plank, a scrambling board, stretched up to the apex of the roof and she went up it like a cat herself, on her hands and bare feet. She could see nothing but the darkness of the roof against the greyer skyline. She got to the very top and sat astride, gripped the tiles with her knees, feeling them sharp through the thin linen of her shift. She heard her harsh breathing and knew that she was afraid. She raised her head and looked at the chimney. Of course, there was no kitten there. She bit her lip as she realised that now she would have to make her way down again, that she had taken a grave risk and for nothing.

'Kitten?' she said to the empty roofs of Piccolo, seeing the streets below them torn by the sea and cluttered with driftwood, the doors banging empty on wet rooms. 'Kitten?'

A tiny little yowl came from the base of the chimney, where the tiles were warmed by the escaping smoke. Tentatively, the little animal rose up and stalked towards her, along the narrow tip of the roof.

'Kitten?' Ishraq said again, utterly amazed.

It came towards her outstretched hand and she picked it up, as a mother cat would, by the scruff of its skinny little neck, and she tucked it under her arm, holding it tightly against her. A muffled mew told her that it was uncomfortable but safe, as she crouched low on the roofer's board and went down again till her questing feet found the ladder, and then went one rung after another, through the hole in the roof into the darkened room until she felt Luca's hands on her waist and he lifted her down and she was safe inside the room with his arms around her.

'I've got it,' she said.

For the first time in long days she heard a chuckle in his voice. 'You're mad,' he said. 'That was the most ridiculous thing to do, the stupidest thing I have ever seen.'

But he did not let her go and for a moment she leaned against his naked chest feeling his warm skin and the prickle of soft hair.

'I was terribly afraid,' she admitted.

She felt his cheek against her hair, and the warmth of his body against her own, and she paused. For a moment she thought that anything might happen, and she did not draw back. It was Luca who steadied her on her feet, then stepped away, releasing her and saying, 'Are you going to let it go?'

'I'll take it to the kitchen and get it some milk,' she said. 'I'll keep it for tonight. If we had not seen it run we would not have known we were in danger. We owe our lives to it.'

He took her hand and guided her through the room full of sleeping men, and closed the door behind them.

'It's an odd thing,' he said. 'Odd that it knew to get up high.'

The kitten struggled in Ishraq's grip and she put it gently down on the floor. The tiny creature shook its head, as if complaining at being held so tight, and sat on its fluffy rump and washed its back feet, and then found a warm corner in the log basket by the fire, and settled down for sleep.

'There's a writer,' Ishraq said, trying to remember her studies. 'Oh! I can't remember his name! Aelianus or something like that. He says that frogs and snakes know when there is going to be an earthquake – they get out of their holes in time.'

'How do they know?' Luca demanded. 'What do they know?'

'He doesn't say,' she said. 'I read him in the Arab library in Spain. I can't remember more than that.'

They walked up the stairs together to the doorway of her room.

'Why was it so important to you that you should save it?' he asked her in a whisper, conscious of the many sleepers in the quiet house – Isolde just the other side of the door. 'Why did the kitten matter, when so much else has been lost? You're not sentimental about animals. Yet you risked your life.'

'I suppose, for that very reason: that so much has been lost,' she said. 'We failed to save the children, we failed to save half the town, we came with all our learning and your mission to understand and yet we knew nothing and when something so terrible happened we could do nothing. We were useless. We did not even save ourselves. We lost Freize, though he was the only one who knew what was happening. But I could at least save Freize's kitten.'

He took her hand and held it for a moment. 'Goodnight,' he said quietly. 'God bless you for that. God bless you for thinking of him.' And then he turned and brought her hand, palm up, to his mouth, and gently put a kiss in the middle, then closed her fingers over it.

Ishraq closed her eyes at the touch of his mouth on her hand. 'Goodnight,' she whispered, and held her fingers tight where his lips had touched her palm.

In the morning, the four of them, with Ree trailing behind Isolde at a faithful trot, went to the church where they helped the harassed priest and clerk to write out descriptions of children who were missing, to post on the gate of the little church. The pieces of paper fluttered in the wind, naming children who might never see their homes again, calling on parents who would never come to find them. A queue of people waited to confess to the priest, and the sense of death was heavy in the little church – it lay over the harbour like a low cloud. More and more people were coming slowly in the little gate to the north of the town, seeking the children who had gone with Johann, hoping that they had escaped the flood. They looked at the slurry of filth and water and the broken timbers in the market square as if they still could not believe that an evil tide had flowed high into the very heart of Piccolo and receded, leaving nothing but devastation.

In the lady chapel alongside the church the little bodies were being prepared for burial. Grim-faced, Luca and Brother Peter noted the clothes, the hair colour, the age, any little oddness of appearance, or brightness of hair, so that the children might be identified if their parents ever came seeking them. When they had looked into every blue, blanched face, and noted every missing tooth and freckled nose, they waved the two wise women forward who sewed the bodies into the newly-made shrouds, and laid them, two to a roughly-made stretcher, ready to be carried to the new cemetery beyond the walls of the town, for burial.

The wise women, who served as folk healers, as midwives and layers-out in the little village, did their work with a steady reverence for the little bodies, but they looked askance at Brother Peter and Luca; and when Isolde, Ishraq and Ree came into the church they turned away their heads and did not greet them at all.

'What's the matter with them?' Ishraq muttered to Isolde, sensing the hostility but not understanding it.

'They'll be grieving,' Isolde suggested.

The new cemetery had been made beyond the church, just outside the walls of Piccolo, on newly-consecrated ground beyond the north gate. It was overlooking the sea, and here the gravediggers stood around, leaning on their spades, beside a great hole, dug deep and wide for all the children to be laid together, just as they had rolled up together in sleep when they were following Johann and believed themselves to be blessed. Isolde took one look as the men laid the little shrouded bodies gently in the bottom of the wide trench, and then led Ree to stand behind the priest, where his robes, billowing in the wind from the sea, hid the view of the grave and the little bodies bundled together.

Father Benito read the service for burial, his voice clear over the constant crying of the seagulls, and the more distant noise of people sweeping their houses, cleaning their wet rooms, and repairing roofs and windows all over the town. Half a dozen people attended the little service, and as they walked away from the gravediggers, filling in the great hole with the dusty soil of the region, the priest promised that he would commission a stone monument to name the children as the pilgrims who walked into the sea. 'If you ever come back here, you will see that we have not forgotten them,' he said to Brother Peter. 'Nor our own losses.'

'D'you know yet how many of the townspeople are missing?' Luca asked quietly.

The priest crossed himself. 'About twenty people,' he said. 'And half a dozen of our own children. It is a terrible blow but this is a community of people who experience terrible blows, very often. In a bad plague year we would lose that number. If there is a storm which catches the fishermen at sea we might lose a ship or even two, five or six fathers lost at sea and five or six families thrown into grief and want. When the Black Death came through here a century ago, the village was emptied – half of them dead in a month, the fields barren of crops because there was no one to plant, the fish spawned in the sea without fishermen! God sends these things to try us; but this week He has sent us a trial indeed.'

'A curse on them not a blessing!' they heard a woman pantingly scream, running up the stone steps, out of the little town gate, and then ploughing breathlessly up the hill towards them, her gown bunched up in her fist, her hair wildly loose, her face ugly with grief. 'Let Satan drag them down to hell! You should have thrown their bodies over the cliff, not given them a grave in sacred ground. Curse them all!'

'What's this?' the priest spread his arms wide and intercepted her as if she were a runaway horse, halfway up the hill. 'What's this, Mistress Ricci? What are you doing running around like this? For shame, Mrs Ricci! Calm yourself!'

She glared wildly around, it was obvious that she hardly saw him. 'They should be flung in the sea not buried with rites!' she cried. 'Beware. They are the storm-bringers! You are honouring our murderers! Demons! Every one of them!'

Half a dozen people, some coming down the hill from the simple funeral, others attracted from inside the village by the noise at the gate, started to gather around. 'Storm-bringers?' somebody repeated, a note of fear in their voice. 'Storm-bringers?'

'Devils,' she said flatly. 'These false children, saying that they were on a crusade! Weren't they storm-bringers all along? Pretending to a holy quest, just to trick us? Were they mortals at all, that they appeared here without so much as a father or mother between them? Led by a boy as beautiful as an angel but with strange sea-green eyes? And we gave them bread, and meat and cheese and they unleashed this horror on us? And now my son is missing at sea and my husband too, and the storm-bringers have destroyed our peace. And you dare to bless them? And bury them like

Christians? Giving them our ground just as we gave them our own kin?'

The priest exchanged one anxious glance with Luca.

'What is she talking about?' Luca asked quickly.

'This is a fishing town, dependent on the sea for their livelihood, dependent on good weather for their safety,' Father Benito answered him. 'They cling to the belief that there are storm-bringers who can make spells and call up bad weather.'

'They believe this as a truth?' Luca whispered. 'A literal truth? They think that people can whistle up a wind, bring down a storm?'

'They have seen such things.' Father Benito spread his hands. 'Inquirer, I can tell you on oath. I have seen such things. I saw a woman call up a storm onto the mast of the ship of a man she hated. I saw it with my own eyes: the woman swore a curse on him as his ship sailed from port, and the one deckhand who swam to safety spoke of cold terrible lights dancing around the mast until the ship went down.'

'We have had a crusade of storm-bringers, God help us,' the woman cried out. 'And then you bury them in holy ground?'

The priest turned to her. 'Mistress Ricci, the children were drowned as innocents. They were on a holy crusade. They were singing hymns as they walked out to sea.'

She shot a pointing finger at Ree. 'All of them?' she demanded, her face twisted with cunning. 'Were they all drowned? Or did some of them cause the wave but then escape scot-free? Is there not, right here, a little girl who was one of the first into town and begging for bread, and yet she ran through the town ahead of the wave, silent – not warning anyone – and now here she is at the funeral of the others? Rejoicing in her work? Taunting us? Who is she? And what's she going to do next? Bring down thunder? A plague? Are snakes going to come out of her hair? Frogs from her mouth?'

'Now, that's enough,' Isolde commanded quietly, stepping forwards to shield the little girl. 'She's just a child. I am sorry for your grief, Mrs Ricci, but we have all lost someone we love. We must comfort each other . . .'

'But who *are* they?' Mrs Ricci looked from Isolde's sympathetic face to Luca. 'And how can you be so sure that they *are* mortal children? All very well for you to say that she is a child, that they were mortal children, but they didn't act like mortal children. They came without parents, from who knows where! Did they not call up the great wave and ride away on it? Like the storm people they are?'

The priest shook his head sorrowfully, raised his hand in blessing and turned away from the angry woman, refusing to answer her questions. He made his way through the little gate into the town, but nothing would discourage Mrs Ricci, and now the wise women were beside her, staring at Ree and clenching their hands in the gesture against witchcraft.

'This is ridiculous,' Isolde drew Ree to her side, then went to follow the priest. At once the three women darted forward and started to close the gate against her. Ishraq stepped quickly forwards and took the weight of the wooden door, pushing back against the angry women, her dark gaze on Mrs Ricci. 'Don't,' she advised briefly. The three women, cowed by Ishraq's gaze and the strong push at the gate, gave way and Isolde and Ree walked through it, Ishraq closely behind them as if on guard.

'No, wait,' a man said, putting a hand out to delay Father Benito as he headed for the church. 'Not so fast, Father. Answer the women. What they say is true. There were children who ran back into town ahead of the flood. How did they know to run? Some of them got clear away?'

'Did they warn the others?' another man asked. 'Did they warn us? No! They didn't!'

Another woman nodded. 'They ran in silence,' she said. 'One went past me and never said one word of what was coming.'

Ree's cold hand crept into Isolde's palm. 'We were just running for fear,' she whispered.

Ishraq stepped up beside Isolde, putting the child between them as if to protect the little girl from the increasingly angry crowd who were now blocking the lane from the church, their voices echoing loudly in the narrow street. Father Benito went on through them, and climbed the steps to the church turning to see more people joining the crowd from the market square, people coming out of their houses, still dirty from their work of salvage and repair, their faces suspicious and fearful.

'Did they not tempt our children into the harbour with their promises? Did they not bear false witness and lure us on? And then the wave came. What about their leader, Johann? Have we seen his body? Or did he go sailing back into the clouds having called up the wave to drown us all?'

'That's right!' someone said from the back of the crowd. 'We don't know who they were, and they came just before the wave.'

'They called up the wave!' someone shouted. 'You're right, Mistress Ricci! They brought the wave down on us!'

'I will have vengeance!' Mrs Ricci raised her voice above the growing murmur of the crowd. 'I swear I will have vengeance for my son and for my husband! I will see the bringers of storms burned as witches and their ashes scattered into their own storm winds.'

Isolde flinched at the words and tightened her grip on Ree, who crept as close as she could get, as if she would hide under Isolde's rough cape. Luca and Brother Peter went up the steps of the church to Father Benito, readying themselves to face the crowd, to try to calm them. Luca glanced across to see Ishraq rise gently to her toes, as if preparing for a fight.

'Now let's all be calm,' Luca said firmly, pitching his voice so that it could be heard over the crowd and the mad crying of the seagulls. 'I am an inquirer, appointed by the Pope himself. I have been sent out into Christendom to make a map of fears, and if your good Father Benito agrees that we should hold an inquiry into this strange and frightening flood then I will do so here.'

The crowd rounded on their priest. 'Call an inquiry!' someone shouted. 'Name the wicked ones!'

Father Benito paused. 'You want me to ask an inquirer of the Holy Father's own order to ask why the sea should surge into Piccolo?' he asked sceptically. 'Why don't I ask him what makes rain? Or why thunder is so loud?'

'You laugh at her grief?' one of the wise women accused him, pointing to Mrs Ricci. 'You won't answer her? You won't even hear us?'

The angry murmur of the crowd rose into a roar of

outrage. Father Benito saw that there was no reasoning with them like this. He glanced at Luca and surrendered. 'Very well. As you wish. Brother Luca Vero – would you hold an inquiry? We should hear what these good women have to say. It will be better for us all if all the fears are spoken aloud and you can tell us if there was anything that we could have done to prevent the flood.'

'There!' Another of the wise women was triumphant. 'We will name the guilty ones!'

'I will inquire into the cause of this wave, and I will tell the Pope what I decide.' Luca ruled. 'If anyone has caused it, I will see that they are charged with causing such a disaster, and I will see that they are punished.'

'Burned,' Mrs Ricci insisted. 'And the ashes blown away on the storm wind that they called up.'

'I will see that justice is done,' he promised, but his level tones only angered her more. She dived towards him and snatched at his hands, shouting furiously into his young face. 'You know there are witches who call up storms? You know this?'

Luca had to force himself not to flinch away from her. 'I know that many people believe this. I haven't found anyone guilty of such a thing myself. But I have read of it.'

'Read of it!' someone said scornfully. 'You've just seen it happen! What book can tell you what has just happened to us? What book was ever written that speaks of a wave that destroys a town, on a sunny day? For no reason?'

Luca looked around; the little crowd around them was steadily growing in number, as more and more people came up from the market square, and stepped out of the doorways of their houses. They were no longer pale with grief, shocked into silence; they were angry and becoming dangerous, looking for someone to blame for their tragedy.

'I think there may be books which tell of this,' he said carefully. 'I have not read them myself, it is the wisdom of the ancients which the Arabs have in their libraries. This is something that we should understand, so as to make ourselves safe. I will consider carefully what you, and everyone else has to say. I will start my inquiry this afternoon, at the inn.'

'You *should* start there indeed,' one of the midwives from the church said spitefully. 'That's the very place to start. You could start in the inn, in the upper room, in the attic bedroom.'

'What?' Luca asked baffled at the sudden rise of hostility in her voice, at the meaning of her accusation.

She raised a pointing finger. The crowd was silent, watching as she slowly turned around until she was facing Ishraq and Isolde, the little girl Ree between them. At once there was a ripple of approval.

'Name them!' someone said.

'Go on!'

'Name the storm-bringers!'

'The upper room,' she said. 'The safe room. Safe for them, up there, calling up a storm; calling up a terrible wave and then sailing up to perch on the roof like seagulls while the flood drowned us mere mortals beneath them.'

'They didn't fly up to the roof!?'

'Didn't they wait out the storm safe and high above the town?'

'I can vouch for these two ladies,' Luca interrupted. 'I was on the roof myself.'

'You said yourself that the Arabs knew how the waves were caused . . .'

'I said they had the books, they are books from the ancients . . .'

'She's an Arab! Isn't she? Does she know Arab learning? Does she know how to call up a wave?'

Ishraq stepped forward to defend herself, her dark eyes blazing, as Luca put up his hand to command silence. 'This young woman is well-known to me,' he said. 'She is in the household of the Lord of Lucretili, a Crusader Lord, a Christian Lord. There is no question that she could have done anything wrong. I can promise you . . .'

There was a sudden swirl of seagulls, disturbed from feeding on the flooded rubbish of the town, and they spiraled upwards into the sky, screaming their wild calls, right above the heads of the crowd.

'The souls of the drowned!' someone exclaimed.

Several women crossed themselves.

'Calling for justice!'

'I can promise . . .' Luca went on.

'You can't,' one of the wise women cut disdainfully through his speech. 'For you don't know the half of it. You were talking to Johann the Pilgrim, blind as a fool, when the two young women were outside the walls of the town calling up a storm in the green lake.'

There was a murmur of real consternation. A woman drew back from Ishraq and spat on the ground before her. Half the women of the crowd crossed their fingers, putting their thumb between the second and third finger to make the old sign against witchcraft, making their hands into fists.

'The green lake?' someone demanded. 'What were they doing there?'

'What is this?' Brother Peter asked stepping forward.

The old woman did not retreat, but her friend joined her and they both stood beside Mrs Ricci, their faces contorted with hate. 'We saw them,' she said so loudly that the newcomers at the very back of the crowd could hear every word of her damning accusation. 'We saw the two young women, dressed so dainty and looking so innocent. Slipping out of town as night fell and coming back all wet in darkness. They went to the green lake and summoned a storm at twilight. And the next day the wave came. The young women called the wave up that night, and next day the bad children led our children into its path.'

'Of course we did not!' Isolde burst out, looking round at the pinched angry faces. 'You must be mad to think such a thing!'

'Mad?' someone shouted. 'It is you that are mad to bring such a thing down on us!'

'Calling up a storm in the green lake, leading our children out to drown. "Thou shalt not suffer a witch to live!"'

'Yes!' a man shouted from the back of the crowd. 'The Bible itself says: "Thou shalt not suffer a witch to live!"'

The mass of people pressed closer to the two young women and the little girl between them. Ree dived beneath Isolde's cloak and clung around her waist, crying for fear. Isolde was as white as the kerchief over her hair. Ishraq stepped in front of her, spread her hands, balanced on the balls of her feet, ready to fight.

Luca spread his arms, raised his voice. 'These are my

friends,' he declared. 'And we have lost our own friend to the sea, just as you have lost your dear ones. You cannot think that these young women would call up a wave that would drown our friend.'

'I *do* think it,' Mrs Ricci hurled the words at him. 'We all think it. It is you who are misled. How will you hold an inquiry if you will not ask the most important questions? What were they doing in the lake?'

Baffled, Luca turned to Isolde. 'What *were* you doing in the lake?'

She flushed red with anger that he should interrogate her before this crowd. 'How dare you ask me?'

His temper flared with his fear of the crowd. 'Of course I ask you! Don't be such a fool! Answer me at once! What were you doing?'

'We were washing,' she said, disdainful of him, of the crowd. 'We went for a wash.'

'Washing!' the women scoffed. 'In the green lake? As night fell? They are storm-bringers, you can see it in their faces.'

There was a dangerous roar of agreement from the crowd and it encouraged the wise women on the attack.

'You will name the storm-bringers?' the woman pressed Luca. 'These women who came with you, and the child who came later, their little accomplice? You will try all three of them?'

'It was the children and the two women who called up the wave. That child would know. You must question her,' a man commanded from the back of the crowd, his jacket dirty with sludge from baling out his house. 'And we will burn all three of them together.'

'Yes!' a new woman agreed with him. 'If they are guilty we will drown all three of them in our own harbour.'

Ree's little hand clenched onto Isolde's steady grip. 'What are they saying?' she whispered. 'What do they think we have done?'

'I assure you these women are innocent,' Luca began. 'And the child also.'

'Then try them!' someone shouted.

'You say that you are an inquirer – hold an inquiry!'

'Right now!'

'I will hold an inquiry,' Luca tried to seize control of the angry crowd. 'I will hold an inquiry this afternoon. A proper inquiry . . .'

'Not this afternoon – now!' the man with the dirty jacket shouted him down.

'I'll hold an inquiry,' Luca insisted through gritted teeth. 'A proper inquiry at the time that I appoint, and Brother Peter will write a report to the lord of our order and to the Holy Father. And you shall give evidence on oath of what you have seen –' he glared at the angry women – 'what you have really seen – not what you imagine. And if there has been any witchcraft or magic I will find it out and punish it.'

'Even if she has seduced you with her witch skills?' Mrs Ricci asked, her voice clear and accusing. 'She, who crept into the men's room in the night?'

Isolde's cheeks burned red for shame, but it was Ishraq who stepped forward and spat out her reply. 'There is no witch, and there is no seduction. There are friends and fellow travellers, Christians and pilgrims and a terrible, terrible tragedy which you make worse by your slurs and scandals. Let the inquirer hold his inquiry without fear or favour and we will all abide by his judgement.'

'Right now, then,' Mrs Ricci insisted.

'Right now,' Brother Peter conceded, frightened by the hostility and the numbers of the crowd. 'We'll go to the inn and meet in the dining room. I'll get some paper and ink from Father Benito. We will hold an inquiry, as we are bound to do, and you shall have your say.'

The man in the dirty jacket suddenly lunged forwards, grabbed Luca by the jacket, thrust his big face forwards. 'Right now!' he shouted. 'We said right now, we mean right now! Not down at the inn! Not when you have fetched paper! Not when you have whispered together and made up a story. Now! Justice for the drowned!'

Luca pushed him away but he was a strong, angry man, and he did not release his grip. Ishraq flexed her fingers and looked around as if to measure how many people might try to drag them down. Isolde saw from her face that she thought they would not escape a beating, perhaps worse. The two young women stood a little closer, knowing that they were hopelessly outnumbered.

'Justice for the drowned!' someone else shouted from the back and then there were more people, running up the narrow streets, shouting and catcalling. 'Justice for the drowned!'

'Right now,' Luca offered. Gently he pushed the big man away, sensing that the whole crowd was on the edge of a riot. 'Where? In the church?'

'In the church,' the big man agreed, and he released Luca and led the way to the church with half the village following, and the other half running through the streets to join them. He looked back at Brother Peter. 'And you write it down, like you should,' he insisted. 'There's ink and paper in the church. And if they are guilty you write down that they are to be given to us, the people of Piccolo, for us to do as we please.'

'If they are guilty,' Father Benito specified.

Ishraq took a look around, thinking that she and Isolde and Ree might be able to break away. Isolde took a firm grip of Ree's hand, lifted the hem of her own long gown ready to run.

'Not so fast,' Mrs Ricci said with an evil smile. 'You're coming too. Don't think you'll get away again to bathe in the water and call down a wave from Hell on us poor Christians, you vile heretic and you vile witch and you vile child.'

Ishraq looked at her, the fury in her dark gaze veiled by her dark lashes, and the three of them submitted to being hustled into the church.

The people filed into the church, ranged around the stone walls and stood in a murmuring hush, waiting for what was to happen next. Luca took a seat in the choir stalls, Brother Peter on one side of him, Father Benito on the other, the witnesses, as they came up to make their statements took the front row of the opposing choir stalls, the light on the altar behind the rood screen shining warmly on them all. The hushed holiness of the place silenced the crowd but they were still determined to see justice done, and one after another, the villagers stepped up to the choir stalls and spoke of their experiences with the crusade and then with the flood.

They reported seeing the children begging and praying. They all agreed that Johann had preached of the end of days and had promised that they would be able to walk dry-shod to Jerusalem. They all reported that he had tempted them, by promising them sight of a beloved lost kinsman. People wept again as they said that Johann had spoken to them personally, described events that he could not possible have known unless he had been guided by the Devil himself, that they had been sure of him as an angel, now they knew he was accursed.

Brother Peter made notes, Luca listened intently, fearing more and more that some terrible wrong had happened in this town and that he had missed it. Remorsefully, he remembered coming into the town at dusk, after riding all day with Isolde, quite entranced by her, noticing nothing about the gateway, the harbour or the inn. He remembered saying goodnight to her on the stairs of the inn, thinking of nothing but the closeness of her and that if she had leaned a little nearer they could have kissed. He thought of the arrival of the children on the quayside and how he had looked up to see the two beautiful girls at their window as they had called down that hundreds of children were on the road; he had heard what they had said, but what he had seen was the two exquisite young women. He remembered warning Ishraq that she should not wear her Arab dress and how he had told her that her skin was the colour of heather honey. He knew now that he had been instantly and completely persuaded by Johann, that he had been determined to join the crusade to Jerusalem, hoping selfishly that he would see his parents again. Distracted, filled with sinful desire, obsessed with his own hopes and fears, Luca blamed himself for being quite blind to the events unfolding before his very eyes, and letting this town be washed through by the flood.

He should have been a Noah, he thought – he should have known that the flood was coming and prepared a safe haven. If he had been a true inquirer, and not a lovesick boy, he would not have been distracted and perhaps he would have seen something: a movement of the sea, the largeness of the moon – something that could have warned him of the disaster that was coming. Luca sat very still, listening intently, filled with shame at his own failure.

'What about the young ladies?' one of the midwives called from the body of the church. 'You are asking about things that we know, that we all know. What about the young ladies and what they were doing?'

At once there was a murmur of suspicion and anxiety in the echoing chancel. 'Call them. And have them answer to you.'

Wearily Luca rose to his feet and looked into the shadowy body of the church. 'Lady Isolde, Mistress Ishraq!' he called. He could see the girls coming slowly from where they had been kneeling at the back of the church and then the quiet patter of their leather slippers as they came up the stone-flagged aisle and hesitated. Solemnly, he waved them into the choir stalls opposite his seat, so that they should take their place like the other witnesses. He looked at them, and he knew he was looking at them as if they were strangers to him: strangers filled with the incomprehensible powers of women.

'And the child,' someone insisted. 'The child who escaped the wave.'

Isolde bowed her head to hide her resentment, and went

back down the aisle and returned with Ree holding her hand.

The two of them sat opposite him, in silence, Ree between them, their eyes on the floor. Luca remembered that when he first met Isolde she was accused of witchcraft and now she sat before him accused of the worst of crimes, once again. He could not help but feel a superstitious shiver that so much trouble seemed to swirl around her, though she always looked, as now, so shiningly innocent. He couldn't help but think that a woman who was truly good would not have one slander against her name, let alone two. This woman seemed to attract trouble as iron bars sown in a field will attract a thunderstorm.

His anxiety about her strengthened his resolve to hold a proper inquiry. He dismissed his feelings for Isolde and stared at her critically, without affection, and tried to see her, as these people saw her: a strange, exotic and danger-ously independent woman.

'You have been accused of working as a storm-bringer,' he said, his voice firm and level. 'Both of you have been so accused, by people who say that you went out of the town as night was falling, to a place called the green lake and that there you called up a storm by splashing and making waves in the lake.'

The two young women looked at him in utter silence. Luca flushed as he imagined that he saw contempt in their level gaze.

'What do you say?' he asked them. 'To these charges? I am bound to put them to you, you are bound to answer.'

'They are unworthy of an educated man,' Ishraq said icily. 'They are the fears of fools.'

There was a buzz, like an angry swarm of bees, at the arrogance of her tone. One of the wise women looked around triumphantly. 'Hear how she calls us fools!'

'Even so,' Luca said, irritated, 'you will answer. And be advised not to abuse these good people. What were you doing at the lake?'

'We went out of the town in the afternoon,' Isolde spoke for them both, her voice very clear and steady. 'We wanted to wash and the landlady didn't have hot water for us, nor a bath that we could carry up to our room.'

'Why would they want to wash? In November?' one of the women said from the centre of the crowd standing before the chancel steps. People murmured in agreement. Ishraq looked around at them scornfully.

'The stable lad had told us of a place where boys went swimming . . .' Isolde went on.

'So what young lady would go there?' someone demanded. 'What young lady would go where the boys go? These must be girls of bad repute, little whores.'

Isolde gasped at the word, and looked at Luca, expecting him to silence the shouts. He said nothing to defend her.

'And the gatekeeper says they went out at night.'

'It was afternoon,' Isolde insisted.

Luca raised his hand on the groan from the crowd and the single shout: 'Liar. Dirty liar!'

There was a scuffle at the doorway, as the door banged, and the porter from the west gate came into the church.

'You tell him,' they pushed him forward till he arrived before Luca, Father Benito, and Brother Peter,

'You are?' Brother Peter dipped his pen in the ink.

'Porter. Gatekeeper Paolo. I saw the women, and I warned them to be back inside the gates before dusk,' he said.

'Was the sun setting as they left?' Luca asked.

'It must have been, for I warned them of the curfew.'

'What did they say?'

'They said they were going for a walk.'

'Why should they lie?' someone shouted. 'If they were going for a wash? Why not say that?'

'And they went out as night fell! Why would they do that?'

'They went out as night was coming, so that no one could see them calling up a storm in the green lake!'

Luca looked at Isolde and saw defiance in her dark blue eyes. She looked as she did when he first met her, a woman against the world, despite her own desire to live at peace in her home. A woman driven to defiance. A woman with no trust in him, nor in any man: a woman at bay.

'Tell these people,' he said. Suddenly he broke into Latin, confident that she would understand him but few other people in the church would. 'Please, please my dearest, trust us with the truth. Tell them that you would not call up a storm. Tell them that you are not a storm-bringer. Ishraq too. Just tell them. For God's sake, Isolde, we are all in trouble here. I can only ask you questions – you have to save yourself. Tell them what you were doing.'

Slowly, Isolde rose to her feet and stepped down from the choir stalls to face the crowded church 'I am no storm-bringer,' she said, speaking simply and loudly so that her words echoed off the stone walls. 'I am no witch. I am a woman of good repute and good behaviour. I am a woman who does not obey a father, since my father is dead, nor do I obey a husband, since I have no fortune and no man will take me without a dowry. I don't obey my brother, since he is false and faithless. So you see me as I am – a woman without a man to represent her, a woman alone in the world. But none of this – *none* of this makes me a bad woman. It makes me an unlucky one. I am a woman who would not knowingly do a wicked act. I cannot prove this to you, you have to trust me, as you trust your mothers and your wives and your sisters. I have to call on you to think of me with generosity, as a good woman of high repute, raised to be a lady in a castle. And my friend here, Ishraq, was raised beside me almost as my sister, she is the same.'

Ishraq slowly rose to her feet, and stood beside Isolde as if she were answering to a tribunal on oath. 'I am a heretic and a stranger,' she said. 'But I have done nothing to harm anyone. I did not call up the wave. I don't believe that any mortal has the power to call up a wave like this. I would never have called up a wave to hurt the children, nor you, and I would never have done anything to put our travelling companion, my friend Freize, in danger.'

Luca, who had been looking down at his papers, praying that the village people would hear the raw sincerity in Isolde's explanation, suddenly flicked his gaze up to see Ishraq's dark eyes were filling with tears. 'He was a true friend, and a loyal heart,' Ishraq's voice was low, choked with tears. 'I think he wanted to be my sweetheart and I was such a vain fool that I refused him a kiss.'

There was a murmur of sympathy in the room from some of the younger women. 'Ah, God bless you,' one of them said. 'And now you've lost him. Before you could tell him.'

'I've lost him,' Ishraq agreed. 'And now I'll never be able to tell him that I loved how he laughed at things, and I loved how kind he was to everything, even a kitten, and how he understood things without learning. He was no scholar but he was wiser than I will ever be. He taught me that you can be wise without being clever. The last thing he did – almost the very last thing on earth that he did – was to send me and Isolde and his friend Luca to safety. That's how we got back to the inn, that's how we knew to get high, up to our room and then to the roof. There was no mystery about it. It was Freize who had the sense to notice that his kitten was crying for fear, and he saw the kitten climbing up to the roof. He guessed that the water would flow back. And I am grieving for him now.

'I have lost the dearest sweetheart that a woman might have. I lost him through my own pride and my own folly and I only knew that he was a fine young man when he sent me to safety and went back himself to save the horses. You have to know that I would never ever have done anything that would endanger him. You can call me a heretic. You can call me a stranger. But you can't think that I would have put Freize in the way of a great wave – I would never have hurt him.'

'Let me through!' a voice from the doorway interrupted and the crowd parted as the stable boy came in, propelled by the innkeeper, red-faced and furious.

'What's this? Brother Peter asked, alarmed by the sudden noise, and then, as he recognised the innkeeper with the landlady behind him, he said: 'Dear Lord, who is this now?'

'He's got something to say,' the landlord said. 'Dirty little tyke.'

The boy, his face as scarlet as his twisted ear, ducked his head before Luca's gaze.

'Do you have something to tell us?' Luca asked. 'You can speak without fear.' To the innkeeper he said: 'Do let him go, that can't be good for him.'

'I followed them,' the boy confessed, rubbing his ear. 'Out of town, and down to the lake.'

There was a whisper of excitement from the packed church.

'What did you see?'

The lad shook his head, his colour deepening. 'They went naked,' he confessed. 'I watched them.'

Oddly, Luca's colour rose too, burning red in his cheeks, in his ears. 'They undressed to swim?'

'They swam and they washed each other with soap. The water was cold. They squealed like little piglets. They washed their hair, they plaited it. Then they got out of the water.'

'Did they do anything,' Luca paused and cleared his throat. 'Did they do anything like making waves in the water, pouring water from a jug, did they say words over the water, did they do anything that was not washing and swimming?'

'They played about,' the boy said. He looked at Luca as if he hoped he would understand. 'They swam and splashed and kicked. They were . . . very . . .'

'Very?'

'Very bonny.' His chin dropped to his chest, his whole body slumped with his shame. 'I watched them. I couldn't look away. She . . .' he made a shrugging gesture with his shoulder towards Isolde, as if he did not dare to point a finger. 'She wore a shift. But t'other one went naked.' He looked up and saw Luca's flushed face. 'Stark naked and she had skin like a ripe peach all over. It was the most beautiful thing I have ever seen. And her . . .'

'You will have to confess,' the priest interrupted quickly, before the boy could continue his description of Ishraq glowing like a peach, naked in the lake. 'You have had unclean thoughts.'

The boy went an even deeper red. He looked imploringly at Luca. 'So bonny,' he said. 'Anybody would have watched. You couldn't look away.'

Luca dropped his eyes to his papers, conscious of his own guilty desire. 'Yes, very well,' he said shortly. 'I think we understand that. But at any rate you saw nothing that made you think they were calling up the wave?'

'They weren't doing that,' the boy said flatly. 'They were just playing about and washing like girls. And anyway, it was the middle of the afternoon.'

'The porter warned them of the curfew?'

'He always warns everyone,' the boy said to a murmur of agreement. 'He always closes the gate early and he always opens it late. He never keeps time. He always does just what he wants and then tells all of us that we are too late or too early.'

Luca looked around the room, testing his sense that the people were satisfied, that he could declare the inquiry over. He saw the angry spiteful faces of Mrs Ricci and the two wise women, but he also saw the exhaustion in the other people, who were grieving for the children and the people they had lost, and now felt that they had wasted their time, accusing girls who had done nothing more than walk out of town in the afternoon for a swim.

'I am satisfied that neither the children of the pilgrimage nor these lady travellers did anything to summon the wave,' he said. His words were greeted in silence, and then a sigh of agreement. 'I shall so report,' he said.

'We agree,' Father Benito said, rising to his feet and looking around his flock. 'This is a sorrow which came upon us for no reason. God forgive us and help us in the future.'

'And the little girl?' the landlady asked. She looked to where Isolde was holding Ree's hand. 'She is cleared too?'

'How can they all three be cleared?' one of the midwives said irritably.

'Because they are all three innocent,' Luca said sternly. 'There is no evidence against them.'

'Ree is innocent of everything,' Isolde confirmed to the landlady. 'Can we find a home for her? She is far from her village and all alone in the world.'

The villagers nodded and slowly filed from the church, some of them stopping to light a candle for loved ones who were still missing. Luca nodded to Brother Peter. 'Perhaps give them all a glass of grappa down at the inn?' he asked. 'For good will?'

Brother Peter nodded and whispered the order to the innkeeper who bustled off with his wife. Brother Peter started to collect up his papers. There was a space and a silence for Luca and the two young women.

'You're cleared,' Luca said to them both. 'Again.'

They smiled a little ruefully. 'We don't seek trouble,' Isolde said.

'It seems to follow you.'

Ishraq heard the criticism in his voice. 'If any woman steps outside the common way then she will find trouble,' she said simply. 'It does follow us. We have to fight it.'

'You are thinking about the wave?' Isolde asked Luca as he watched Brother Peter reading through his notes.

'This is no report,' Luca said, frustrated, flicking at the papers with his fingertips. 'This is nothing. This is a village scandal, a few old women frightening themselves. But the question that they ask is the right one. What caused such a thing? What could make such a great wave happen? I can say that it was not you two – washing in a lake – but I can't tell them what it was. And most importantly, I can't tell them if it could happen again. *Could* it happen again? Tonight, even?'

Isolde crossed herself at once at the thought of such a terror, and Luca lowered his voice so the people leaving the church would not hear.

'I have been thinking of this too, and I think it may have been an earthquake, the fall of a mountain or a mighty cliff, perhaps far far away,' Ishraq said, surprisingly. 'Perhaps it caused a wave, just one great wave, as a bowl of water will make waves and spill over, if you were to throw a stone into it.'

Brother Peter rose to his feet and smiled at the prosaic image, typical of a woman who cannot imagine the earth as void and empty, and darkness upon the face of the deep; and the spirit of God moving over the waters, as the Bible itself describes. 'The ocean is not a bowl of water,' he corrected her gently. 'It does not move with waves because someone throws a stone. It is not rocked in a basin for you to wash dishes in.'

'I am not saying that it is. But small things sometimes work the same way as larger. The wave may have been caused by an earthquake, a great falling of rock. Just as you can make a wave in a bowl of water if you throw in a pebble.'

'That's true,' Luca said. 'But what made you think of this?'

'Plato describes the drowning of the country of Atlantis in just such a way,' she said. 'He says that a great earthquake caused a great wave which drowned the island.'

'Plato?' Brother Peter repeated sceptically. 'How has a girl such as you read Plato? I've heard of him, but I've read nothing that he wrote. There are no copies of anything he wrote.'

'No, not that you could read, not translated into Italian; but we Arabs have his books. A few of them have been translated from the Greek into Arabic. I read a little part of them in Arabic when I was in Spain, with Isolde and her father, and I was allowed to attend the university. Plato is a philosopher who talks about great mysteries such as the wave, and has strange understandings.'

'You were privileged,' Brother Peter said irritably scooping up the papers and stoppering the bottle of ink. 'A heretic and a woman to read such a thinker. You must take care that it does not strain your nature, putting too much pressure on you. Women cannot think of abstractions..'

She gave a small shrug. 'My brain is well enough so far, though I thank you for your concern. At any rate, Plato says that the drowning of Atlantis might have followed a great movement of the earth. It made me think that this might be a natural occurrence, not an act of God, nor of the devil, nor of storm-bringers – if there are such people. Perhaps it occurs naturally, from the world of nature. Though why God would make a world where such a thing could happen, is another question.'

Brother Peter knew himself to be on firmer ground. 'Ah, you ask an important question. It is because the perfect world that God first made was destroyed by sin in the garden of Eden, when the woman ate the apple.'

Isolde exchanged a quick smiling glance with Luca. They both knew that Ishraq and Brother Peter would be quarrelling within a moment.

Ishraq looked at him quite blankly. 'What is wrong with eating an apple?'

'Because it does not mean an apple. The apple signifies knowledge.'

Luca winked at Isolde.

'The woman wanted knowledge?'

'Yes,' Peter said, adopting his teacher's voice. 'But it was God's will that the woman and her husband should be innocent of knowledge.'

Ishraq looked as if she did not need his instruction. 'I would have thought an all-seeing God could have foreseen that a woman would want knowledge,' she said. 'Why should she not? Why should I not? Would any woman want to live in ignorance? Would any man? And what does it benefit God to have people so ignorant that they are like these poor peasants – believing that people call up storms and the devil takes the time and the trouble to make them unhappy?'

Brother Peter was almost too irritated to speak. He picked up his papers, bowed to the altar and turned away.

'There is no point trying to explain such things to you,' he said. 'You are a heretic and a girl.' It would have been impossible to say which he thought was worse.

'The Lord Lucretili believed that a girl could study, without straining her nature,' Ishraq insisted. 'Women like Hypatia of Alexandria taught Plato to her students without illness. So when Lord Lucretili was in Spain he sent me to study at the university of Granada. Education is important to us heretics. There are many Arab women who are educated. We Moors believe that a woman can study as well as a man. We do not think that it is godly for a woman to be an ignorant fool.'

'But he did not send his daughter, Isolde, to learn heretic knowledge? He took care to protect her,' Brother Peter said pointedly.

'I wish he had!' Isolde interrupted.

'The lessons were in Arabic or Spanish,' Ishraq said. 'Lady Isolde speaks neither. And besides, she was raised to be a Christian lady ruling her lands.'

'But how would we ever find out?' Luca asked, almost to himself, going down the aisle to the open doorway, and looking downhill to the harbour where the quietly moving sea with its ugly burden of wreckage, looked as if it had never raged inland. 'How would we discover if the earth had moved and caused the wave? If it happened far out at sea, or even under the sea? If no one was there to see it happen? How could we ever discover the cause?'

Father Benito walked beside him. 'You know, the people of the village tell a story of a great earthquake that threw down the harbour walls – all this was about a hundred years ago – and then there was a great wave that washed all the boats out to sea and destroyed all the houses two deep back from the harbour. The bell tower of my own church was thrown down when the ground shook. It was rebuilt; we have the stonemason's costs still in the church records. That's how I know it to be true.'

Ishraq nodded towards Luca. 'An earthquake followed by a wave,' she remarked.

'A hundred years ago?' Luca pressed Father Benito. 'Exactly a hundred?'

'More,' he said quietly. 'The earthquake was in 1348. And after the wave the Black Death came to the village. First the ground shook, then the wave came, then the plague. God forbid that this wave brings the pestilence also.'

'The Black Death?' Brother Peter queried.

The priest nodded. 'It was the worst in Friuli, but they felt it as far away as Rome. It shook this village. I have the accounts of the church rebuilding, which is how I know the dates. It was almost impossible to get the stone masons to repair the tower, for within months of the wave, they were all dead.'

'I shall write this in my report,' Luca said. 'Perhaps we should see it as a warning. Do you think you should store grain, and food? In case a pestilence follows this wave, as it did a hundred years ago?'

Father Benito crossed himself. 'God forbid,' he said. 'For last time they had to dig great plague pits in the graveyard to take the bodies. I wouldn't want to have to open them again. They buried half the village, more than a hundred people, old and young. And the priest himself died. God spare me.'

'God help us all,' Luca said solemnly. 'Perhaps this is, as

they say, the end of days.' No one answered him, and he turned and went down the hill to the quayside alone.

Brother Peter and the two young women watched him go. Father Benito murmured a blessing, closed the church doors, and went quietly away to his damp house.

Brother Peter sighed and led the way down the hill to the inn on the quayside. 'I suppose we had better get a ship and move on,' he said. 'There's nothing we can do here any-more. We'll sail across to Split as we planned.'

'Are we giving up on Freize?' Isolde asked bleakly. 'Are we not looking for him any more; not waiting for him?'

'We could leave a message for him, as to where to find us, if he were ever to return. But I can't believe that he survived the flood,' Brother Peter replied. 'What would be the point of us waiting here?'

'For fidelity!' Isolde exclaimed. 'Because we can't just go on!'

Ishraq shook her head. 'No. We may as well leave. It does Luca no good to wait and watch here. We'll have to find a boat and go on with our journey. Can you find someone to take us, Brother Peter? Would you like me to go and ask?'

'A few ships came into port this morning, which seem to have escaped damage. I'll find someone. Shall we set a time and go tomorrow?'

'In the morning,' Ishraq said. 'I suppose you'll all want to attend mass before we sail. We can go after Prime.'

Brother Peter looked curiously at her as they went together down the cobbled steps. 'Don't you want to con-fess your soul and attend the service now that you have seen God work in such a mysterious way? Should you not turn to our God, now that you have been in such danger? I could explain our beliefs to you. I could convert you.'

Ishraq smiled at him, indifferent to his concern. 'Ah, Brother Peter, I know you are a good man and would like to save my soul. I don't know what caused the wave. But it doesn't inspire me to pray to your God.'

~

Isolde agreed that they should leave the following day but she could not bring herself to tell Luca. 'Will you tell him?' she asked Brother Peter. 'I can't bear to do it.'

He waited until the hour before dinner while they were all four sitting in the dining room before a smoky fire of damp wood, and then he said quietly, 'Brother Luca, I think we can do nothing more in this town and I will send my report tomorrow. I will write that we can find no certain explanation for the wave, though some wild thoughts from pagan and heretical writers have been mentioned.'

Luca barely raised his head.

'And I have found a master who will take us on his ship tomorrow. We can go after Prime.'

'We stay,' Luca said instantly. 'At least for a few more days.'

'We have a mission; and there is nothing more to be done here,' Brother Peter repeated steadily. 'We will send your report tomorrow, we can warn Milord and His Holiness that we have seen a powerful sign of the end of days. We can warn them that a previous earthquake was followed by a wave that was followed by the pestilence called the Black Death. But we serve no one by waiting here – and anyway, if a plague is coming we should leave.'

Isolde reached out and put her cool hand over Luca's clenched fist as it lay on the table. 'Luca,' she said quietly.

He turned to her as if she might have answers to his agonising questions. 'I can't go,' he said passionately. 'I can't just sail away from here as if nothing is wrong. I can't just continue on. Freize came with me, he was following me on this quest. He would never have been here but for love of me. I don't see how to do it without him. If I had been washed out to sea, he would not have left me. He would not have run for his safety and left me behind.'

'He would want you to complete your mission,' Isolde said, trying to comfort him. 'He was so proud of you. He was so proud that you had been called to this work and that he could serve you.'

At the thought of Freize's joyful boasting, Luca nearly smiled, but then he shook his head. 'You must see, I have to stay here until . . .'

'We will leave instructions and money that his body is to be buried if it is washed ashore,' Ishraq said, surprising them all with the brisk clarity of her tone. 'If you are thinking of that; we can provide for him, as you would wish. But I was speaking to one of the fishermen and he says there is a strong current a little further beyond the harbour and perhaps Freize and all the children have been washed far away. Their bodies may never be found. Perhaps we should think of them all as buried at sea. Brother Peter could bless the waves as we sail to Split.'

Luca rounded on her in anger. 'You speak of his burial? The burial of my friend Freize? Blessing the waves? You have given him up for dead?'

She gazed at him steadily. 'Yes, of course. Weren't you

thinking the very same thing, yourself? Isn't it the very thing you have been afraid to think for days?'

He flung himself from the table and wrenched open the door. 'You're heartless!' he flung at her.

She shook her head. 'You know I am not.'

He paused. 'How can you talk about blessing the sea?'

'I thought you would want to say goodbye,' she said.

'How dare you say that I must think of this?'

'It is your life's work to think of difficult things.'

Isolde gasped and would have intervened but she saw the steady way that Ishraq held Luca's angry glare, and she fell silent. Luca's temper burned out as quickly as it had come. He breathed out a shuddering sigh, came back into the room and closed the door behind him and leaned back against it as if sorrow had weakened him.

'You're right of course,' he said. 'You're right. I just don't want it to be true. I'll leave instructions with Father Benito in the morning and – Brother Peter, perhaps you will write to our monastery and tell them what has happened and ask them to tell his mother? I will write myself later . . .'

Isolde rose and put her hand in his; she laid her cheek against his shoulder. Brother Peter watched them without comment, though his expression was completely disapproving.

'And we'll take ship tomorrow,' Ishraq pursued.

'Ishraq!' Isolde exclaimed. 'Be at peace! Leave him alone!'

Stubbornly, Ishraq shook her head. '*He's* not at peace,' she said, nodding to Luca. 'And you crying over him doesn't help him at all. Better that we do something, rather than sit here mourning. In my religion Freize would have been buried by sunset on the day that he died. We'll always remember him whether we take a ship to Split now or the day after. But,' she nodded at Luca, 'this is not a young man who should be left to mourn for a long time. He has had too many losses already. Grief must not become a habit for him.'

Isolde looked up into Luca's strained face.

'She's right,' he said bitterly. 'I can do nothing here but weep for him, like a girl. We'll go tomorrow, after Prime.'

~

They went to their rooms to pack their things, but they had almost nothing to pack. Everything but the clothes they were wearing had gone down with the ship. They had bought new rough cloaks from the tailor in the little town but new boots or hats, or a writing box for Brother Peter would have to wait till they got to a bigger town. The manuscripts which Brother Peter and Luca carried to advise them on legends, folklore and previous investigations were irreplaceable. They would have to buy new horses when they got to Split, and a new donkey to carry their goods.

'How far do you think it is from Split to Budapest?' Isolde asked idly, looking out of the window of their bedroom. 'I am so tired of travelling. I am so tired of everything. I wish we could just go home to my own home and live on my own lands, where I belong. I wish that none of this had happened.'

'You can't wish to be back in the nunnery,' Ishraq objected. 'You can't wish to be under the command of your brother.'

Isolde turned her face away and shook her head. 'I wish

I were a girl in my father's care again,' she said. 'I wish I could be home.'

'Well, Freize said that we would be about a week on the road,' Ishraq replied trying to cheer her friend. 'And the only way to get your own home back is to get your godfather's son to support you. It's a long journey, but with luck it leads us home at last.'

Isolde turned into the room. 'I don't know how we'll manage without him. I can't imagine setting out on a journey without him.'

'Without him complaining?' Ishraq suggested with a faint smile. 'Without him endlessly complaining about the road, and about the mission, and about Brother Peter's secret orders?'

Isolde smiled. 'We'll miss all that,' she said. 'We'll miss him.'

~

It was a quiet group that assembled for dinner. Much of the company had left the inn since the burial of the bodies of the children, and travellers on the coastal roads had heard of the disaster that had hit all the fishing villages along the coast and were skirting the blighted areas and travelling inland. Nobody had much appetite and there seemed to be nothing much to say.

'Where is Ree?' Isolde asked the landlady. 'Is she in the kitchen with you?'

'She's worked like a little cook, and now she's eating her dinner as good as gold,' the landlady said, pleased. 'That was a good thought of yours, my lady. That was kind Christian work.'

'What did Lady Isolde do?' Luca raised his head in momentary interest.

'She took me to one side and she prayed with me and Ree together. She showed Ree my linen room and the child saw the beauty in it. She'll make a good kitchen maid and a good housemaid. I was spared from the terror of the flood, locked safe in my linen room; I can't help but warm to a girl who admires it. She can stay here with us. Lady Isolde has offered to pay for her keep for her first month and then she'll earn her wages. I'll look after her.'

'That was well done,' Luca said quietly.

Isolde smiled at him. 'It wasn't hard to see that they might help each other. And Ree will have a good home here and learn a trade.'

'That's good,' Luca said, losing interest.

'Split tomorrow,' Brother Peter said, trying to be cheerful. 'We'll probably get in about dawn if we leave early.'

Isolde directed her words to Luca. 'And then Zagreb.'

There was a clatter of noise in the stable yard and a cheerful 'Halloo!' from outside. It was an incongruous yell in a town gripped with mourning. The innkeeper opened the kitchen door and said, 'Hush, don't you know what has passed here? Keep the noise down. What do you want?'

'Some service!' came the joyous shout. 'Some stabling for the bravest horses ever to swim for shore! Some dinner for a great survivor! Some wine to toast my health in! And news of my friends. The two beautiful lasses and the brilliant young man? And the sour-faced priest that travels with us? Are they here? Have they gone on? Swear to me that they are safe as I have been praying?'

Luca went white, as if he thought he was hearing a ghost and then he exclaimed, 'Freize!' and leapt up from the table, overturning his chair, and dashed down to the kitchen, and out through the back door to the stable yard.

There, standing at the head of his horse and holding the reins of four others, with the tired donkey behind them, was Freize: sea-stained and dirty, but alive. As he saw Luca outlined in the light from the kitchen, he dropped the reins and spread his arms. 'Little Sparrow, thank God you're safe! I have been riding for miles fretting about you.'

'I! Safe! What about you?' Luca yelled and catapulted himself into the arms of his boyhood friend. They clung to each other like long-lost brothers, slapping each other's backs, Luca patting Freize all over as if to assure himself that he was alive. Freize caught Luca's face in his hands, and kissed him roundly on both cheeks and then wrapped his arms around him again.

Luca thumped his shoulders, shook him, stepped back and looked at him and then hugged him again. 'How ever did you—? How did—? I didn't know where you were – why didn't you run for the inn with us? I swear I thought you were right behind me – I'd never have left you on your own!'

'Did you get up on the chimney like the kitten?' Freize replied to the torrent of questions. 'Are you all safe? The girls? Both girls?'

As the two young men spoke at once, Ishraq and Isolde came running out of the inn door and threw themselves on Freize, hugging and crying and saying his name. Even Brother Peter came out into the yard and thumped him on the back. 'My prayers!' he cried. 'Answered! God be praised He has brought Freize back to us. It is a miracle like the return of Jonah onto dry land from the belly of the fish!'

Ishraq, tucked under Freize's arm with Isolde clinging to his other side glanced up. 'Jonah?' she asked. 'Jonah swallowed by a great fish?'

'As the Bible tells us,' Brother Peter said.

She laughed. 'The Koran also,' she said. 'We call him Jonah or Yunus. He preached for God.' She thought for a moment and then recited:

'*Then the big Fish did swallow him, and he had done acts worthy of blame.*

Had it not been that he (repented and) glorified Allah,

He would certainly have remained inside the Fish till the Day of Resurrection.'

Brother Peter's delight faded slightly. 'It's not possible,' he said. 'He was a prophet for God, our God.'

'For our God too,' Ishraq said, pleased. 'Perhaps, after all, they are one and the same?'

~

The innkeeper paddled around the waters in his cellar for a special bottle of wine, two special bottles, three, as more and more people came to hear the extraordinary story and drink Freize's health. Even those who had lost brothers or sons at sea were glad that at least one life had been spared. And his survival gave hope to those who were still waiting. The landlady brought some cheese and chicken to the table, some bread fresh-baked in the re-heated oven, and half the village piled in to watch the restored Jonah eat his dinner and hear how he had been saved from the terrible destruction.

'I saw the wave and I was running for the inn after you

when I heard the horses kicking down their stalls on the ship, so I ran back to them . . .' Freize started.

'Why didn't you come with us?' Isolde scolded him.

'Because I knew that the little lord would care for you two, but there was no one to care for the horses,' he explained. 'I saw you set off at a run and I splashed across the harbour to where the boat was stranded. I got on board – Lord! the boat was sitting on the harbour floor – and I thought that I would set them free, let them run away, and catch them later. But as I was trying to get close enough to cut the ropes, talking to them and telling them all would be well, the world made me a liar indeed for I looked over the shoulder of the horse on the seaward side, and I saw the great wall of water, as high as a house racing towards us and already in the mouth of the harbour. I had seen it shining like a white wall, a long way off, but it came faster than I had dreamed.'

There was a little groan from the people who had lost their children, at the thought of the great wave. 'I did nothing,' Freize, admitted. 'God knows, I was no hero. Worse than that. I ducked down between one horse and another and I fairly buried my face in Rufinos's mane. I was so afraid I didn't want to see what was coming. I thought it was my death coming for me, I don't mind admitting. I could hear a great roar, like a beast coming for me. I closed my eyes and clung to a horse and cried like a baby.

'I could hear it – dear God, a noise that I hope I never hear again – a grinding sliding screaming noise of the water storming towards me and eating up everything in its path. It hit the little ship like a hammer blow on a wooden box and threw us up in the air like we were a splinter. I had my arms around Rufino's neck like a child crying on its mother's lap. I'm not ashamed to say I was weeping in terror, as we went up and up and up. I could feel the moorings tear away, and I could feel the back of the boat stave in and next thing we were roaring away, boat and horses and me, with the wave rushing us inland like little ducks on a flood.'

'What could you see? Did you see the children?'

'God bless and keep them, I saw nothing but the sky and the land ahead of us and then the boiling water like a pan of grey soup, and I heard nothing but the roar of the waters and my own frightened cries. The horses wept in fear too, and the little donkey; we were seven sorry beasts, as we stormed over dry land, the world buckling and folding underneath us, and I thought the world had ended and it was another great flood and I, a failed Noah, with none of my kind on board, and no preparation done.'

He paused and nodded at Luca. 'I really *did* think it the end of the world and hoped that somewhere you were safe and taking note.'

Luca laughed and shook his head, as Freize went on. 'Then, and this was a bad moment, the wave sort of took a breath, like it was a living devil and thinking what would be the worst thing that it could do, and I felt the tide turn beneath what was left of the boat and we started to run back out to sea again, back the way we had come, but bumping and grinding against things that I could not even see, and crashing against things in the dark. That was a terrible moment; that was as bad as before, worse. I thought I would be halfway to Afric and on only half of a boat. Then the keel caught: I could feel it spin against something, and then it grounded and I was fool enough to hope that I would step out on dry land, when a rush of water hit us again and the boat tipped over, throwing us into the sea and into darkness and everything was rushing around me, and great trees were turning over and over crashing around my frightened head and I was never knowing whether I was upwards or downwards or simply drowned.

'I kept tight hold of Rufino and I felt that he kept tight hold of me and that we were better when we shared our fears together. When the boat tipped over I was flung towards his back and gripped on like a child, legs around his belly, arms around his neck and whispered to him that he had better get us out of danger for I was no use to man nor beast, being a great coward.

'When the boat had crashed it had smashed itself and so he was freed, all the horses' tethers were free, and I could feel Rufino take great leaps as he swam in the flood. And glory to God and to the horse in particular that he bobbed and swam and struggled, and neighed out loud as if he was saying his prayers. I clung to him and sometimes he was washed from under me, and I was clinging to him and swimming beside him, but then I got my legs around him again, and then I felt him struggling in mud, not in water, and then I heard his hooves ring on stone, and though I had no idea where we were, at least I knew we were on land.'

'Praise be!' someone said.

'Amen,' Isolde replied fervently.

'Indeed,' Freize said. 'And bless the horse. For I would not have lived through that, but for the strength and wisdom of a dumb beast. So you tell me who is the wiser?'

Ishraq could see Brother Peter biting his tongue to stop

himself replying that the horse, any horse, was undoubtedly wiser than Freize.

'And then when we were sure we were on land again, and hoping that the sea was never coming back, I looked around me and found that they had all stayed together, like the sensible beasts they are; even the little donkey who likes to play the fool had stayed with us. I gathered up their halters and I climbed back on Rufino, without saddle or bridle, and, though we were all so weary, I rode a little way uphill, for though I could see the water was seeping away, I was still very afraid of it. As soon as I thought we were high enough and dry enough I told my five horses and the little donkey that we would spend the night and rest, and try for Piccolo in the morning.

'Well, we were further away than I knew, for we have been walking all this long while back to you and I've seen many sad sights all along the way. Good houses ruined, good fields destroyed by salt, and more drowned animals and good people than I could bear to see. All the villages I passed by are filled with sad people seeking their own, and burying their dead. Everywhere I walked they asked me had I seen this child, or that woman, and I was sick to my heart that I had to say that I was alone in my ship like a poor ill-prepared Noah, and saw no one and nothing from the moment that the great wave came.

'And I didn't stop, except to sleep at nights, which I did once in a farmer's damp barn, and once in a wrecked little inn, for I was so anxious to come back here and find you. All the way I have tormented myself that the wave was too fast for you and that I had saved five horses and a little donkey, God bless them; but lost the most precious man in the world to me.' He looked at Luca. 'Little sparrow. Did you perch all night on the roof?'

Luca laughed shakily. 'I have been sick with grief for you. I thought you were dead for sure.'

Freize wiped his mouth with the back of his hand. 'I was a Noah,' he said grandly. 'A Noah of six beasts, and all of them geldings, so of no use to anyone. But I did ride my ark in a great flood. If I had not been so weak with fear I would have been impressed by the adventure. It was the strangest thing. And when I have stopped being so afraid of the memory it will make a very good story and I shall tell it at length. And when I have forgotten that I cried like a coward I shall give myself many good speeches and be the hero of my story. You have it now as it was – before improvements. You have it as a true history and not a poem. I am not yet a troubadour, I am a mere historian.' He turned to Isolde. 'And you, my lady? I have been fretting about you, without your squire at your side to guard you. You were not hurt?'

She gave him her hand and he kissed it. 'I'm just so very pleased to have you with us again,' she said simply. 'We have all been praying for you. We had special prayers said for your deliverance, and every day we have been looking and looking out to sea.'

He flushed with pleasure at the thought of it. 'And the horses are well,' he assured her. 'Shaken, of course, and tired – oh they are weary – poor beasts. I doubt they'll go very willingly on board a ship again, but they are fit to travel.' He turned to Ishraq. 'And you were safe? You got quickly to the inn. I trusted you to see the danger and run. I knew you would understand.'

She nodded gravely at him. 'Safe,' she said.

'And Brother Peter. I am glad to see you,' Freize volunteered.

'And I you.' The clerk extended his hand and shook Freize's hand with unmistakable warmth. 'I have been afraid for you, on the flood. And I have missed you these last days. I have regretted some hard words that I said to you. I am more glad than I can tell you, to see you safe and back with us. I prayed for you constantly.'

Freize flushed with pleasure. 'And the children of the crusade? Were they all lost? God bless them and take them into His keeping.'

'Some were saved,' Isolde said. 'Saved by you. The ones that you warned and sent back to the village got as far as the church and were safe. They're travelling home, while the little girl Rosa, with the hurt feet, who you sent back, is here and will serve as a kitchen maid at the inn. But many of them, most of them, were taken by the sea.'

'It's been a terrible disaster,' Luca said quietly. 'We buried some of them this afternoon. We were going to leave tomorrow. We would have left you messages, where to come. But now we'll wait here a few more days, and you can rest.'

'No, we can go. I can sleep on the ship,' Freize said, 'if someone can promise me that such a wave will never happen again. If you promise me that the sea will stay where it ought to be, I'll get on board and sail tomorrow. I think God has sent me a sign that I will not die by drowning.'

Brother Peter shook his head. 'Nobody knows what it means, or what caused it,' he said, not looking at Ishraq. 'So nobody can say if it will ever come again. But it has not happened in this generation, not even for a hundred years. We can only pray that it never happens again.'

'Is there no way of knowing?' Freize asked Luca. 'I admit that I'd cast anchor more happily if there was any way of knowing for sure.'

Luca frowned. 'It's the very thing I have been puzzling about,' he said. 'The horses seemed to know.'

'They did know,' Freize said certainly. 'And the kitten knew too.'

'And there was a terrible noise, and the sea went out, drained away, before it came in.'

'The wave itself didn't rear up out of nothing,' Freize was thinking out loud. 'It was rolling in, as if it might have come from some distance, as if it might even have swelled and grown out at sea. If anyone had been far out at sea they might have seen it beginning.'

Luca nodded, and a few people crowded around Freize to ask more questions and he answered, pausing only to drink wine, happy to be in the middle of the crowd and the centre of attention. He did not speak again to Ishraq, nor she to him, until almost everyone had gone. Brother Peter was putting his cape around his shoulders to go up the hill to the church for the night service, and Luca, Isolde, and Freize were following him. Ishraq saw them out of the front door of the inn and was closing the door on the cold night air, as Freize turned back to speak to her.

'You were safe?' he asked. 'I knew that you would get Isolde out of danger.'

'I'm safe,' she said. 'But I was very afraid for you.'

He beamed. 'Afraid for me? Well, we agree on that. I was afraid for myself.'

'It was a brave thing to do – to go back to free the horses.'

He shook his head. 'To tell you the truth, I don't think I'd have done it if I'd known the wave was coming so quick. I'm no hero, though I am sorry to say it. Very sorry to have to confess it to you.'

'I have something for you,' she said smiling. 'Hero or not.'

He waited.

From the inner pocket of her cape she produced the sleepy little kitten. Freize cupped his big hands and she put it gently into them. He took the kitten up to his face and inhaled the scent of warm fur, as the little thing stretched for a moment, and then wound its golden tail over its white nose and snuggled down clasped in his big hands.

'You saved it for me?'

'I woke in the night, last night, thinking of you and remembering it, and I got out of bed and went up the ladder to the roof in the darkness, and fetched it down from the chimney pot.'

'You went up and down the roof in darkness?'

'I should have remembered it before.'

'Was it not dangerous?'

'Nothing like you in the flood.'

'You were thinking of me?'

'Yes,' she said frankly.

'Worrying about me?' he suggested

'Yes.'

'Perhaps crying for me? A little? When nobody was looking?'

She smiled a little, but she did not look away or pretend to shyness. She made a small nod of assent. 'I cried for you

190

and I told the whole village that I was sorry I had been unkind to you.'

'Perhaps you were wishing that you had kissed an honest man when he asked you kindly, and not thrown him down in the mud, that time in Vittorito?'

Again, the tiny nod told him that she had thought very kindly of him and regretted the missed kiss.

'You could always kiss me now,' Freize suggested.

To his surprise, she did not refuse him, though he had expected her to box his ears for asking. Instead she stepped towards him and put one hand over the soft kitten in his cupped hands, as if to caress them both. She put her other hand on the nape of his warm neck, and drew his head down to her, and she kissed him, tenderly and fully on the lips so that he inhaled her breath, and tasted the soft dampness of the tender skin of her mouth.

~

Ishraq waited in their shared room for Isolde to come back from church and took her cape as she entered, and stood behind her as she sat on the wooden three-legged stool. Ishraq untied the ribbon in Isolde's blonde hair and ran her fingers through the plaits, pulling them loose. Slowly, luxuriously, she combed the beautiful golden ringlets till they lay heavy and smooth over Isolde's shoulders, and then plaited them back up for the night. The girls changed places and Isolde combed and then plaited her friend's thick dark hair, twisting the curls around her fingers.

'Isn't it a blessing that he is safe?' she said quietly, 'I had lit half a dozen candles for him in the church and then I was able to give thanks.'

Ishraq bowed her head under the gentle caress. 'Oh, yes.'

'He came running after us up the hill to church and he looked filled with joy.'

'Yes, I expect he did.'

'Did you give him his kitten?'

Ishraq nodded.

'Was he very pleased?'

'Yes.'

Something in Ishraq's reserve warned Isolde, who gave the fat dark plait a little admonitory tug. 'What are you not telling me?'

Ishraq turned to face her friend. 'How do you know that there is something that I am not telling you?'

'Because his face was alight with joy. Because you are saying nothing – but you look the same as he did. So what passed between the two of you?'

Ishraq hesitated. 'You won't like it,' she guessed.

'Of course I won't mind. Whatever it is. Why would I mind? Did he promise you his service for life, like he did to me?'

'Oh no. He doesn't think of me as a grand lady. He doesn't want to be my squire. He asked me if I was sorry for throwing him down in the mud at Vittorito. And I said I was sorry.'

'You apologised?' Ishraq was amazed. 'You never apologise!'

'Well, I said sorry to him.'

'Is that all?'

'I said I wished that I had kissed him that time and not tripped him up.'

'Ishraq!' Isolde was playfully shocked. 'What a thing to say to him! What can he have thought?'

'Oh that was nothing. He asked me could he kiss me now?'

'Well, he was bound to. And I hope you refused him kindly?'

'Oh,' Ishraq said nonchalantly. 'I wanted to. So I kissed him.'

Isolde was genuinely shocked. She dropped the comb and stared at Ishraq's reflection in the little mirror. 'You kissed him?'

The girl nodded. 'Yes. Yes, I did.'

'How could you allow him? I know you were happy that he came back safely – we all are – but how could you forget yourself so? How could you permit him? A servant?'

'I didn't really allow him. I didn't "permit him", as you say.'

'He never forced you?' Isolde was horrified.

'No! No! It was I who kissed him.'

This was even worse. 'But Ishraq, your honour!'

The girl met her friend's stunned gaze. 'Oh! Honour!'

'What do you mean?'

'I suddenly felt, I suddenly thought, that nothing mattered more to me than that I had thought him dead, and that I was so happy that he was alive. I had thought he was lost and here he was – just as he had always been. And I was so glad of that – nothing else seemed to matter.'

Isolde shook her head. 'If you were so happy for him, you could have given him a favour or a gift. You could have let him kiss your hand. But to lower yourself to kiss him! What about your honour as a lady?'

'I am sick of all of this,' Ishraq said impatiently. 'Like in the church today – people doubting our reputation just because we were going to wash where the boys swim. As if all that matters is how a lady behaves around boys! I want my honour to be about me as a person, not me as an object with boundaries and gateways, as if I were a field – someone can touch my hand, someone can see my face, someone else can't even speak to me. If my honour is a real thing then it can't depend on whether a man sees my face, or touches my hand, or kisses my lips. If I am an honourable woman then I am an honourable woman like a man is an honourable man – whatever I wear, however I appear. It is about my respect for myself – not how the world sees me, not what events happen. I *know* that I am an honourable woman, I don't stoop to sin, I don't embarrass myself, I don't do things that I know to be wrong. I know I am a good woman whether I wear a veil or keep my hair plaited out of sight. I felt that I could, in honour, give him the kiss that he once asked for, and that I wanted to do so.'

'A lady should be untouchable until marriage,' Isolde stated the absolute rule that they had both been taught from childhood. 'Her husband should know that she has known no other man, that no other man has been closer to her than to kiss her hand. He must know that she has felt no desire, permitted no touch.'

'It's not true,' Ishraq said roundly. 'You are a lady, a great lady, and you will make a great marriage with some high lord. But you will have known love and you will have felt desire.'

'I won't!' Isolde insisted. 'I would never admit to it.'

'But there is more to life than trying to fit inside men's idea of an honourable woman!' Ishraq exclaimed. 'We didn't come away from the castle and then run away from the nunnery to live as if we were still enclosed.'

Isolde was scandalised. 'We should live as we were brought up to live! Not like loose women on the road, not as if we had no hopes of ourselves, no standards, no self-respect!'

'Not me,' Ishraq declared boldly. 'I am out of the castle, I am out of the nunnery. I'm not going to wear a hood any more, I'm not going to wear a veil. I am going to dress as I please and do what I think right and I am going to kiss who I want to, and even lie with someone if I want to. My honour and my pride are in my heart, and not in what the world says.'

Isolde was genuinely distressed. 'You can't throw away your reputation, Ishraq. You can't become a loose woman, a shamed woman.'

'Nobody shames me,' Ishraq said proudly. 'But I will choose my own path and who I love and who loves me.'

'When we were in church, before Luca, accused of being storm-bringers, we told everyone that we were women of good reputation!' Isolde cried out. 'It was one of the things that saved us. Everyone could see that we wouldn't have gone running after boys to the green lake; everyone knew that we said that we were ladies of high regard, of good name. You risk everything if you behave lightly. It's a terrible thing to do.'

'We were saved in the church because the stable lad said that we had done nothing but swim,' Ishraq argued. 'All that about being the Lady of Lucretili might impress a few peasants but it means nothing. If the boy had not proved that we left the town gate in daylight and gone for a swim they would have burned us as storm-bringers whether we were virgins or not. We have to fight for our way in the world; nobody is going to give us safe conduct because we try to be ladylike.'

'You won't be a fit companion for me, and Luca would be horrified,' Isolde stormed. 'Luca does not want to travel with a girl who has lost her honourable name. He would not tolerate you in his presence, if he thought you were dishonoured. He would send you away if he knew you had kissed his servant.'

'No he wouldn't, for he knows what it is to want someone to hold you, to want the comfort of love. When he was in his sorrow on the quayside I held him in my arms.'

'What?' Isolde nearly screamed.

'I held him for pity when he was weeping, and I was not shamed. He did not think I was dishonoured. I was not shamed when he kissed me.'

Isolde gasped. 'He kissed you?'

'Yes. He was not horrified. He didn't think me dishonoured.'

'He kissed your lips?' Isolde's voice was shrill.

'No! Not like that! How can you think such a thing? He kissed me tenderly, gently, on my forehead.'

'How do you mean?'

Ishraq was irritated. 'What do you think I mean? He held my face in his two hands and he kissed me on my forehead, practically on my hood. I hardly felt it. It was almost on my hood.'

'It can't have been on your hood if you felt it! If it had

been on your hood you would not have known he had done it. So was it on your forehead or your hood?'

'What difference does it make? What difference does it make to you?'

'Was it on your forehead?'

'Why would it matter? He's obviously in love with you. I held him in my arms like a sister, I held him while he wept for his friend, and then, when he came into the inn, he gave me a kiss of tenderness: we were both grieving for Freize.'

'You were hardly grieving very much, if you were kissing another man.'

Ishraq looked incredulously at her friend, and then crossly got to her feet, pushing the stool out of the way under the bed. 'What on earth is the matter with you about all this?' she said rudely. 'You are screaming like a stuck pig.'

'I am so shocked by you!' Isolde's voice quavered as if she were about to cry.

'Shocked by what? By my holding a young man in my arms who was grieving for his friend? Or by my kissing a young man when he had just come back from the dead?'

'And him! How *could* he? How can we travel with them – how can we travel at all – if you are going to be like this? How can we face them tomorrow knowing that you have kissed not just one but both of them!'

Ishraq almost laughed and then looked again at Isolde's distressed face, saw even in the flickering candlelight the shine of tears on her pale cheeks. 'Why you're crying! Isolde, this is ridiculous. What's the matter with you? Why are you so upset?'

'I can't bear that he should kiss you!' burst out the girl. 'I hate it. I hate you for allowing it! I hate you!'

There was a stunned silence. Both girls were deeply shocked at the words.

'This is about Luca. Not about me or Freize, not about my honour. It is about Luca.'

Isolde sat on the bed and put her face in her hands and nodded.

'So you are in love with him,' Ishraq observed coldly. 'This is serious.'

'No! Of course not! How can it possibly be?'

'You are jealous that I held him in my arms, and that he took my face in his hands and kissed me on the forehead.'

'Shut up!' Isolde rounded on her friend in a fury. 'I don't want to hear about it, I don't want to think about it. I don't want to have to imagine it, I wish you had not done it, and if you do it again – if you even think of doing it again – then we will have to part. I can't stay with you if you are going to become some sort of . . .'

'Some sort of what?' Ishraq demanded icily.

'Some sort of whore!' Isolde spat out in her rage.

Ishraq was shocked into silence, then she got into bed, pulled up the covers of the bed as far as they would go, up to her chin and turned over as if ready for sleep. 'If you were a man I would have thrown you down for saying such a name to me,' she said to the limewashed wall. 'But as it is, I see that you are a stupid jealous girl who fears that the man she loves is being taken from her.'

Isolde gasped, but could not deny it. She sat on the edge of the bed and put her face in her hands.

'A jealous girl, a stupid girl,' Ishraq went on bitterly,

still with her back turned. 'A girl truly dishonoured by thinking such things of her friend and saying such a word to her friend. And you are wrong, so wrong. I would not take the man you loved away from you, even supposing that he would be willing. I would not do such a thing to you, for I never forget that we love each other like sisters, and that our love should matter more than what we might feel for a man. A passing man,' she said driving the point home, into the silence of the darkened bedroom. 'A man that you met just a month ago. A man who is promised to a monastery and to an order and is not free to kiss anyone, anyway. A young man who probably cares for neither of us.

'But you have put your stupid girlish feelings for him above your love for me. And then you accuse *me* of being dishonoured! And then you call *me* a foul name! You're no sister to me, Isolde, though I have lived my life thinking of you as dearly as a sister. But at the first sight of a handsome young man you become a rival. A stupid rivalrous girl. You're not fit to be my sister, you don't deserve my love.'

She heard a sob behind her, but she refused to turn around.

'And it is you who are dishonoured,' she said fiercely. 'For you are in love with a man who is not free, and who has not spoken to your family to ask for your hand in marriage. So you are a fool.'

She was answered by a little shaky gasp.

'Goodnight,' Ishraq said frostily, and closed her eyes and fell, almost at once, asleep, as Isolde got on her knees at the foot of the bed and prayed to God for forgiveness for the sin of jealousy, for speaking cruelly and wrongly to her dearest friend; and then – reluctantly – owning the truth to herself: she prayed for forgiveness for the terrible sin of desire.

In the morning the two girls were pointedly polite to each other, but hardly spoke at all. Luca and Freize, in the joy of being reunited, completely failed to notice the icy atmosphere. Brother Peter regarded the young women critically, and thought to himself that they were – like all women – as changeable as the weather, and as inexplicable. He would have thought they would be overjoyed to have the favourite Freize back with them again – but here they were sour-faced and silent. Why would God make such beings but for the trouble and puzzlement of men? Who could ever doubt that they were a lesser being to the men that God had made in His image and set over them for their guidance? What could he do but thank God for preserving him from their company by keeping him safe in a religion governed by men in an order exclusively male?

As Freize went down to the harbour to confirm the arrangements for them to sail, Luca, Brother Peter and Isolde went up the hill to the church for Terce, the third service of prayer in the day. Isolde made her confession to the priest and then kneeled in prayer, her face buried in her hands throughout the mass. When it was over, and the men had said farewell to Father Benito, she was still kneeling. They left her to follow them and walked back to the inn.

Freize greeted them on the threshold of the inn, his face grave. 'We can't take a ship to Split,' he said. 'I found a man who has just come from there. He'll be the first of many. The town is all but destroyed, the country for miles around laden with broken boats and upturned trees, wrecked houses and drowned barns. The place was hit by a greater wave than we were; it is far worse than here. There's no house standing for miles around, and nothing to eat that has not been spoiled with salt water. We can't go to that coast at all.'

Luca shook his head at himself. 'I should have thought of that! What a fool I am! Of course we won't be the only town that had the wave. If the sea moved, then every town on the coast would have been affected.' For a moment they could see him furiously thinking, then he turned to Brother Peter. 'If we knew which town was worst affected then we would know which town was closest to the source of the wave,' he said. 'If Ishraq is right, and it *was* like a pebble in a bowl, then the wave is deepest nearest to where it starts and gets more and more shallow as it rolls away. If we knew where the wave was greatest we might at least discover where it came from.'

'That's true,' Brother Peter said. 'But . . .'

Suddenly, shockingly, the warning bell of the lookout on the harbour wall started to sound, a single jangling bell, an urgent clangour, terrible for the whole village, terrifying for those on the quayside.

'Not again!' Brother Peter exclaimed. 'God save us from another wave.'

'Where's Isolde?' Freize demanded urgently. 'Where did you leave her?'

'At the church,' Luca shouted. 'Get up there, get to higher ground!'

Everyone tumbled out of the inn, the innkeeper among them.

'Why are they ringing the tocsin?' Luca demanded of him. 'Is it another wave?'

'No!' the innkeeper said. 'Look, see they're raising the signal.' He yelled above the pealing bell, so the people clamouring in the yard could hear. 'God bless us, it's not a wave, it's a slave galley. That's the bell for the warning. That's the bell that warns of a slave galley. They've raised the signal on the harbour fort. Don't run for high ground. It's not the sea, it's a raid! Take your places! Guardsmen! Take your places in the fort!'

Luca's face grew dark with anger. 'A slave galley? Raiding now? When the people have just lost their children to the sea?'

At once the men of the village started to run to the squat little fort that guarded the harbour, shouting to each other that it was not a wave but the warning bell for a slave galley. The women raced for their homes calling for their children. They could hear doors slamming from all over the village as frightened families bolted themselves inside. Isolde came running down from the church. 'Father Benito says there is a slave galley coming into port!' she said breathlessly. 'He saw it from the tower.'

They crowded into the inn where the innkeeper was lifting a formidable hand gun out of a cupboard, with a box of gunpowder. Freize stepped back from the dangerous-looking instrument. 'Won't that be too wet to fire?'

'Couldn't I dry it quickly on the fire?' he asked.

'No!' Freize said hastily. 'No! Much better not.'

Luca turned to the two young women. 'You'd better go to your room and lock yourselves in. We'll go down to the harbour fort and do what we can to stop them landing.'

'The laundry room,' the landlord advised. 'Go with my wife and the little maid. You can mend laundry while you wait. Nobody will ever find you there.'

When the two girls were about to argue Luca raised his hand. 'You can't come with us. What if they were to see you and take you? Go and lock yourselves in as this good man says.'

Jealously, Isolde saw that he turned to Ishraq, trusting her to cope in this new emergency. 'Take a weapon in with you, in case they come,' he said to her quietly. 'Knives from the kitchen, an axe from the yard. And don't open the door till you know it's safe.'

'Of course,' she said quickly, and led the way upstairs.

'Go,' he said quietly to Isolde. 'I can do nothing, unless I know you are safe.'

'And Ishraq,' she said, testing him. 'You trust her to defend us.'

'Of course,' he said, and was then puzzled when she turned on her heel, without another word to him, and ran upstairs without even wishing him good luck.

Luca, Freize and Brother Peter followed the innkeeper down to the harbour.

'We too should get into safety,' Brother Peter said anxiously. 'We're not equipped to fight.'

'I'd use my bare hands against them,' swore Luca. 'I'd go after them with a hammer.'

Freize exchanged one fearful look with Brother Peter and hurried after his master.

The innkeeper had paused on the quayside and was shading his eyes, looking out to sea. Men pushed past him, hurrying to the little round fort that guarded the entrance to the harbour, where they were handing out pikes. Half a dozen men were heaving on a wooden capstan. With a great groaning creak it yielded and slowly hauled a sunken chain out of the water to stretch across the harbour mouth, and bar the entrance.

'It's not like a raiding ship,' the innkeeper said, puzzled. 'I've never seen them approach so slowly before. And it's coming in under a white flag. Perhaps they were damaged out at sea. It's coming in too slowly and there are no cannon on deck, and there's a white flag at the spur. It's not an attack.'

'Could be a trick,' Luca said suspiciously, squinting to see the distant outline of the ship that was coming slowly, cautiously, closer. 'They would stoop to anything.'

They hurried on to the little fort. An older man was there, shouting orders. 'Is it a raid?' the innkeeper asked him. 'Captain Gascon, is it a raid?'

'I'm ready for one,' was all he grimly replied. 'Tell me what they're doing.'

Luca stepped to the edge of the quay, and got his first

clear sight of the ship that had sailed through his night-mares ever since he had learned that his mother and his father had been captured. It was a narrow ship, lying very low in the water with oars stretching out either side, scores of them, in two banks, one above the other, rowing slowly now, but moving absolutely as one. Over the noise of men running to get weapons and taking their places in the tower behind him he could hear the steady beat-beat-beat of the drum keeping the rowers to a slow tempo. A wicked spike extended from the prow as if it would gouge the very land itself, a white scarf billowing from the killer blade in a tem-porary gesture of peace.

The first sail was down, tightly lashed, but he could see at once that the second sail, in the middle of the ship, had been torn down and had brought the mast down with it. They had cut it away, but the ropes were still trailing over the side; and the broken stem of the mast was jagged and raw. At the stern of the ship, on a raised platform, the master of the galley himself held out a broad white sheet in his upraised arm, so that the signal for parley flickered like a flag at front and back. They came slowly towards the chain, as if they feared nothing, and then, as the rhythm of the drum changed they did an extraordinary manoeuvre, feathering the oars all together, so that the ship moved nei-ther forwards nor back, despite the swift inward current, but stayed, rocking in the churned water of the harbour, waiting before the chain, as if they could dream that any town in Christendom would ever willingly admit them.

'What are they doing?' shouted the captain, frantically loading the only weapon they had – an old culverin – inside the fort.

'Holding still before the chain,' Luca replied. 'As if they think that we would ever lift it to them.' He felt his heart thudding fast at the sight of the ship that was such a terror to every port and riverside village in Europe.

Every year the Ottoman slave galleys or the Barbary corsairs took thousands of people into captivity; whole towns had been abandoned because of the raids, villages destroyed. The slaving raids were a curse and blight on every coast in Europe. They raided from Africa to Iceland, creeping up quiet rivers and inlets at night, falling on isolated farmhouses and stealing people away. Now and then they would sail into a town, steal all the treasures and burn all the wooden houses to the ground. Families, like Luca's own, had been torn apart by the brutal kidnaps. For Luca, safe in the monastery, the news that his father and his mother had gone missing was worse than if he had been told that they had died. For the rest of his life he feared that perhaps his mother was working as a house slave in a Muslim household, perhaps – or far worse – slaving to death in the fields, or brutalised by her owner. His father was probably serving in a galley like this one, chained to the oars and rowing every day all day, never raising up from his seat but sitting in his own dirt with the heat of the sun on his back, trained like an obedient mule to pull and pull when commanded, till his strong heart gave out under the strain and he died still rowing, and they unchained him and threw his wasted body over the side.

'Luca,' Brother Peter said shaking his shoulder. 'Luca!'

Luca realised he had been staring blindly, filled with hatred, at the galley. 'It's just that – for all I know – my father is slaving on one of these,' he said. 'I'm going to get a pike.'

The captain came out from the fort, the ancient culverin in his hand, a slow burning fuse in another. 'Hold this,' he said, thrusting the handgun into Brother Peter's unwilling hands.

'I really can't . . .'

'What do you want?' the captain shouted over the water, cupping his hands around his mouth. 'What do you want? I have cannon trained on your ship.'

'Do you?' asked Freize, surprised.

'No,' the captain said. 'A town like this can't afford a cannon. But I'm hoping he doesn't know that.'

'Anyway, they can sail after they have been holed,' Luca said bitterly. 'You could have a cannon and fire it and hit him and still he would come on. They can stay afloat when they are filled with water. They are all but unsinkable.'

'Can I give this back to you?' Brother Peter asked faintly, proferring the weapon and the smoking fuse. 'Really, I have no skills . . .'

Silently Freize took the weapon from the clerk.

'I need a mast and a new sail,' the shout came back across the water in perfect Italian. 'I will pay a fair price for it.'

The captain looked at Luca. 'You can see they need a mast.'

'Could still be a trick,' Luca said. 'Don't let them in.'

'How did your mast break?' the captain bellowed.

There was a little silence. 'A terrible wave,' came the reply. 'You will have had it here, *Inshallah*. We have seen its path all along this coast. You and I, we are all equally powerless against the greatness of the sea. We are all sailors.

We all need help sometimes. Let us in to your harbour to repair our ship. And I will remember that you have been a brother of the sea to me.'

Brother Peter crossed himself at the name of the Muslim god.

'Did you see any children in the water? Any children swimming?' shouted Captain Gascon, the commander of the fort.

'Allah – praise be His holy name – help them, yes, we saw them; but we were running before the wind and our sail came down. We could reach only two of them. We pulled them on board and have them safe. You can have them if you will give us a mast and a sail.'

'Show them,' prompted Luca.

'Show them to us,' the captain of the fort shouted.

The master of the ship bent down and spoke to someone in the waist of the ship. He lifted and half pushed two children to stand in the prow. They clung to each other and turned white, frightened faces towards the shore.

The captain exchanged one look with Luca.

'We've got to get the children back,' Luca said.

'Why should we help you?' Captain Gascon shouted. 'You are our enemy.'

The master of the ship made a little gesture with his hands, commanding the slaves to keep feathering the oars, holding the galley just clear of the chain, as the drum beat still thudded. 'Because we are all men who have to face the sea,' he said simply. 'Because we wish to put our enmity aside, since the greater enmity of the sea has been shown to us. If you sell us a mast and a sail we will pay you well for them. And we will return these children for free.'

'Would you agree to never come here in war again?' the captain asked. 'No raids.'

The man shrugged his shoulders. 'You are not to know, but I'm not a slave taker. I am on a journey, not raiding. I don't raid anyway.'

'Can you command that the slaving galleys don't raid our village?'

'I can request it of them.'

'Then swear to me that you will urge the slaving galleys never to come here again.'

'Not for a year,' the man bargained.

'Ten years,' the captain of the fort demanded.

'Two.'

'Five.'

'*Heras*. All right,' he said in agreement. 'Five.'

'And instead of payment for the mast, make him release all the slaves from the galley,' Luca suggested.

The captain hesitated.

'You don't need money,' Luca said. 'We don't need paying for a mast and a sail. This is a great opportunity. Let some of those poor devils get home to their families.'

'Do you have any Christians at the oars?' The captain yelled.

'Of course.'

'Any Italian men?'

A brief shout for help came clearly across the water and then they could hear the sound of a quick blow.

'We may have some,' the man at the stern of the galley said cautiously. 'Why?'

'You must release them all to us, and we will give you mast and sails for free.'

210

'I cannot release them all, or we cannot row home,' he said reasonably.

'You can sail!' Luca shouted, interrupting the negotiations as his anger overcame him. 'You can sail with the mast and sails that we will give you! Those men must be freed.' He found he was shaking with rage and that he had stepped out of the shelter of the fort. 'I'm sorry,' he said to the captain, stepping back. 'I should not have interrupted.'

Luca rejoined Freize. 'I can't bear it,' he said in an undertone. 'My own father might be on that damned ship. That might have been his voice that called out that he was Italian. That might have been him who was struck.'

'God help him,' Freize said quietly. To the captain he said, 'Probably best to make them wait outside the harbour and we bring the mast and sails down the spit, so they don't come inside the chain. Probably safer not to let them in too close to the town. They may carry the plague, as well as being a people who are not well known for their reliability, in the friendship line of things. Not that I wish to be unpleasant.'

'You will row back down there,' the captain ordered gesturing to the seaward side of the fort. 'You can tie alongside at the very end there. You must stay where we can see you and all your men must stay on board the ship. We will bring you the mast and sail and you will release all the Italians you have on board. Agreed?'

There was a low groan from the captives of other kingdoms.

'Listen to them!' Luca said fiercely. 'Hear them!'

'I will release ten Italian men,' the master of the galley said. Still the drum sounded, regular as a heartbeat. The sea raised the galley up and down and the master of the ship swayed easily standing on the prow deck, as graceful as a dancer as the rowers kept the ship exactly where he had commanded it to be: still on a moving sea.

'No, all of them,' the captain said steadily. 'You stole these men from us, now you need our help. You must restore all the Italians to us.'

There was a brief silence.

'Or go,' Luca shouted. 'Though the wave is going to rise again, and this time you will not survive it. It will wash you to hell.'

At once they could hear the master of the ship laugh. 'What do you know of the wave?' he demanded.

'We have great scholars here,' the captain of the fort said with dignity. 'This is an inquirer, from Rome. He understands all about the ways of the sea, of land and of the heavens.'

'Has he read Plato?' the commander of the slave ship taunted. 'Has he read Pliny?'

Hopefully the captain of the fort looked at Luca. He gritted his teeth and shook his head.

'Do they agree to the price for the mast or not?' Freize prompted.

'Do you want our help?' the captain demanded. 'For we have named our price.'

The master of the galley said something quietly to himself. Then aloud, he said, 'I agree.' He gave an order and at once the oars dipped and rowed on only one side of the ship while the other side of rowers held it steady. It was an extraordinary piece of seamanship; Luca acknowledged the masterful control of the galley, even as he stared at them with hatred. The ship turned almost on itself, and glided to where the captain of the fort had directed them. The oars that were beside the quay folded themselves in, like a monstrous skeletal wing, so that the craft could come close to shore, and two men leapt on shore and took up the ropes, prow and stern.

'Go to the sailmaker,' the captain ordered his men inside the fort. 'Get a lateen sail off him. Tell him we'll all settle up later. And you, run to the shipyard and get them to bring a mast down here. As fast as you can. Tell them to hurry. Tell them why. I want those scoundrels back out at sea and away from here as soon as possible.' To Luca and Brother Peter he said, 'Will you come and see that the rowers are freed?'

'I'll come,' Luca said.

'I go with him,' Freize added.

Brother Peter hesitated. 'We are travelling with a young woman who is under our protection,' he said. 'She is not obedient to the orders of the Church nor to our command; but she does know languages. I believe she has read – er – Plato. She may speak their language. It might be useful to have her with us, in case they try to cheat.'

'A Muslim woman?' the Captain was scandalised. 'You men of the church are travelling with a heretic?'

'She's slave to the lady that we are escorting to her godfather's son,' Luca said quickly.

'Oh, a slave,' the captain said. 'That's all right then. Can you fetch her?'

'It brings her into danger,' Luca said quietly to Brother Peter. 'What if they try to take her?'

'She's enslaved already,' the captain said reasonably.

'Why would you care? And your friend is right, she can listen to their talk, and warn us if this is a double-cross.'

'I'll fetch her,' Freize offered, handing the culverin to the captain, and setting off to the inn at a trot, coming back with Ishraq.

She was almost unrecognisable. She had been dressed by the landlady in the clothes of the stable lad. Her long hair was caught up under his floppy hat, and she was wearing his dirty trousers, baggy shirt, and jerkin. The hat was pulled so low over her face that there was no way of seeing that she was a beautiful girl. Only her slim ankles showing above the clumsy heavy shoes betrayed her, to anyone who was looking closely. She stood behind Freize as if she were a frightened youth.

'This?' the captain said, his idea of a beautiful girl in Luca's private harem disappearing quickly.

'This,' Luca said. To Ishraq he said, 'Keep right out of the way and if it goes wrong at all, then run back to the hiding place in the inn. Get yourself to safety and we will follow. Save yourself before anything else. But listen to what they say. You speak Arabic, don't you?'

'Of course,' she said quietly.

'Warn us if they are pretending to agree with us, but planning something among themselves. The moment you hear them plotting something, just touch my sleeve, I'll be watching for a sign from you. They say that they need our help but these are devils. Devils.'

From the shadow of the hat her dark eyes regarded him. 'These are my people,' she said quietly. 'These that you are calling devils.'

'These are nothing to do with you. They are devils,' he

said flatly. 'They took my father and my mother from their own safe fields and I don't know where they are now, or even if they are alive.'

She started to put out her hand to him, and then she remembered Isolde's jealous rage and tucked both her hands firmly in the jacket pockets. 'I'm ready,' she said.

Freize stood one side of her and Luca the other. From the sailmaker's loft came four men, carrying a heavy rolled sail on their shoulders. Further down the quayside a dozen men carrying ropes slung under a long mast, were walking in slow step towards the fort.

The captain of the fort came forwards to meet them. 'Are you all carrying knives?' he asked. They nodded in silence. 'Keep them hidden until I give the word,' he said. 'If they keep the peace then we will too. If anything goes wrong fall back on the fort.' To Ishraq he said. 'Warn us at once if you suspect anything.'

She nodded. 'I understand.'

He glanced at Luca. 'Are you ready, Inquirer?'

Luca nodded, and they led the way past the fort to where the quayside sloped down to the sea and the galley was held to the harbour wall by two waiting men. One of them was a tall broad man from the coast of Benin, his black face completely impassive, his dark eyes scanning each one of them as they walked towards him. The other was a tall white man, blond-haired and blue-eyed. The master of the galley stood in the stern of his ship, the drummer beside him.

The master was a young man, little more than eighteen, richly dressed in a pair of wide navy brocade pantaloons with beautiful red leather short boots. He had a richly embroidered white linen shirt, the sleeves billowing, and a surcoat over the top, encrusted with precious stones. At his side he wore a belt with a long curved sword and on his head – strangest of all for Luca – was a tight small white turban with a stone and the white floating plume of egrets' feathers at the front. His skin was a light brown, his eyes dark, almost black, and squinting now against the bright sky as he looked up at the quay as the Christians arrived, followed by the men carrying the sail and the long mast. He stood like a young man filled with joy in his own strength and confidence, accustomed to command, unbeaten. He was, as even Luca could see at once, dazzlingly handsome.

Luca, the captain of the fort, Freize and Ishraq came to the brink of the quay so that they could see down into the slaving galley; it was a pitiful sight. Every oar had two men chained to it, and there were forty, perhaps fifty oars. That was only the first deck. Below the enslaved rowers was another deck with another set of men chained to their oars, dressed in rags, burned brown as dried nuts from the constant blaze of the sun, sitting in their own filth, dully awaiting the order of the pounding drum. Luca gave a horrified exclamation and stepped back, cupping his palm over his nose and mouth against the stench, trying not to retch.

'Will you help us to fit the mast?' the master asked.

Ishraq listened carefully to his accent, looked from the one man onshore to the other, strained to get a sense of their purpose, to see if there was double-dealing planned here. Unnoticed, she eased her feet out of the ill-fitting shoes. If she was going to have to run or fight, she was not going to stumble.

'First, you will release the Italians,' Luca said, his anger in every clipped word.

'Are you in command here?' the young man asked politely, bowing his head a little. The great ruby in his turban winked in the sunlight. 'Are you the one that he said was an inquirer? From Rome?'

'I am visiting the town. The commander of the defence is this captain,' Luca explained.

'You are a traveller?'

Luca nodded.

'Appointed by the Pope?'

'I am a Papal inquirer,' Luca said. 'But it is no business of yours. What are you doing here?'

'I have been inquiring too – I take an interest in coastal defences.'

Ishraq eased towards Luca. 'He's a very senior commander,' she muttered. 'See the ruby in his turban and the jewels in his coat.'

'Where are you going to?' Luca asked.

'Homeward bound,' he showed them a taunting smile. 'We call it home now. You called it Constantinople, but we call it Istanbul. Do you know why?'

At the new name that the conquering infidels had given to the Christian city of Constantinople, Brother Peter hissed in horror and crossed himself. The commander laughed at the gesture. 'We named it from the Greek.'

Luca, who had not been taught Greek, gritted his teeth on his own ignorance.

'The Greek *istimbolin* means "in the city". We are in the city now and we will never lose it. So we have called it In-the-city.'

'What's your name?' Luca asked.

'Radu Bey,' he replied. 'Yours?'

'Luca Vero.'

'Priest?'

'Novice.'

'Ah, I know who you are,' he said with sudden understanding. 'You're one of those commanded to make inquiry for the secret order. You will be a servant of the Order of Darkness.'

Luca exchanged a quick shocked glance with Brother Peter. 'What do you know of the Order of Darkness?' he demanded.

'More than you would think. A lot more than you would think. Am I right?'

'I don't discuss it with you.'

'Do you know your commander? Do you know any other inquirers?'

Luca kept his face impassive.

'I think not,' the commander said in Arabic, quietly, almost to himself. 'It's just how I would do it.'

'He said "I think not ... it's just how I would do it,"' Ishraq translated in Luca's ear.

'First, the children,' Luca said, as the Piccolo men, sweating, dumped the long heavy mast beside the folded sail.

'Will you take them, whether they want to come with you or no?' Radu asked. 'Will you take them against their will?'

'No, of course not. But why would they choose to go into slavery with you?'

'Because they are not going to be enslaved. They're going to be janissaries. The greatest soldiers in the world.

218

They could rise through my army, they could become commanders.' He smiled at Luca, inviting him to see the joke. 'When we conquer Italy, they could be the ones riding at the head of the invading army, the triumphant army. Either one of them could rise to be governor, and come back to his home as a lord. He could march into his own village, he could live in the castle in the place of the Christian lord. They may prefer this future to coming back to plough the fields and muck out stables for you.'

Luca ignored him and called directly to the children. 'Do you want to come ashore? I will see that you get back to your homes. You have been saved from the flood by a miracle. Do you want to come home now and go back to your father and mother and serve God?'

'They are brothers,' Radu remarked, watching them. 'And their father beat them every day, and their mother starved them. That's why they ran away in the first place. I don't think they'll want to go back home.'

'I can put you into a monastery,' Luca offered. 'You can live and work in the Church. That's how I was raised, and Freize my friend here. It was all right. We ate well, we were educated.'

'But you didn't learn Greek,' the slave galley commander taunted him.

'That hardly matters,' Luca said, irritated.

Clearly the boys did not know what to do.

'My brother and I were both taken by the Ottomans,' Radu remarked to the boys. 'We might be an example to you. We chose different routes. He went home to the Christians and is now a great commander; one of the greatest. You could take his path and rise as well as he did. You could go with these men; I am sure they would put you in a safe place.

'But I stayed in the Empire and I am as great a commander as my brother. I eat better than him, I am certain that I am better dressed, and I am on the winning side. The Ottoman Empire is over-running the world, our frontiers expand every year. Now you two can choose. By luck – by the breaking of a mast and the loss of a sail you are free to choose. Not many boys get such a choice. It is a moment of destiny – fate – funny that it should come to two such little boys as you.'

'We'll go with you,' the eldest boy said. He looked up at the handsome face. 'You promise that we can stay together and that we will not be made slaves?'

'You will live with a family of Turks in the country, and they will feed you and educate you. You will have to work hard but you will be trained as soldiers. You will be forbidden to marry or take up any trade but soldiering. When you are big and strong enough, you will join the army and serve the Sultan Mehmet II, as I do. His command runs from Wallachia to Armenia and there's no doubt that you will march into Christendom, to the very gates of Vienna and beyond, to Paris, to Rome, to Madrid, to London. Every year we advance. Every year the Christians are defeated and fall back before us. You will be on the winning side under my command. The Christians say themselves that the end of days is coming for them. They predict that the world will end: we know that it will be us who ends it for them.'

'We will never be defeated,' Luca said fiercely. 'You lie to the boys. We will never be defeated and you will never ride into Vienna, for we are under the hand of God.'

'*Inshallah*, we are all under the hand of God,' the Muslim said quietly. 'But clearly, even you must see, that us both believing this makes no difference to who wins the battles. At the moment, as you must see, we are winning.'

'We will never renounce our faith!'

'We don't ask you to. You can believe what you like. You can even pray as you like. But we will rule all of Christendom.'

'Come home!' Luca exclaimed, holding out both hands to the boys as if he would have them jump on shore.

The eldest boy shook his head. 'Thank you very much,' he said with careful politeness, 'but this man saved us from the flood and will teach us to be soldiers like him. We'll stay with him.'

'Don't you want to see your home again? Your mother and your father?'

'Not at all,' the boy said clearly. 'They treated us worse than their hounds. We will make a new home.'

Luca stepped back, looked at Brother Peter. 'I have no words,' he said wretchedly. 'I have failed these children twice over. Once when I could not foresee the wave, and now I cannot stop them selling their souls to the devil.'

Radu smiled. 'Cheer up, Inquirer! The galley slaves won't choose to stay with me. They are all yours, poor wretches. Now, I'll have to unchain them. I will have to take my men and go down among them.'

The commander of the fort, Captain Gascon, glanced at Luca, who was still silent, looking at the children. 'You can go down slowly and unchain them,' Gascon ordered, tightening his grip on the gun. 'No tricks.'

Radu Bey nodded to the man with the drum who

unsheathed a massive blade, and stepped down behind him, on guard. He barked an order in Arabic. Luca glanced at Ishraq who nodded and whispered, 'He said: "Who is Italian?"'

Several men raised their heads and called out: '*Eccomi!*'

One man responded, a little after the others.

'*Dove sei nato, pretendente?*' snapped Radu Bey.

The rower stumbled to understand the simple Italian sentence. '*Napoli,*' he stammered, naming an Italian town, but speaking unconvincingly late with a Spanish accent.

'I don't think so,' Radu Bey said simply, and the man dropped his head to his oar and gave himself up to despair.

'We have to release them all,' Luca exclaimed, watching this doomed exchange. 'All the slaves. We have to attack the galley and get them free.'

'We can't,' the captain of the fort shook his head. 'There are too many of them.' He nodded to the ship; seated among the slaves were free men, the janissaries of the Ottoman army, ready to row or fight as the captain ordered. All down the centre of the ship were their comrades, armed with great scimitars and cutlasses, handguns stuck casually in their belts. 'They'll have cannon mounted in the prow,' he said. 'Rolled back out of sight for now, but it will be armed and ready to fire. They've lost a mast but they can still take this ship out to sea at fighting speed. I'll be happy if he just keeps to his word and we get the Italians off without trouble.'

'My father may be enslaved on one of these hellholes!' Luca said, anguished.

'Let's do what we can here today,' Freize advised quietly. 'See if we can get some men freed, then think about the rest.'

Radu Bey had been moving steadily and quietly among

the ranks of the oarsmen, turning one key and then another. The freed men rose carefully to their feet, wary of the armed men around them, and put their hands on their heads, turning around as they were bid and walking through their fellows without looking to either left or right. Seven men from the upper deck went unsteadily up a narrow gangplank to the quayside, and then three came up from the lower. As they touched the stone of the quayside some of them fell to their knees to thank God. One man's legs buckled from being seated at his oar for so long that he sank to the ground, and he could not rise up again.

'Get them away,' the captain of the fort said to the men who had brought the sail. 'Take them to the hovel where they put the lepers, and get them washed and fed and kept there.'

'That's my side of the bargain,' Radu Bey said, indifferent both to the men crying with relief on the quay and those groaning in the galley. 'Will you help fit the mast?'

'We won't set foot on your ship,' Gascon replied. 'We'll leave the sail and the mast here and you can fit it yourself. If you're not gone by sunset I will turn the cannon on you, as you wait here.'

'We'll be gone,' Radu assured him. 'And we won't come back, as I promised. Will you sell us some food?'

'I'll send some down to you, and fresh water. Give water to these poor devils.'

'I should like to go onto the ship,' Brother Peter suddenly said, surprising everyone. 'I should like to go among the rowers with the priest and hear confessions of the men, and bless them.'

Radu laughed abruptly. 'What for? Do you think you will

raise them from the dead? For these men think they are dead and gone to hell. Don't come down, priest. We'll eat you instead of bread.'

Brother Peter hesitated. 'I should bless them,' he insisted.

The commander of the galley did not even bother to reply. The fair man who was holding the rope on the shore laughed. 'Half of them are converted to the Muslim faith anyway,' he volunteered, speaking Italian with a strong English accent.

'Are you English?' Luca exclaimed.

'Captain Marcus, English privateer, advising General Radu Bey.'

'Are you enslaved?'

'Oh no. I am paid. I am going to command my own galley next year. I am a free man, a commander, serving the Empire. I'm a volunteer, a mercenary.'

'How can you do this to your fellow Christians?' Brother Peter demanded, trembling.

'It's a hard world,' the man said cheerfully. 'I used to ship slaves from Ireland for the French. Then I was on an English privateer preying on the Spanish. I don't mind the nationality, I do mind being on the winning side. Right now, I am on the winning side. The Ottoman Empire is unstoppable, take my word for it.'

'I shall send my men on shore for the mast,' Radu interrupted, snapping his fingers as half a dozen men came forwards and waited for their orders. 'Can I come onshore to dine?' Radu spoke directly to Luca. 'Will you ask me to dinner?'

'You are the enemy of my country, and my church, and my family,' Luca replied.

'So think of me as on parole,' Radu Bey suggested. 'Why not bring some food and set a table here, and we can dine and talk while they are repairing the ship.'

'You'll have to disarm,' Luca said, looking at the wicked curved sword.

'Of course. And you have to swear not to kidnap me. We have to dine as friends and then part as enemies.'

Luca hesitated.

'I know Plato,' Radu Bey said temptingly. 'Pliny too. I have a manuscript with me that I take everywhere I go. It talks about this coast, it tells of a wave. The ancients knew about this. It's in Arabic, but I'll read it to you over dinner.'

'It tells of a wave?' Luca repeated.

'And it has a map.'

'I'll get the table set,' Luca ruled, tempted beyond bearing at the thought of the ancient learning.

'Take care,' Gascon whispered to him.

'If they know how to tell that a wave is coming, we have to learn the secret.'

~

While the servants came out from the inn under Freize's watchful supervision, and set up the trestles and board midway along the quayside, Ishraq went back and released Isolde from the hidden laundry room and told her that Luca was dining with an infidel.

'How could he?' Isolde demanded. She peered out of the doorway of the inn to where Luca was standing at the end of the quay, watching Radu strip himself of a small arsenal of weapons and lay them down on the cobble stones.

Ishraq hesitated. She could not describe the power and

charm of Radu, glittering in his beautiful clothes on the boat that could move so swiftly and powerfully in the water, hold still like a bird of prey, hanging in the water like a peregrine falcon hangs in the air, or fold its oars like wings to come close to the harbour wall, docile as a collar dove.

'Luca wants to talk to him,' she said. 'He wants to know all about Arab learning.'

'He's walking very close to sin,' Brother Peter said, coming upon the girls. 'And danger.'

They watched Radu unsheath the curved blade of his sword, and from his belt produce two daggers. From a pocket inside his surcoat came the assassin's weapon, a stiletto, and from a holster tied inside his pantaloons a beautiful miniature hand gun. He laid it all on the cobbles at Luca's feet with an air of quiet pride at the armoury he carried.

'Will you dine with him?' Isolde asked Peter.

'Not I! My conscience would not allow it.'

'Freize will serve,' Ishraq reassured her. 'And he is carrying a knife, and he will be watching all the time.'

'Why would Luca not just send him away?' Isolde fretted. 'An infidel! A slaver!'

'Because Radu said he had a manuscript,' Ishraq answered. 'He taunted Luca that he had not read the philosophers. Luca wants to know what caused the wave. Radu says that he knows.'

'He's prepared to risk his life for this knowledge?' Isolde asked incredulously.

'Oh yes,' Ishraq said as if she too thought that knowledge was worth almost any risk.

Freize came quickly down the quayside and saw them at

the door, peering out. 'I was looking for you,' he said to Brother Peter. 'The little lord wants you to come and write down all that the infidel lord says. He wants a note of the manuscripts.'

Brother Peter hesitated. 'I won't break bread with such a man.'

'Nobody is asking you to dine,' Freize said, irritably. 'He is asking you to be his clerk. To write things down. And since you came with us to be a clerk, since we were forced to travel with you and have you every step of the way because they told him he had to have a clerk, it seems only reasonable that you should be a clerk now. On account of the fact that I can serve dinner and save him from being beheaded by the foreign lord or poisoned by the foreign lord or dragged into that damn boat by the foreign lord; but I can't write, so I can't write down the endless lies that the foreign lord says. But you can. And so you should. And so you will.'

Brother Peter stared stubbornly into Freize's angry face. 'I shall not. I will not be dictated to by an infidel.'

'You're a clerk!' Freize bellowed. 'You are supposed to be dictated to.'

'I will not sit at his table.'

'Do it standing!'

'I'll go,' Ishraq volunteered. 'I can do it.'

She dived into the inn and came out with paper, a quill pen and an ink pot.

'You can't go,' Isolde said at once.

'I have to.'

'It's dangerous.'

'Luca needs me.'

'And what do I do?' demanded Isolde, irritated beyond

227

bearing. 'What am I supposed to do, while you are there with Luca? Suddenly, you are the only one that can be of any use? When is he going to need me?'

'Go to your bedroom window and keep watch for us,' Freize advised. 'Watch the sea in case another galley happens to come along. And if you see anything, scream like a banshee. I don't trust them any more than you do.'

He turned to Brother Peter. 'Does your precious conscience allow you to keep watch for us? While we are half a step from danger and you are safe away, yards away, down the quayside?'

'Yes, of course.'

'Then you stand half way between the inn and the fort, and if you hear her scream, raise the alarm and turn the men out of the fort to help us.'

Isolde hesitated, longing to be at the table with Ishraq.

'Go on,' Freize said. 'Ishraq has to come because she speaks the language and she can write. But he'd want to keep you out of the way.'

'Oh, I know she is quite indispensable,' Isolde turned abruptly, without a word to Ishraq, and went up the stairs.

~

Freize and Ishraq followed the servants carrying baskets of bread and bottles of oil and wine and water. Luca glanced around and saw them coming, then turned his attention to the galley.

Radu, now completely unarmed, brought a box covered in oiled pony skin from his ship. He held it before him so that Luca could see there was no trick, and walked towards the table that the servants were setting up. 'Two manuscripts,' he said quietly. 'Only two. I chose to bring these with me because they are about this coast. I have been sailing along it and comparing what I see to what they saw more than a thousand years ago. These are copies of ancient writings held in our libraries. We have the greatest libraries in the world, and translators and philosophers working all day, every day.'

Luca had a sudden pang of envy that he had no teacher and no books to guide him, and that the greatest library he had ever seen had been at his monastery where they had three manuscripts and a Bible chained to a desk. But first he had to ask Radu something else.

'I want to find a man and a woman. I believe they were taken on a slaving raid.'

Radu started to unwrap the waterproof cover. 'Really? Taken recently?'

Luca gulped. 'Years ago, four years ago. My parents.'

'Do you know what ship was raiding? The name of the commander?'

'I don't even know if he took them or killed them.'

'It's hard to trace people after a long time,' Radu said indifferently. 'But sometimes it can be done. There are thousands of slaves taken every year, but it can be done. You will want to ransom them, I suppose? You need to speak with Father Pietro, in Venice. He buys slaves from us when their families raise the money; he's accustomed to finding people. Every year he buys a few thousand unnamed slaves with money given from your church and returns them to their homes.'

'He does?' Luca blinked. 'I've never even heard of him.'

'Of course. Someone has to trade between us. We are two

mighty trading empires, and there are all sorts of people coming and going all the time. There are many middle agents, but he's the best that I know. You are always kidnapping our people and we yours. He deals in the sales of holy relics too. We can't make them fast enough for you. You have an unending appetite for human bones, it seems.' He laughed. 'We could almost think you gnaw on them like dogs. Fortunately, we have an unending supply from our endless victories. What name is it?'

'Vero,' Luca said. 'My mother and father. Where would I find Father Pietro?'

Radu smiled. 'On the Rialto of course. Slaves are a trade like any other. I should think you can buy anything there.' He shouted towards his boat. 'Anyone heard of a man named Vero?'

'Guilliam Vero,' Luca prompted.

'Guilliam Vero. Taken about four years ago. Rowers, you can speak!'

One head went up. 'On Bayeed's ship,' he said. 'Two years ago.'

'There you are,' Radu said indifferently. 'Father Pietro may be able to trace him for you, if he's not dead already.'

'Who is Bayeed?' Luca asked urgently. 'Where is his ship?'

Radu shrugged. 'I don't know Bayeed. He'll be a slave raider, and where his ship is right now, no one knows – could be anywhere, working the Italian coast, perhaps Spain, or France. They raid and then take their stock back home for sale. You'll have to ask Father Pietro.'

'Is the man sure? The slave who knows my father. Can I ask him?'

'He's sure. No one speaks to me unless they are sure. You can't ask him.'

Luca exclaimed with frustration but Radu Bey was untroubled. He pulled out a chair from the table and sat himself down, looking around him as if he was pleased with this unexpected dinner on land.

The soldiers were coming off the galley now, one by one up the gangplank to take the measurement of the rough-cut mast. They brought with them woodworking tools. They would pare down the mast to fit it exactly to the place on the deck. Below them on the ship, other men were cutting away the broken spars and throwing them into the water.

'Alive,' Luca said. He was shaking with emotion. 'My father is alive.'

Radu looked at him without sympathy. 'I suppose it's hard to lose a parent if you love him,' he said indifferently. 'My father gave me as a hostage, to Sultan Murad. I never saw him nor my mother again. I've never been home. My father traded me and my brother for his throne. I don't forgive him for that. I might have done the same in his position; but I'll never forgive him for giving the two of us away. His own sons.'

'I've spent years praying that my parents were still alive and that I might see them again.'

'Yes, I suppose you will have done,' Radu said without concern.

'My father!' Luca was choked with emotion. He shaded his eyes with his hand. 'Excuse me, I had thought that I would never see him again. You have given me hope.'

The servants from the inn put food on the table, some meats, some bread, cheeses, smoked fish, fresh stewed fish, a bottle of wine. Radu held out his hands and one of the servants poured water into his palms for him to wash, and gave him a towel of linen to dry them. He served himself liberally and then passed his plate to Luca. 'Forgive me. I will eat with a better appetite, if you would taste everything they have brought for me. I don't wish to be an impolite guest but equally, I want to survive this dinner.'

'Very well,' Luca said.

Radu waited patiently while Luca took a spoonful of everything.

'The wine, if you will forgive my suspicious nature,' Radu gestured to the bottle. Ishraq stepped forward and poured a small amount into a glass and handed it to Luca.

He took a sip. 'Don't you refuse wine? I thought you could not drink alcohol?'

'Not when I am at sea, or on campaign.' Radu watched Luca for signs of poison, but all he could see was a young man struggling to take in extraordinary news.

'If I could get him back, if I could find her, then I would be an orphan no longer.'

'Stranger things have happened,' Radu said cheerfully, and seeing that Luca showed no signs of illness, he started to eat with relish, watching the work on his ship and now and then glancing back at the quayside to see that he was safe from a landside attack. Ishraq stood behind Freize and watched the Ottoman with a steady, unwavering gaze.

'I am sorry. You have quite unmanned me,' Luca said recovering himself. 'I can hardly believe that my father lives. My father, that I thought was lost to me, still lives. Praise be to God.'

Radu, chewing on a chicken leg, nodded. 'You understand that life on the galleys is hard? Few men live beyond a few years. He might have died since this man saw him, he might be dead now, might die before you get him ransomed.'

Luca nodded. 'But I have been without hope, and you have given me hope.'

Radu laughed shortly at the thought of being the bearer of good tidings to a sentimental Christian, and reached for some stewed fish. 'I am glad to be – what do you call it? – a herald angel. And your mother?'

'Will I be able to find her?'

'Perhaps more easily than him. If she is working for a master he will know her name, he might even have taken pity on her and offered her to be ransomed back. Unless she is in a harem and her master has taken a fancy to her. Was she pretty? Fertile? You might have half a dozen brown-skinned brothers and sisters.'

Luca's fists clenched on the table. 'She is my mother,' he said warningly. 'I won't hear a word . . .'

Behind him Freize tensed, readying himself for a fight but Ishraq stepped swiftly forwards, her hat pulled low over her eyes. 'More wine, Sires?' she lifted the bottle and deliberately clunked it against the back of Luca's head in passing. 'Sorry, Sir.'

'Clumsy fool,' Luca gasped, recovering himself. He took a breath and turned to Radu. 'We won't speak of my parents. You will not speak of my mother. Now, to business. The manuscript. You don't object that my clerk's lad makes a note of what we say?'

Radu shook his head. 'Not at all.' He looked at Ishraq who pulled out a stool to sit down, and dipped the quill in the ink. For a moment their eyes met: dark into dark. 'Interesting boy,' he said. 'An Arab?' He said a few rapid words in Arabic. Ishraq did not allow herself even a flicker of response, though he had said to her, 'Are you an Arab boy? Do you want me to free you?'

'Half-caste,' Luca said indifferently. 'The child of a slave.'

'Does he understand Latin?'

'No,' Luca said. 'Only enough to write what I say, that's all he's good for.'

'You should teach him,' Radu advised. 'It's amazing what a bright boy can learn.'

'Were you a bright boy?'

Radu smiled. 'My brother and I were more than bright, we were brilliant boys. Our father gave us to the Sultan as hostages for his alliance and though he did not intend it, he sent us to perhaps the only court in the world where we would be educated by the best in the world. We were raised with Sultan Murad's son Mehmet, we were taught with him – five languages, mathematics, geography, philosophy – in short: the meaning of the world and how to describe it.'

'And now?'

The smallest shadow crossed Radu Bey's face – Ishraq saw it, but nobody else did. 'My brother went home. He inherited my father's throne and agreed to hold our homelands for the Ottoman Empire, but he was faithless and turned against us. He's overthrown now – in exile, but he'll be gathering an army I don't doubt, and hoping to hold the frontier against us again. He is dead to me. I doubt I'll ever see him again. He chose the wrong side. He is my enemy. Our fates have led us in opposite directions: he is a great

234

Christian commander, and I am one of the greatest commanders that my friend the Sultan Mehmet can put in the field.'

'And you carry manuscripts with you everywhere that you go? You study?'

'I read, all the time, and then I read some more. This is the way to understanding. I believe that one day we will understand everything.' He smiled. 'Shall I read what Plato says about earthquakes? It's translated from the Greek into Arabic. I'll translate it as I read for you, as best I can.'

Carefully, he unwrapped the manuscripts that were written in beautiful Arabic letters on scrolls of vellum. Meticulously he spread them out, and with a glance at Ishraq, started to read. 'Now, this is the bit you will find interesting: Here ... he talks about a great island in the Atlantic, a huge country, bigger than Libya and Asia put together ... and he says, hmm ... "*There occurred violent earthquakes and floods; and in a single day and night of misfortune all your warlike men in a body sank into the earth, and the island of Atlantis in like manner disappeared in the depths of the sea. For which reason the sea in those parts is impassable and impenetrable, because there is a shoal of mud in the way; and this was caused by the subsidence of the island.*"'

'Earthquake and the land sinking?' Luca confirmed. 'An army of men sinking down into the earth? A great island sinking down into the sea and then nothing but a shoal of mud where it had been?'

'It sounds as if there was an earthquake so great that it swallowed up an army. An earthquake which caused the sea to drown a huge country.' Radu read on. 'Plato is telling of this because Socrates has been talking about an account of a city with earthquakes and floods.' Radu's smooth voice paused. 'That's about it.'

'Earthquakes and floods? As if they come together?'

Radu nodded. 'Also, one of our own Arabic thinkers suggests that the earthquake moves the land under the sea. If you can imagine it, the land beneath the sea rises up, and the water is forced to flow away from it.'

Luca made sure he did not look at Ishraq, who kept her head bowed over the paper, rapidly writing.

'What else does he write about, Plato? What else does he say?' Luca was transfixed.

'He writes about everything, really.' Radu saw Luca's entranced face. 'Ah, you must get hold of a manuscript and have a Greek translate it for you.'

'I could learn Greek,' Luca said eagerly. 'If I were to have a manuscript in Greek I could understand it. I can learn languages quickly.'

'Can you?' Radu Bey smiled. 'Then you should come to our library in Istanbul. There is so much there, I can't begin to tell you. Plato, for instance, talks about all of the real world that can be observed. He is very interesting about things that he has seen and heard about.'

'And?'

'And he talks about the real world that sits behind the things that you cannot observe. That there is another reality we do not touch. A world that we can't eat like food, a world that doesn't trip us up, like rocks. There is a reality which is more real, that sits behind all this.'

'So how would we ever see it?'

'That's the very thing. This is the unseen world behind the real one. We wouldn't see it, we would only know it. We would understand it with our minds, not with grabbing hold of it and looking at it.'

'The things that we can see and taste are of no help to understanding?'

'They are shadows on the wall. Like a child making shapes in candlelight. The real thing is the candle, not the shadow. But all the child observes is the shadow.'

Luca looked at Radu as if he would lay hold of him and shake information out of him. 'I want to understand!'

Radu wiped his mouth and then started to roll up the manuscript again. 'Come to Istanbul,' he offered. 'Come with me now. There are students there who can speak in your language; they will take you into the library. You can read the documents we have, you can study. Are you a mathematician?'

'No!' broke from Luca in frustration. 'Not as you would mean!'

Radu smiled. 'Plato studied with his tutor Socrates, and in turn he taught Aristotle. You are not a mathematician yet because you have to try to understand things alone. This is not a single thing that you can learn. It is about a body of knowledge – one man builds on another man's learning. You need to understand those who have gone before you – only then can you ask questions and learn yourself.'

Luca rose to his feet, his hands shook a little and he tucked them into his robe so that the sharp-eyed Ottoman soldier could not see that he was deeply tempted at the thought of a library of mathematical manuscripts. 'This has been an interesting meeting for me; but I have to remember that you are the enemy of my faith, of my country, and of my family.'

'It is so. But you could change your faith, and your country, and your family is anyway lost to you.'

'I could not change my faith,' Luca said shortly.

'Perhaps all faiths are shadows on the wall,' Radu Bey said crinkling his dark eyes as he looked up at Luca. 'Perhaps there is a God like firelight, but all we can see is the shadows that we cast ourselves when we walk in front of the fire. Then we see great leaping shadows and think that this is God, but really it is only our own image.'

Luca's eyes widened slightly. 'I will pray for your soul,' he said. 'For that is terrible heresy.'

'As you like,' Radu Bey said with his handsome lazy smile. 'Did you write it all down, boy?'

Ishraq kept her head down. 'I did, milord.'

'Heresy and all?'

Ishraq stopped herself from looking up and smiling into his warm dark face. 'Yes, sir.'

'Well, leave your papers here and carry these to the ship for me,' he said carelessly. He passed her the wrapped box of manuscripts and to Luca he extended his hand. They gripped each other, hand to elbow, and felt the power in each other's arms.

'You are too good to chase around a failing country asking ignorant people what is going wrong in their poor lives,' Radu said quietly to Luca. 'You are too intelligent to be employed studying the night-terrors of old ladies. I know your commander – he has pledged his life to the wrong side and he will find the price is too high. He will sell his soul, thinking that he is doing the work of God, but he will find the world changes and he is left far behind. Come on board with me now and we will sail for Istanbul, for the libraries and for the study you can do.'

Luca released him. 'I keep faith,' he said, a little breathlessly. 'Whatever the temptation.'

'Oh, as you wish,' Radu Bey said gently, then turned and walked towards the ship.

Ishraq shot a quick glance at Luca, and at his nod, followed Radu Bey down the quayside carrying the box of manuscripts. Quietly, over his shoulder, the Ottoman threw a sentence to her in Arabic, 'If you are a slave I will free you. Come down to the quayside at sunset and jump into the ship and we will take you away. If you are a girl, as I think, you will be safe. I give you my word. If you are a scholar, no – I know you are a scholar, girl or boy – you should come with me to Istanbul where you can study.'

Carefully, she said nothing.

'Your master is a fool to choose ignorance over learning,' he said. 'He chooses to stay with the side which is losing. He chooses to stay with a God who can foresee only the end of days. Will you remember me, when you see me again?'

Startled, she blurted out in Arabic: 'Yes!'

He turned and smiled at her, his heart-stopping good looks quite dazzling in the midday sunshine. 'Remember me well,' he said. 'And when you see a man who reminds you of me – and I think you will see a man that you would take for my very twin brother – then remember that you are in the most terrible danger, and that you should come to me.'

'I cannot come to you,' she said, recovering herself and speaking in Italian. 'Ever. Never.'

He spread his hands and made her a little smiling bow. 'I think there will come a day when you pray to come to me,' he said, and took the parcel from her hands and stepped down to the prow of his galley. 'Sister mine, these Christians, are not half as kindly as they seem. I know this for I was born and bred by them, and abandoned by them, just as you have been.'

'I'm not abandoned,' she said, suddenly urgent that he should hear her. 'Nobody abandoned me.'

'They must have done,' he said. 'Your father must have abandoned you, or your mother. For here you are, with skin like honey and eyes like dates and yet you are in service to a *Franj*, and you don't acknowledge your people, nor come home with us when we invite you.'

'I'm with my people,' she said stubbornly.

'No, you're not, they're *Franj* – foreign to us.'

There was a little silence.

'You are skilled,' he said. 'You've been well-taught; you walk like a fighter and you write like a scholar.'

She said nothing.

'You are working for people who think that you are going to hell,' he pointed out.

She handed the box to him and stepped off the raised deck to the quay.

'When the day comes that you see a man who looks like me, you should turn your back on him and come to me,' he repeated his warning. 'Otherwise you will see terrible things, you will do terrible things, you will look into the abyss itself. You will start to believe that you are in the hell that these Christians have invented.'

She pulled her cap over her eyes, she turned her collar

up, as if against rain, and she turned and walked away from him – though she would rather have been walking to him.

~

The village watched the Ottoman galley all day through the shuttered windows of the quayside houses, and from the arrow-slits of the fort, as the men planed the mast to fit, set it in the boat, rigged the stays and the sail, and then, finally, as they had promised, cast off at sunset and started to row out past the little fort and the dripping obstacle of the chain.

'Stop that ship!' The shout echoed in the narrow streets over the clatter of hooves as a horse and rider scrabbled down the cobbled steps towards the port. Luca whirled around, on guard against fresh danger.

'Stop that ship! In the name of the Holy Father, stop it!'

After one moment of hesitation, Luca ran to the fort, waving his arms. 'Stop the ship! Someone is coming!'

The horse burst from the shadow of the buildings, the rider bent low over his neck as the sparks flew from the horse's hooves skidding on the stone cobbles. He flung himself to the ground and shouted, 'I command you to stop it!'

The men spilled out from the fort, demanding to know what the matter was now.

The stranger threw himself at Luca. 'Stop it! That ship is commanded by the greatest enemy to Christendom!'

'How could we stop it?' Captain Gascon demanded irritably. 'It's under sail and they are rowing? We have no way to stop it.'

The stranger stamped his feet in his rage. 'That ship is commanded by a devil!'

241

'The ship is gone,' Luca exclaimed. 'And, anyway they have no cannon here. We can't bombard it. And it was under a flag of truce. Why d'you want it held? What is your authority?'

Then he saw the dark blue robe, the piercing black eyes inside the shadow of the hood, and realised they were terribly familiar. Brother Peter, beside him, dropped to one knee. 'Milord,' he said simply.

Luca hesitated. 'Is it really you, my lord?'

The man looked past them both to the slave galley as the wind filled the sails and the rowers lifted their oars, and then shipped them. As if he were mocking them, the tall figure standing at the raised stern of the ship released a standard in gorgeous irridescent blues and greens with great golden eyes, a long ribbon of precious cloth of gold meticulously embroidered to look as if it were overlaid with peacock tails, the symbol of nobility in the Ottoman empire, the standard of a great man of a conquering country.

'Was that Radu cel Frumos?' the lord demanded. 'Answer me! Damn you! Was that Radu cel Frumos?'

'He called himself Radu Bey,' Luca said carefully. A quick glance at Brother Peter, who was still on one knee, his hand on his heart, assured him that the furious hooded man, glaring after the vanishing ship, was the lord who had recruited him to the Order of Darkness. Luca knelt beside Peter and put his hand on his heart.

'Greetings, lord.'

'Get up,' he spat, not even looking down at them.

'I'm sorry that we didn't know you wanted him detained,' Brother Peter said quietly. 'He was here with his ship after an accident with the mast. If we had known ... But they were heavily armed, and we had no cannon or anything more than the local guard.'

'You will know in future. If ever you meet him,' Milord snatched his breath, and fought for patience. 'If you ever meet him again, you are to entrap him if you can and send for me. If you cannot capture him then kill him outright. He is my greatest enemy. I will never forgive him for opposing me – at every turn he is my antithesis. He is second in command to Sultan Mehmet II. He breached the walls at Constantinople. He is head of their army. He is the worst enemy of Christendom that I can name. There is no one I would rather see captured than him. There is no one I would rather see dead at my feet. He is an agent of Satan. He alone is a sign of the end of days.'

Luca and Brother Peter exchanged one uncomfortable glance and rose to stand before him.

Out at sea the gorgeous flag dipped in ironic salute and was taken in. The three men watched the ship grow smaller and smaller as it went swiftly away on the darkening sea, and then the early evening twilight enveloped it.

'So, he is gone laughing at us,' the lord said. 'He treats us like land-bound fools shouting after a ship sailing away. But you will remember this. And next time – for there will be a next time – you will not let him treat you so.'

'Never,' Brother Peter assured him.

The lord took a moment to recover his temper. 'I have read your report on the Children's Crusade, and on the great wave,' he said to Luca. 'My path crossed with your messenger as I was riding here to see the Crusade set out. You can tell me more after dinner.'

'It's a poor inn,' Luca warned him. 'They are still repairing and drying out.'

'No matter. Were you on your way to Split?'

Luca shook his head. 'No, Milord. That side of the sea was even worse hit by the great wave than this has been. It's destroyed. We can't go that way; there are people fleeing from there to come here, poor as it is. We were going to write to you for new orders.'

The lord paused, thinking. 'You can go overland, north towards Venice. There's something I want you to look at there.'

He passed the reins of his horse to Freize without another word and turned and went into the inn.

'Venice is it now?' Freize asked the horse dourly. 'Rides in here like one of the horsemen of the apocalypse and the other three are coming along behind in their own time, and tells us we're going to Venice. Well and good. Well and good, and you and I are nothing but dumb animals as you know, and I should remember.' He stroked the animal's neck and the big head turned to gently sniff at him. 'So do you know what he's planning?' Freize asked conspiratorially.

He waited as if he really thought that the horse might speak to him. 'Confidential?' he said. 'That's understandable, I suppose. But never tell me that he doesn't confide in you?' When the horse was silent, Freize patted its side and undid the tight girth. 'Ah well. A man who keeps a secret from his horse is a secretive man, indeed.'

~

In the inn, Ishraq and Isolde who had been watching from the tap room window as the ship set sail, melted away up to

244

their room as the strange lord called for the innkeeper. He ordered a glass of wine and a fire lit in the dining room, commanded the best bedroom available for himself, refused completely to share with other travellers, agreed a price for his exclusive use, and then, finally, sat down in the great chair and pulled off his riding boots and said that he would dine alone, but that Luca and Brother Peter should come to him after dinner.

'Who is he?' Isolde took Brother Peter by the arm as he bowed his way out of the dining room, and closed the door on the stranger with an air of relief.

'He is the lord commander of our Order.'

'What's his name?'

'I cannot tell you that.'

'What is his authority, then?'

Brother Peter looked almost afraid. 'He is high in the trust of the Holy Father,' he said. 'He is trusted with discovering the end of days. The Order walks on the frontier of this world and the next, patrolling the frontier of the Christian and the infidel worlds. There is no man in greater danger. There is no man more fearless.'

'Is he wealthy?'

'Of course.'

'How many men does he command?'

'Nobody but him knows. And only he knows.'

'How long have you worked for him?'

Brother Peter thought. 'Five years,' he said.

'What is the name of the Order?'

'Some people call it the Order of Darkness,' he said cautiously.

'Is that the name he calls it?'

He smiled. 'I don't know what he calls it.'

'So it has another name?'

'Probably many.'

'Is Luca sworn to it?' she asked. 'Sworn as a celibate soldier, or inquirer, or whatever it is?'

'Not yet,' he paused. 'You have to serve, you have to prove your worth, and then you are sworn to it,' he said. Unaware of what he was doing, he touched his hand to his upper arm.

'They mark you?' she guessed acutely.

His hesitation told her that she was right.

'Show me,' she said instantly.

He hesitated.

'Why would you not show me? Are you ashamed of your loyalty?'

'Of course not!' he said, stung. Carefully, he rolled up his sleeve and on his upper arm, inscribed into his flesh in a dark tattoo, he showed her the sign of the Order.

She was silent as she looked at it, the dragon eating its tail, the symbol of eternity and the suggestion of circularity – a fear that feeds on itself. 'Is Luca marked like this? Has the lord had him scarred too?'

'No. Not yet.'

'Will he have to swear himself to the Order and then be marked?' she asked, knowing the ways that men bind themselves to each other.

His silence told her that she had guessed correctly.

'Brother Peter. I am asking you this in very truth, not as an inquisitive girl; but as a soul in waiting for the Holy Kingdom. Luca is one of the special children of God: do you not think that he should be free in the world? Don't you think that he should be free to travel and study and call no man master? Don't you think that he is a special young man with a purity of vision and a wisdom that should not be bound to any other man? Don't you think that he is gifted and that he should be free?'

He shook his head. 'You might think that. You might think that he should be free to study and learn, hone his skills, but these are not ordinary times. If these were ordinary times I might agree with you but these are the end of days. The Order may save us from the end of days or it may guide us through. The Order needs men like Luca. He understands things at first sight. He can calculate with numbers as quickly as most men can form words. He may have the gift of tongues and be able to speak any language. Don't you distract him or try to lead him away. He is vital to the work of the Order. I have seen many inquirers and never one who understands as quickly and compassionately as Luca Vero.

'You have asked me many questions and I have answered you so that I can tell you this: the work of the Order is the saving of the world itself. It could not be more important. The only thing you should do is to help Luca in his work for the Order. Anything else is the work of Satan. Remember it.'

She bowed her head. He had a moment's fierce joy that she listened to his instruction. 'I know there is nothing more important than his work,' she said humbly. 'And besides, I don't have any influence over him.'

Brother Peter nodded, and went upstairs to find Luca.

~

Luca and Brother Peter spruced themselves up in the attic bedroom as well as they could, given that all the clothes they had were those they were wearing during the flood or had since bought from the limited stores of the tailor of Piccolo.

Luca took his boots down to the kitchen to beg for some oil to polish them. 'I'll meet you in the dining room,' Brother Peter promised. 'It will look better if we arrive after each other, than if we go in together. Will you tell our lord that you spoke with the infidel?'

'Why not?'

The clerk shrugged. 'Clearly, my lord is no friend to him. The moment that he saw him he called for us to arrest him.'

'The infidel knew the history of the wave. I had to ask him about it. I had to be able to report what might have caused it.'

'Will you tell Milord that I would not come with you to write down what the infidel said?'

'If he asks me directly. But I thought you were obeying your conscience? I would have thought you would have been proud to tell him that you refused to speak with his enemy?'

Again Brother Peter shrugged. There was no way of telling whether he would be commended for his discretion in avoiding the infidel, or condemned for failing to do his duty as Luca's clerk.

'This is nothing!' Luca asserted. 'Whether we spoke to him or we avoided him is nothing to the rest of it! We nearly died. We saw the Crusade. We were on our way to Jerusalem, walking on the bed of the sea. We were driven back by a wave as big as a church steeple that drowned everything in its path. Extraordinary things are happening all around us nearly every day.'

Brother Peter heaved up a pair of ill-fitting breeches and fastened the rope from his gown around them to hold them up around his thin hips. 'I've never known him come out from Rome to an inquiry before,' he confessed. 'It makes me nervous.'

Luca hesitated. 'He has never come out to meet an inquirer at his work before?'

'Never.'

'Why would he come for me?'

'That's what I am asking myself.'

~

Freize was to serve the dinner and was in the kitchen, helping the flustered landlady spoon up a meat stew onto trenchers of fresh dark bread. Ishraq and Isolde were to dine in their room. 'I'll carry up the food for the ladies,' Freize offered.

'I've come down for it,' Ishraq said from the doorway. 'And I'll bring the things down again. I knew you would be busy in the kitchen.'

'Lord love you and bless you,' the landlady said. 'And him a gentleman from Rome and everything damp still.'

'It's fine,' Ishraq assured her. She took their two bowls of stew and some rough bread and started for the stairs. Freize held the door open for her.

'What did he say to you?' he asked her quietly as she went past him.

Her head came up. 'What did who say?'

'The infidel nobleman. He spoke to you in his foreign language. He took you aside to the boat, when you were carrying his package for him. I saw you go with him, but I have no skill in languages. But I saw him speak quietly. I didn't know what he said to you – nor what you said to him?'

'I didn't understand him,' she said quickly. 'He spoke too fast.'

'So what did you reply?'

'That I couldn't understand him.'

There was a second, a split second when Freize saw her dark eyes slide away from him, and he knew that she was lying. 'Seems to be an important man,' he said easily.

'Very learned, from what he was saying to Luca,' she said indifferently, and went from the room and started to climb the stairs.

'Are you serving dinner, or flirting with the young lady?' the landlady demanded from her place by the blazing fire where she was spooning fat over a roasting duck on the spit.

'Flirting,' Freize replied instantly. 'Firstly with the young lady and now – thank the lord she has gone – I can start on my greater quarry: yourself. Shall we go to your laundry room? Shall we say to hell with the duck and will you lock me in and ravish me among the sheets?'

~

The lord from Rome ate better than he could have hoped in a village recovering from a disaster, and pushed back his chair and bit into a fresh apple. Luca, and Brother Peter arrived with the fruits and sweetmeats to stand before the dining room table and report as best they could about the Crusade, about the wave, about the slaving galley, and waited for his opinion.

He sat at his ease, in a robe of beautiful dark blue cloth but with the hood over his head so that his face was in shadow. 'I've heard of this Plato you speak of,' he said. 'And I've read him. But only in Greek. We have a manuscript in Rome but it's an imperfect copy. They had a better one in our library in Constantinople, but that's now in Muslim hands with the rest of the wealth of Christendom, all our great library now owned by the infidel. Brother Peter, you can give me a copy of what the infidel said.'

Brother Peter nodded his head. He did not explain that the copy had been made by Ishraq.

'And now I hear you are travelling with two ladies?' the lord said. 'They arrived with you, and they are still here?'

'I have tried over and over again to send them with another party,' Peter exclaimed. 'Circumstances have prevented them leaving us.'

'Who are they?' the lord addressed Luca, ignoring Brother Peter.

'The Lady Isolde of Lucretili, and her servant Ishraq,'

Luca confessed. 'They escaped from the nunnery, as you know, and we met with them on the road. They were in some danger as they were travelling alone. They travel with us for safety, only until they can find another party to join. They were very helpful at Vittorito, as I reported, and again here. The Lady Isolde spoke so well that she all but averted a riot by some ignorant people who were making accusations of storm-bringers. And Ishraq is unusually learned. She was very helpful with the infidel ship; she speaks Arabic.'

The lord shrugged as if he did not much care about the ladies, but since the light did not penetrate his hood to illuminate his face, Luca could not tell if he approved or not.

'That's all right,' he said indifferently. 'You wrote to me already that the slave is skilled?'

'She's not a slave but a free woman,' Luca explained. 'Half Arab but raised at the Castle of Lucretili. She speaks languages and she studied in Spain. The former Lord of Lucretili seems to have planned to train her up as a scholar. He let her read medicine, and study Arab documents. She is very skilled in many things as you will have seen from my report.'

'What's her faith?' the lord asked, going to the main, the only, question.

'She seems to have none,' Brother Peter said heavily. 'She does not attend church but I have never seen her pray as a Muslim. She speaks of God with indifference. She may be an infidel, a Muslim or even some sort of pagan. But she's not Christian. At least, I don't think so.' He hesitated and then said the words that would protect her from an inquisition and a charge of heresy. 'We consider her as a Moor.

She obeys Christian laws. She does not bring herself into scandal. She behaves modestly, like a maid. I can find no fault in her.'

Luca looked at his newly-polished boots and said nothing about Ishraq coming into the mens' room in her nightgown and cape and going up the ladder for the kitten, and coming down again into his arms.

'And where are they going? Didn't you write that they were going to Budapest?'

'Lady Isolde is the god-daughter of the late Count Wladislaw of Wallachia. She wants to ask his son to help her gain her inheritance from her brother. The new Count is at the court of Hungary – his kingdom has been captured by a pretender.'

'Does she know him?' he asked with sudden intensity. 'Count Wladislaw? The son or the father? Has she ever seen him?'

'No, I don't think so.'

The lord laughed shortly as if this were amusing news. 'How things come about!' he said. 'Well, they can travel with you if they wish, and if you have no objection. For I want you to go to Venice. That lies on their way since they can't go to Croatia in the wake of the wave. You can start tomorrow. If anything occurs, or you hear of anything on your way, you must stop and investigate; but when you get to Venice there is work for you to do. There are stories of much gold on the market.'

'Gold?'

'In coins, gold coins. It is of interest to me because someone, somewhere has obviously found gold, a lot of gold, mined it, and is pouring it into the Venice markets. Or perhaps someone has a store of gold that they have found or thieved, or released. Either way, this is of interest. Also, the gold appears in Venice in coins, not in bars – which is unusual. So there is a forger there, somewhere, tucked away in the Venice ghetto, making very good quality English nobles, of all things, from a new source of gold. Beautiful English nobles with their old King Edward on a ship on one side and the rose of England on another – but they're perfect.'

'Perfect?'

He reached inside his robe and brought out a coin. Luca took the heavy gold weight in his hand and turned it over looking at the beautiful engraving, the handsome rose and the lettering around the edge.

'Notice anything?'

'Shiny,' Luca said. 'Beautiful.'

'Exactly, it's too heavy and unworn. Nobody's clipped them, nobody's shaved them. They've not been passed around and half a dozen petty crooks tried to scrape a paring off them. They're all full weight.' In the darkness of the hood Luca could glimpse a small smile. 'They're too good for this world,' he said. 'And that's the very thing of interest to us: something which is too good for this world.'

'You want me to investigate?' Luca asked. 'You want me to look for a forger or a coiner?'

'I have reason,' the lord said, without explaining it to him. 'Get there, mingle with people, buy and sell things, handle the coins, change money, gamble if you have to . . .'

Brother Peter raised his head and repeated, '*Gamble?*'

'Yes, go and see the money changers, do whatever you

have to do to get hold of a lot of these coins and look at the quality. If there is a forger doing extraordinarily good work, then I want to know. Identify him, and write to me at once. Pass yourself off as a young merchant with money to spend on trade coming in. Talk about taking a share in a ship: buy things, spread money around, handle a lot of money, let people know that you are wealthy. Hire a couple of manservants, take this pair of women with you, if they will go. If they will agree to it, pass yourself off as a family, thinking about buying a house in Venice. Brother Peter and you can seem as brothers, one of the women, the Lady Isolde, can appear as your sister, her servant can travel with her. Make up a story, but put yourself in the market for gold coins.'

'You want us to lie?' Brother Peter confirmed, quite hor-rified at these instructions. 'Perform a masquerade? Receive forged coins and gamble with them?'

'Trade?' Luca asked. 'Game?'

'For the greater good,' Milord said without a flicker of discomfort.

'Let me make sure that I understand,' Luca specified. 'You want us to set ourselves up, lie about who we are, pretend to be people that we are not, so that we attract these gold, probably counterfeit, coins. We become a false thing to attract a false thing.'

'Inquirer, you know as well as I that two false things probably create a real thing. Go and pretend your way to a truth. See what you see when you are behind a mask.'

Luca and Brother Peter exchanged a look at these extraordinary instructions. But then Luca spoke of his own interest: 'The infidel lord said that there was a man on the Rialto who might be able to trace my father,' he said hesitantly. 'When we go to Venice, I must find him. I will do it at the same time as I look for this gold. I promise I won't neglect my work for you, but I have to speak with him.'

'I thought your father was dead?' Milord asked casually.

'Disappeared,' Luca corrected him, as he always corrected everyone. 'But the infidel lord had a galley slave who said that he had seen my father on a ship commanded by a man named Bayeed.'

'Probably lying.'

'Perhaps. But I have to know.'

'Well, maybe you can buy him back with this mysterious gold,' the lord said, a smile beneath his hood. 'Perhaps you can do the work of the Lord at a profit to the church.'

'We will need funds,' Brother Peter remarked. 'It will be expensive, a masque like this.'

'I have funds for you. The Holy Father himself is pleased with your work. He commanded me to make sure that you have funds for this next inquiry. I will see you both again, after Prime, tomorrow morning. I leave then. Now I would talk with Brother Vero.' He paused. 'Alone.'

Peter bowed and went out.

Peter opened the dining room door abruptly on Ishraq and Freize who were outside in the hall. Ishraq, with the empty dinner dishes in her hands, was openly eavesdropping though pretending to be on her way to the kitchen. Freize was apparently on guard.

'Can I help you?' Brother Peter asked with weighty sarcasm. 'Either of you?'

'Thank you,' said Ishraq promptly, not at all embarrassed at being caught listening at the door. 'You're very kind.' She handed him the heavy board.

'And we were hoping to know – where next?' Freize asked.

'You know where next,' Brother Peter said irritably, taking the burden of the dishes and heading towards the kitchen. 'Since you have been listening at the door, I assume you know where next: Venice. And Milord says that the ladies may come with us and pretend to be of our party. We are to appear as a merchant family, you two are to appear as servants.' He paused and looked disapprovingly at the two of them. 'In order to pass as our servants, you will have to work. You will have to carry dishes perhaps. I do hope it's not an inconvenience to you.'

He dumped the plates on the kitchen table, ignored the flustered thanks of the innkeeper's wife, and went up the stairs to the attic bedroom room he shared with Luca and the other travellers. Ishraq and Freize were left alone.

'A breath of air?' Freize suggested, gesturing to the front door and the greying sky and sea beyond.

She went out before him and he offered her his arm to walk along the quayside in a quaint careful gesture. She smiled and walked beside him, arm in arm, like a young betrothed couple. She noticed that she liked his touch, his closeness, the warmth of his arm, the gentle support as they walked across the cobbles. She felt comfortable with him, she trusted him to walk beside her.

'The thing is,' Freize confided, 'the thing is, that I heard you with the infidel lord, on the quayside earlier today, and it's somewhat disturbing, to know that he spoke to you kindly and that you responded. I know that he spoke to you in a strange language – perhaps Arabic. And I know that you answered. Then, when I asked you, you told me that he said something you couldn't understand. Now, I don't want to call a young lady a liar; but you can see that I would have some concerns.'

She was silent for a moment.

'What I want to know is what he said and what you replied. And also: why you told me that he spoke too fast for you to understand?'

They took half a dozen steps before she replied to him. 'You don't trust me?'

He shook his head. 'I'm not saying that. All I'm saying is that I heard him speak to you in a foreign language, and I heard you reply in the same language. But when I asked you, you denied it.' He hesitated. 'It would make anyone wonder. We don't need to talk about trust. Let's talk about wonder.'

She paused, releasing his arm. 'You brought me out here to question me?' she accused him.

'Sweetheart mine, I have to know. Don't get all agitated with me. I have to know. Because he is the enemy of the little lord's Milord. You heard him. He said he was the worst enemy in the world. So I have to take an interest. I am sworn in love and loyalty to the little lord, and he is sworn to the rather quiet lord in the blue hood, and so I am bound to want to know what you are saying to his most deadly enemy.'

'You don't trust me,' she said flatly. 'After all that we have been through.'

'Sweeting,' he said apologetically. 'Usually I am the most trusting man in the world, ask anyone! I am a great lummock of trust. But here, in these circumstances, I am filled with doubts. I have been thrown about on a great wave, I have been nearly drowned, and now I am troubled by our new acquaintances.' He spread his big hand to show her his reasons for concern, counting on his fingers. 'I don't trust the infidel lord. That's one. I thought him a most dominant and glamorous character and I have a craven aversion to dominant and glamorous men, being myself humble and ordinary except for moments (I remind you) of great heroism. Two: I don't trust the little lord's lord, whose face I have never yet seen, but who seems to frighten Brother Peter out of his wits. He has the ear of the Pope – and that makes him rather important, and I have an aversion to important men, being myself very humble, except (I remind you) for my moments of greatness. He turns up without warning, and he has the best linen and the best boots I have ever seen. That troubles me, since I don't expect to see a man of the church in the linen of a lord. Three: I don't always trust your lady given that she is flighty and easily disturbed, and a woman and so naturally prone to error and misjudgment, and today she has been like a caged wolf. I don't know if you have noticed but she is not even speaking to you? And four: I barely trust myself, what with floods and handsome infidel and miracles, moody girls and well-dressed priests, and so many things that I comprehend as well as the horse – well not as well as him, actually. So don't, I beg you, take offence that I don't trust you. You are just one of many things that I can't trust. You're number five on my list of fears and worries. Dearest, I mistrust and fear a whole handful of things. Believe me, I doubt everything else long before I would ever doubt you.'

She was not diverted by his list, as he hoped she would be, but turned frosty-faced, without saying a word, and stalked back towards the inn. Freize, watching her, thought that he had never before seen a woman who could walk like an irritated cat.

He saw that he had offended her, and very deeply, and went after her with two long strides and caught her at the door. 'Don't be angry with me,' he said softly into her ear. 'Not when you were so sweet to me when I came back to you through the flood. Not when you can be so kind to a little thing like the kitten, and so loving and tender to a big thing, a big foolish thing like me.'

She was not to be persuaded. 'Well, it doesn't matter anyway, since you are going to Venice,' she said coldly. 'Perhaps my lady won't want to come with you to Venice. Perhaps we'll go at once to Budapest and leave you, then you can doubt someone else.'

'Ah no,' he said quickly, putting his hand in hers to swing her gently round. 'Of course it would matter. Wherever we were going. But you must come with us to Venice. You can get to Budapest from Venice as easily as from here. And besides, the lord in the hood is giving us money to set up a house in Venice. You would like to do that. We shall set out our stall as a prosperous family. Your lady can live as she should, as a lady in a beautiful palace with lovely clothes for a little while. We can all get a bath in hot water – think of that! You can buy some lovely clothes. Perhaps we shall make a fortune. Perhaps you will like Venice.'

'It hardly matters what I like,' she said irritably. 'It's only ever what she likes.'

'I know. But you'll make friends again,' he counselled gently.

'What do you mean?'

'You'll make up your quarrel.'

'We haven't quarrelled. What do you think we are? We're not stupid girls to have a quarrel over nothing. We have never quarrelled in all our lives. You don't begin to understand us. You don't have any idea about me.'

'He's a handsome young man,' Freize said gently, showing no sign of his amusement at her indignation. 'He's bound to cause a bit of a yowling in the cat basket. Bound to set the little kittens scratching at each other.'

He nearly laughed out loud to see her chin come up and her temper flare in her dark eyes. But then he admired how she caught herself, and acknowledged the truth of what he was saying.

'Well, we've never quarrelled before,' she explained.

'The two of you were never on your own with a handsome young man before,' he returned. 'There was no real cause.'

She giggled. 'You make us sound rather ... ordinary.'

'Little cross hens in a hen house,' he said comfortably. 'Very, very ordinary. But at least you have me to fall back on.'

'When would I fall back on you?'

'When he prefers her to you. When he makes his choice; if it's not you. When you are down to the bottom of the barrel. And have to scrape.'

Again he saw her colour rise. But she managed to laugh. 'Ah, but you swore loyalty to her already. I'm not such a fool that I don't know that everyone always prefers her to me. Everyone always will.'

'Don't you believe it,' he said tucking her hand in his arm again. 'I worship her from afar. I have promised her that she can call on me as her squire. I have offered her my fealty, of course. But you . . .'

She was ready to be offended. 'Me? Don't you worship me from afar?'

'Oh no. You, I would bundle up behind the hayrick, lift up your skirts, and see how far I could get!'

He was ducking before she even swung at him and he laughed and let her go as she turned in the inn door.

And she was laughing too, as she went up the stairs to the bedroom that she shared with Isolde to tell her that they were all to go to Venice, and that they could stay with the two young men for a little while longer, whoever was in love, whoever was preferred, whatever might happen.

~

The evening grew steadily darker. Luca and his lord spoke quietly of the cause of the wave, of the learning of the ancients, and of the signs of the end of days, and then Luca left the lord to pray alone, and go to his solitary bedroom.

In the kitchen the fire was banked down, Freize dozing before it, seated in a wooden chair with his booted feet cocked on the chimney breast. He started up when he heard the dining room door close. 'I waited up to see you to bed,' he said, rubbing his eyes and yawning.

'I think I can get up the stairs safely,' Luca remarked. 'You don't need to tuck me in.'

'I know,' Freize said. 'But it's so good to be together once more. I wanted to say goodnight.'

'Where are you sleeping?' Luca asked. 'Our bedroom is packed tight with guests. And Milord won't share.'

'She said I could bed down here,' Freize said, gesturing to the pallet bed of straw in the corner of the kitchen where the kitten was already fast asleep. 'I'll be warmer than all of you.'

'Good night,' Luca opened his arms and the two young men hugged. 'Dear God, Freize, it's good to have you back again.'

'I can't tell you what it means to be safe on dry land and know that you and the girls are safe,' Freize said. 'I was even glad to see that miserable monk.'

Luca turned and went quietly up the stairs, and the door creaked and then there was silence. Freize shucked off his boots and loosened his belt, gently moved the kitten to one side, and stretched himself out on the pallet bed. He put his hands behind his fair head and readied himself for sleep.

Half dozing, he heard Milord go quietly up to his bedroom and the click as he dropped the latch on his door. The kitten settled itself across Freize's shoulder and Freize fell deeply asleep.

He was drifting in and out of pleasant dreams when the tiniest noise jolted him into wakefulness. It was a hiss, like the sound of a sleeping snake, a whisper of cloth. He opened his eyes but some apprehension of danger warned him to lie completely still. Through the open kitchen door he could see the darker hallway of the inn, and beyond that, the open front door. Even then, he did not move but lay watching and saw two dark silhouettes against the starlit sky. One was a woman; he could see her slight shoulders and her bare feet, the gleam of silver on one toe. The other was a man completely robed and hooded in black. Freize recognised at once Luca's lord who Brother Peter had called Milord and who had insisted on sleeping alone.

It was Ishraq who stood with him, and it was her whisper and the susurration of her chemise under her cape that had woken Freize. She paused in the doorway, her hand on the lord's arm, and Freize saw the lord turn his hooded face towards her, but could not hear his reply.

Whatever he said, whatever he murmured so quietly that Freize's straining ears could make out no words, it satisfied the girl, for she released his arm and let him go. He stepped out onto the quayside; Freize noted that he walked like a dancer, his boots made no sound, he was as quiet as a cat, and he disappeared into the darkness in the next second. The girl stood for a moment longer, looking after him but as he went from shadow to shadow in the darkness he disappeared as if by magic.

Carefully, she closed the door, holding her finger under the latch so that it did not make the slightest noise. She turned towards the kitchen. Freize snapped his eyelids shut so that she could not see the gleam of his eyes by the ebbing firelight, and sighed a little, as a man deeply asleep. He felt her watching him. By her complete silence he knew that she was standing still and studying him, and he felt, despite his attraction to her, despite his affection for her, a chill at the thought of those dark eyes looking at him from the darkness, as her companion, her accomplice went quietly down the quayside, on who knew what mission?

Then he heard the first stair creak, just a tiny noise, no more than the settling of an old house, drying out after a flood, and knew that she had slipped up the stairs, and a little draught of air told him that she had opened and closed her bedroom door.

Freize waited for moments, listening to the silence, knowing that the two of them, the young woman and the dark lord, could move as quietly as ghosts. What the hooded lord was doing, speaking to Ishraq whom he had declared a complete stranger to himself, and then creeping out to the dark quay, he could not begin to imagine. What Ishraq was doing, silently closing the door behind him, acting as his porteress, he could not think. He lay still, turning over treacheries and uncertainties in his mind and then he sat up in his pallet bed, pulled on his boots in case of an emergency, and spent the rest of the night dozing in the chair by the fireside, on guard – but against what, he did not know. At some time, just before dawn, he thought he was on guard against fear itself, and that he could hear it, quietly breathing at the keyhole.

The inn was stirring at dawn, the lad who slept in the stable yard bringing in wood for the kitchen fire, the innkeeper's wife coming down yawning to bake the bread which had been rising in a pungent yeasty mound all night long, and the innkeeper running up and down stairs with jugs of hot water for the guests to wash before they walked up the hill to attend Prime at the church. The church bell was starting to toll when Freize started at the sound of a shout from the top of the stairs.

He was out of the kitchen and racing up the stairs, two at a time, to the door of the lord as Luca came tumbling downstairs from the attic room. The door stood open and the lord was there, his hand held out, shaking slightly. As Luca and Freize came towards him he turned his face away from them, pulled the hood over his head to hide his face, and then showed them what he had in his hand.

'Radu Bey,' Luca said at once recognizing the standard in the lord's hand. It was a perfectly circular beautiful piece of fabric, richly embroidered in gold and turquoise, green and indigo to look like the eye of a peacock's feather, the symbol of nobility in the Ottoman empire, the colour of the standard that Radu Bey had laughingly unfurled from his galley while Luca's lord had shouted impotently for his arrest.

'How?' Luca stammered. 'What does it mean? Where did it come from?'

'I found it this morning, pinned on my heart. On my heart! It was fastened to my robe with a gold pin. He sent a killer to pin this on me, as I slept. He pinned it over my heart. This is his warning. This is a message from Radu Bey telling me that he has put his mark on me; he could have put his dagger through my heart just as easily.'

The lord thrust the perfectly circular, beautiful badge into Luca's hand. 'Take it!' he swore. 'I can't bear to touch it. It is as if he put a target on my heart.'

'Why would he do such a thing?'

'To warn me. To boast that he could have killed me. It's how they work. It's what they do. They warn you, and the next time they come, they kill you.'

'Who?' Freize asked. 'Who came?'

'The Assassins,' the lord said shortly. 'He has set an Assassin on me.'

'An Assassin?' Brother Peter asked, coming down the stairs. 'An Assassin has been in the inn?'

Isolde and Ishraq, disturbed by the noise, came out of their attic bedroom, and stood at the doorway, their capes thrown over their night gowns. 'What's happening?' Isolde demanded, coming down the stairs.

Luca turned to her. 'Someone got into the inn last night, and left Milord a message. A threat.'

Freize was watching Ishraq, on the steps above them all. She was quite still, her face impassive; she was looking at the lord.

'How did he get in?' Isolde asked.

Slowly, as if she felt his gaze upon her, Ishraq turned her eyes to Freize, and looked at him, her dark eyes revealing nothing.

'They can climb walls like cats, they can run along rooftops,' Milord said, shaken. 'They study for years how to enter a room in silence, how to kill without warning and leave again. They are trained killers, they take a target and hunt him down until he is dead,' he broke off. 'This is a warning for me.'

'Did he come in the window?' Luca strode across the room and swung open the shutters and one side squeaked loudly. 'No, you would have heard that.'

'The front door is never locked,' Freize volunteered. 'He could just have let himself in.' Ishraq's gaze was steady on his face. 'And out again.'

She raised her eyebrows slightly and turned a little away.

'What does it mean?' Luca asked the lord. 'Why would he do this?'

'It means that I am under sentence of death,' he said. He exhaled and gave a shaky little laugh. 'I am a dead man walking,' he said. Beneath his hood they could see his faint bitter smile. 'The Assassins have a command to kill me. They will send one of their number, and then another, and then another, until I am dead, or until they are counter-manded.'

'What are the Assassins?' Isolde asked, coming down the last steps, Ishraq following her. 'Who are they?'

'They are an order,' Brother Peter replied. 'More like a Guild. They take talented youths very young, they teach them all the arts of warfare, all the arts of spying, all the dark arts of deception and weaponry. And then you can hire them: you give them a target and pay them, and they send one Assassin after another until they have fulfilled their mission and their victim is dead.'

'Why did he not kill you then?' Ishraq asked bluntly.

'They did this to Saladin,' Brother Peter explained. 'They put a target on his heart while he slept, fully guarded in his tent, to warn him that if he went on he was a dead man.'

'What did he do?'

'Retreated,' Brother Peter said shortly.

'They are infidels; but they threatened Saladin?' Luca asked, puzzled. 'They threatened their own kind?'

'They honour their order before anything,' Milord replied. 'They will accept any target, of any faith, of any nation. They serve themselves, not religion or race.'

'But why would this galley slaver want to kill you?' Isolde asked, puzzled.

He spoke to her directly for the first time. 'He's no galley slaver,' he said. 'He is one of the greatest men of the Ottoman Empire, he is commander of all the armies, he is head of the janissary soldiers, the elite fighting force. He's the right-hand man of the Sultan Mehmet, who has just triumphed at Constantinople; they are sworn to each other for life. He stands for everything that I fight against – the victory of the Ottoman Empire over Christianity, the invasion of the Arabs across Europe, the rise of terror, the end of the world.

That was the man you had here, and you let him go. Now he warns me that I will not be as lucky if I fall into his hands. He taunts me. This is a game to him. A game to the death. He will know I have commanded you to kill him. This is his way of telling me that he has ordered my death too.'

There was a horrified silence.

'What will you do, Milord?' Luca asked quietly.

The man shrugged, recovering himself. 'I'll go to Prime,' he said. 'Breakfast. Talk with you and Brother Peter, and go on my way. Continue my struggle. Fight for Christ.'

'Will you defend yourself?'

'If I can, for as long as I can. But this tells me that I will die. I won't stop my work. I have sworn an oath to lead the Order of Darkness to guard against fear itself, and I will never give up.'

Luca hesitated. 'Should we not come with you? Should we not defend you against this threat? You should have someone with you all the time.'

His voice was bleak. 'It is a fight to the death,' he said. 'My death or his. And neither my death nor his death is as important as your mission. When I die, a new lord will take my place, you will still have work to do. For now, you go to Venice and trace the signs of the end of days. And I will keep myself as safe as I can.'

He looked at the peacock badge in Luca's hand. 'Get rid of that,' he said. 'I can't bear to see it.'

Silently, Ishraq put out her hand and took it from him. Freize watched her as she tucked it into the pocket of her cape.

~

The three men and Isolde went up the hill to the church. Freize saw them go from the inn doorway, as Ishraq started up the stairs to pack their few things ready to leave.

'You didn't hear anything, in the night, I suppose?' Freize asked her neutrally.

She turned on the stair, looked him straight in the face, and lied to him. 'No. I slept through it all.'

'Because he must have come up the stairs and stood on the landing floor just below your bedroom, and gone into the room beneath yours.'

'Yes. But he went past the kitchen door too. Did you hear nothing?'

'No. If he had killed the lord, it would have been most terrible. He is my lord's commander. I am bound to defend him. Luca is bound to guard him.'

'But whoever it was, didn't kill him,' she pointed out. 'He never intended to kill him. He took him a message, he left the message, and went away again. It is Milord who speaks of death and threatens death. All I saw was a badge from a standard.'

'A message from our enemy,' Freize prompted her. 'And not any old message. A death threat from our enemy.'

'From *your* enemy,' she said. 'To the lord of your lord. But I don't know that I like Luca's commander very much. I don't know that he is my friend. I don't know if I am on his side. I don't know that he is my lord. I don't know if his enemy is my enemy. I don't even know if he's a very good lord to Luca. Perhaps you should think of that, before you ask me how I sleep?'

~

The four walked back from Prime and they all ate breakfast in the inn kitchen while Milord ate alone in the dining room. When they had finished eating, the two young women went up to their attic bedroom to prepare for the journey.

'What will you do with that?' Isolde asked, seeing Ishraq put the gloriously embroidered peacock eye standard in the bottom of her little bag.

'Keep it, I don't know,' she said.

'Luca's commander was very afraid,' Isolde observed. 'He wanted it out of his sight.'

'I know.'

'Perhaps you should burn it.'

'Perhaps I will.' Ishraq hesitated. 'But I don't understand why Luca's lord was so troubled. He was unhurt, after all.'

'If it was an Assasin who pinned it on his chest for a warning . . .'

'It was no Assassin,' she said. 'It was Radu Bey himself, and Luca's lord must have admitted him to his room in secret. For I saw Radu Bey come out. I myself let him out of the front door.'

'Why didn't you say?' Isolde asked.

'Because Luca's lord had met him in secret and then made up this story about an Assassin. I didn't know what it meant. Now I doubt Luca's lord.'

'He is appointed by the Pope,' Isolde pointed out.

'That doesn't make him a good man,' Ishraq reminded her. 'There are many appointed by the Pope who persecute and destroy. And there is more between him and Radu Bey than we know. And, as he left, Radu Bey warned me.'

'Of what?'

'He asked me had I ever looked in Milord's face, and I

said that he is always hooded and in shadow. And he laughed and said that a man of God does not work in darkness. He said that when I see his face I will understand more. He said . . .' she broke off.

'What?' Isolde asked, lowering her voice as if she feared that Milord might be listening to them.

'He said never to let him come too close.'

'Why?'

Ishraq shook her head. 'He didn't say. He said not to let him touch me. Not to let him . . .' she hesitated. 'Not to let him kiss me.'

'He's sworn to a monastic order!' Isolde objected.

'I know. But it wasn't because it would be a sin,' Ishraq tried to explain. 'He said it as if . . . as if it would be dangerous. As if his touch might be . . . dangerous.'

There was a frightened silence. Then Isolde shook her head. 'We can trust no one,' she said.

'We can trust Luca, and Freize,' Ishraq said. 'We're safe with them. And I know that Brother Peter is a good man. But I don't trust Luca's lord nor his Order.'

'We can trust each other,' Isolde suggested, tentatively. She stretched out her hand to her friend and Ishraq stepped into her embrace. For a moment they stood together, then Ishraq stepped back. 'We can trust each other,' Ishraq ruled. 'And we have to. For I think we are alone together in a very dangerous world.'

~

After his breakfast, Milord came down to the inn kitchen and gave Brother Peter a set of sealed orders, and a heavy bag of cash. 'And a note to the Jewish moneylenders in

Venice,' he said. 'You will want for nothing while you search for the forgers.' Brother Peter tucked the sealed orders into his jerkin; Freize rolled his eyes to heaven.

'Will you guard the money for me, Freize?' Brother Peter asked.

'I'll carry the orders too if you like,' Freize grinned at him.

'No. I don't think that giving them to you would be to put them in safekeeping. I'll keep the orders myself, and open them when I am commanded and not before. But I'd be glad to know that you were guarding the purse.'

Freize nodded, secretly pleased at being trusted. As Brother Peter handed over the heavy purse of gold, the lord turned to Luca. 'I'll talk with you privately before I leave,' he said, and led the way into the dining room.

The stable lad was laying the fire. As the two men came in, he ducked his head in a bow and scuttled out. Luca closed the door behind him as the lord seated himself before the table, his back to the light, and gestured to the opposite chair. 'You can sit,' the lord said.

Luca obeyed and waited.

'You have seen a lot,' the man said to him. 'You have completed four inquiries and seen some of the horror and the strangeness of the world in these dangerous times. And you have looked without flinching.'

'I flinched when I saw the wave,' Luca confessed. 'I was very afraid.'

'Fear is not a problem. Fear before something that is truly fearful is what will keep you alive. I was afraid when I found Radu Bey's badge on my heart pinned by an Assassin. There are fearful things in this world, objects of

275

terror. What I cannot tolerate among the men of my Order is fear of things before they happen, fear of things because they might happen, fear of things that probably won't happen. You don't suffer from fears like that?'

'I'm not afraid of shadows on the wall,' Luca said.

The dark eyes looked at him acutely. 'What do you know of shadows on the wall?'

'Radu Bey, the infidel lord said . . .'

'Oh, he is well read indeed,' the lord said crushingly. 'I am sure we could all learn from him. He has had great teachers. He has given up his own soul, his immortal life so that he should know of this world. Look at his allies! He works with the Order of Assassins: what does that make him if not an Assassin himself?'

Luca was immediately silent, as the lord recovered his temper.

'No matter. He is not important to us now. I am watching you, Luca Vero, and I am encouraged by what I see.'

Luca bowed his head, feeling absurdly pleased at the praise.

'You are in obedience with my commands? You acknowledge the rule of the Order?'

'I do.'

'You understand the work that we are sworn to do, and you continue to do it?'

Luca nodded.

The lord drew his rosewood box towards him. 'If you bare your arm, I will mark you with the first sign of the Order. As you progress I will complete the marks until the seal is completed, and then you will be a full member and may know me, know me by name, you will see my face, and you will know and work alongside other knights of the Order.'

Luca hesitated; he had a strange reluctance to take the mark on his arm.

'You don't want to? You hesitate before this honour?'

'Is this like priestly vows? For I am not sure that I am prepared.'

The lord smiled. 'No. Not really. Is that why you delay?' He laughed to himself. 'You are a young man indeed! No, in our Order you are not sworn to poverty – I am sending you to Venice as wealthy as a lord. You are not sworn to chastity – your private life is your own concern, between you and your confessor. I don't concern myself with any sin or vice unless it affects your work for the Order.'

Luca blinked.

'Remember that you did not complete your novitiate. You are not bound by the vows of a priest; you can choose to take your vows later.'

'I was not sure . . .'

'My Order only requires obedience. You must be obedient to me and to my commands and to our mission, which is to guard the frontier of Christendom from the devil, the pagan and the heretic. You will be an inquirer and a servant of the Order. How you obey the commandments is between you and your confessor and God. Do you submit to the Order?'

'Yes, my lord,' Luca bowed his head.

There was a small gleam of a smile, and then the hooded figure moved to the newly-lit fire and took a taper from the flame. One by one he lit all the candles in the room and carried each one of them to the table, so that they were shining on Luca as he sat in broad daylight. In the rosewood box the lord had a set of bronze instruments like a set of embroidery needles, and a small pot of what looked like black ink.

'Bare your arm,' he said quietly.

Luca rolled back the sleeve of his robe, and stretched out his arm.

The lord took up a needle, sharp as a stiletto blade. 'Whether you find your father or not, you have a family in this Order,' he said quietly. 'Whether you speak with the Muslim lord or not, you have no lord but me. Whether you travel with the woman or not, your heart is given to your work and to the mapping of fears and the tracing of the end of days. Whatever else you see on your journey, my command is that you look into the very jaws of hell itself and tell me their measurements. Will you do this?'

He pressed the point of the needle to Luca's skin, inside the forearm, halfway between the crook of the elbow and the wrist, and Luca recoiled as he saw the blood well up and felt the sharp scratch.

'I will,' he gasped. He clenched his fist against the pain and watched as again and again the little blade cut and then scratched, opening up the skin, marking him lightly with a tickling sharp pain, making a shape, an unmistakable shape on the pale skin.

The pain deepened, as the cuts took a form. It was the tail of the dragon, exquisitely drawn by a knife on soft flesh. That was all: the first marks of the Order, the scaley tail outlined in the scarlet of Luca's blood.

Luca looked at the drawing in blood, the detail in crimson, then the lord dropped his hooded head to Luca's wound. Luca gasped as the lord's soft mouth came down on his flesh. He felt the prickle of the stubble on his lord's chin and upper lip, erotic as a kiss against his sensitive flesh. He felt the man's teeth nibble the inside of his arm, felt the touch of his warm tongue on his raw skin. Luca felt the blood well into the lord's mouth, as he sucked the flowing blood from the little wounds, then he felt the cool wetness of the man's saliva as the lord raised his head and pulled his hood forwards over his face so that Luca only glimpsed for a moment his mouth, stained red, and the gleam of his black eyes.

Without comment, the lord lifted his head and took a tiny brush, dipped it in the pot of ink, and painted, with meticulous accuracy, over the lines he had cut, the wounds he had sucked. Then, he took a linen napkin from inside the box and pressed it against the red marks, now darkened with black ink. He raised his head and looked into Luca's face. The younger man was pale and his brown eyes were darkened, his breath quick and shallow. The two of them stood in silence, as if something very strange and powerful had taken place.

'There,' said the lord, quietly. 'I have marked you with my symbol. I have tasted your blood. You begin to belong to the Order. You begin to be mine.'

THE END

AUTHOR NOTE

I think any reader will be able to see the immense pleasure I have had in writing this book, which has given me the chance to imagine the characters of a wholly fictional story against an historical background. Luca, Freize, Isolde and Ishraq seem to be growing, almost of their own accord, into the people they will be later in the series. In this novel we see Freize's courage and sense of humour coming to the fore, and also the complexity of Luca's feelings: about his childhood, about his vocation, about the two young women.

These two are becoming clearly differentiated individuals; I am getting more and more interested in where Ishraq's questioning mind and Eastern background will take her, and the way Isolde's sense of privilege and nobility is being tested by being endangered and frightened in the hard world she encounters. The discussion between the two young women about whether it is better to be free or to restrict your own behaviour in accordance with the conventions, is one that medieval people discussed, as have subsequent generations. The debate about appropriate behaviour for women continues to this day.

This novel also sees the emergence of characters who are going to matter a lot in future episodes. Luca's shadowy master is even more ominous in this story, though we see for the first time what his battle against the Ottoman Empire has cost him. We are going to see more of Milord and understand the deep enmity which will rob him of his compassion. His arch-enemy, and mirror image, is Radu Bey, a glamorous, powerful and thrilling character who is going to return in later stories and dazzles Luca and Ishraq with his learning and good looks.

The legend of a children's crusade is one that persisted throughout the medieval period and had its roots in the many short-lived musterings of young people and poor working people who were known as 'boys' or 'girls' regardless of their ages. There were many instances of small armies of the poor and powerless who marched to a nearby town, attacked a ghetto, or besieged a church, and were soon disbanded or paid off. Historians now think that there was no major crusade by children to the Holy Land, but legends persist of such an expedition, and some people continue to believe that there were at least two significant attempts by children and young people to go to the Holy Land on crusade - and I draw on those here.

The tidal wave that swept these children away is also fictional, but there *was* a tremendous earthquake, as Father

Benito reports in this story, which was centred on Friuli in 1348, and indeed there has been another earthquake in that area in recent years. The philosophers of the period did not understand how an earthquake could cause a flood, but they did believe that it might cause the plague: the earthquake of 1348 released foul odours, and was followed by a terrible plague, as Father Benito tells Luca.

People did indeed believe that storms could be called up by stormbringers, and that they went to secluded lakes and pools and splashed the water to summon storms. It is easy for us, who have the resources of scientific research and global communication, to wonder that people should believe in such fantasies; but for people whose lives were in danger almost all the time, it was easy to believe in unseen and threatening powers.

At the end of this novel Milord gives the five travellers a new commission: they are to go to Venice, the great trading centre of the medieval world and try to trace a new currency. The story of this inquiry, *Fools' Gold*, will be the next book in the Order of Darkness series.